CARRY ME HOME

A COMING HOME NOVEL

JESSICA SCOTT

Thirty One Fox Books

USA TODAY BESTSELLING AUTHOR
JESSICA
SCOTT
CARRY
ME
HOME
A Coming Home Novel
"Jessica Scott should be on every reader's list."
— Brenda Novak
New York Times Bestselling Author

Home' is one of those books" ~ **Stacey | Absorbed in a Book**

"Jessica Scott should be on every reader's list." ~ **Brenda Novak** *New York Times* **Bestselling Author**

Claire Montoya has never met a rule that wasn't meant to be broken. Being in a woman in the Army means she has to be tougher and smarter than everyone around her. She good at being a soldier but ignores the quiet longing for something more - belonging.

Evan is a man full of dark secrets and a thousand regrets. He finds solace in the rules and someone like Claire who doesn't know how to spell the word grates on his last nerve. He must have been out of his mind the night he thought he was attracted to her.

They've both avoided mention of that night but now, thrown together to help prepare a close friend for her upcoming deployment, they're forced to confront their shared past. And together, they face a choice and a chance and finding a place they've both been longing for...a place called home.

Previously published as
ALL I WANT FOR CHRISTMAS IS YOU

THE COMING HOME SERIES
Because of You
I'll Be Home for Christmas: A Coming Home Novella
Anything For You: A Coming Home Short Story
Back to You

Come Home to Me: A Coming Home Novella*
Carry Me Home*
A Place Called Home*
Take Me Home*
Homefront
After The War
Last One Home*

Note – these books are fiction. Any resemblance to real people or events is purely coincidence

Author's Note
The Coming Home series and Homefront series were originally published as separate series. I have rebranded them to get things organized as they were originally intended.

Come Home to Me: A Coming Home Novella* was originally published as part of the Homefront series

Carry Me Home* was originally published as Until There Was You as part of the Coming Home series

A Place Called Home* was originally published as All for You as part of the Coming Home series

Take Me Home* was originally published as It's Always Been You as part of the Coming Home series

Last One Home* was originally published as Find My Way Home as part of the Homefront series

DEDICATION

To Patty & Darcy
Thank you for so many reasons.

THE COMING HOME SERIES

Because of You

I'll Be Home for Christmas: A Coming Home Novella

Anything For You: A Coming Home Short Story

Back to You

Come Home to Me: A Coming Home Novella*

Carry Me Home*

A Place Called Home*

Take Me Home*

Homefront

After The War

Last One Home*

THE FALLING SERIES

Before I Fall

Break My Fall

After I Fall

Catch My Fall

Until We Fall

NONFICTION

To Iraq & Back: On War and Writing

The Long Way Home: One Mom's Journey Home From War

BOOKSHOTS

Dawn's Early Light

Author's Note

The Coming Home series and Homefront series were originally published as separate series. I have rebranded them to get things organized as they were originally intended.

Come Home to Me: A Coming Home Novella* was originally published as part of the Homefront series

Carry Me Home* was originally published as Until There Was You as part of the Coming Home series

A Place Called Home* was originally published as All for You as part of the Coming Home series

Take Me Home* was originally published as It's Always Been You as part of the Coming Home series

Last One Home* was originally published as Find My Way Home as part of the Homefront series

PROLOGUE

Fort Hood, Texas
July 2005

Captain Evan Loehr was having a bad day. Granted, it could have been worse. It could always be worse. But as he pulled his Stetson out of its carrying case and dusted it off, he contemplated the consequences for blowing off the mandatory fun of tonight's hail and farewell. He was not in the mood. Not in the least. Not when he was eight weeks out from leaving on his third deployment and was up to his neck in maintenance issues and, well, other issues that he'd never in a million years thought he'd have to deal with as a company commander.

There were things he simply did not want to know about his soldiers.

But his battalion commander said they were going to the hail and farewell, so Evan was going to the hail and farewell. The brutal Texas summer sun blazed overhead, baking the earth and melting the asphalt beneath his shoes. He hoped like hell there was air-conditioning in the bar.

More, he hoped none of his more illustrious soldiers decided to attend tonight's shindig. He'd been in command for less than a month, and so far at least one of his troopers had spent a night in jail every single weekend.

Stepping into the bar, he walked into a blanket of darkness, tinged with cigarette smoke and a bouncy country song blaring at him from all sides. The dance floor was surrounded by a low wall and illuminated with flickering strobe lights. He couldn't believe they were having a military function at a bar where there would be civilians. Normally military functions like these were in separate rooms at somewhat classier establishments, not in rowdy country bars. He wasn't entirely sure it was a good idea, but then again, he wasn't in charge of planning the event. Evan made his way to the bar, needing something a hell of a lot stronger than a beer to get him through tonight.

⚜

"You realize it looks bad for you to hang out with your old enlisted buddy, don't you?"

Claire Montoya looked up at her oldest friend, Sergeant First Class Reza Iaconelli, whom she was no longer supposed to be friends with now that she'd earned her commission two years before. "You're the only person—officer or enlisted—in this brigade I know. I don't really care what it looks like."

"Yeah, well, my commander might have something to say about that if he gets the wrong idea. The guy must have been potty trained at gunpoint."

"That uptight, huh?" Claire grinned and sipped her beer. She'd been in the Reaper Brigade Combat team for all of three weeks, and Reza was the one person she trusted to have her back. "Where is your illustrious commander, anyway?"

"Working, as always." Reza grinned, and it was pure evil. "You'll never guess on what."

Claire braced for the worst. She could only imagine. "Do I want to know?"

He tossed back the rest of his beer. "Apparently, there are eight new cases of chlamydia in our company. So the battalion commander has tasked him to find out A, where they came from, and B, what he's going to do to prevent any more outbreaks."

Claire choked on a swallow of Dos Equis that went down the wrong pipe. It was a long minute before her lungs were clear and she could breathe again, let alone talk. "That is wrong on so, so many levels," she said when she could speak.

"Speak of the devil." Reza turned and pointed his beer at someone behind Claire. She twisted on the edge of the wall that circled the dance floor, prepared to meet someone starched and rigid. "Evan Loehr, Claire Montoya. You two mingle. I'm getting another beer."

She was going to kill Reza. He was forever trying to get her to hook up the way he did: with all the discretion of a dog in heat. She stared daggers into his back as he walked off. He never quite understood why she wasn't into dating. Her track record with men sucked, and she was not about to add to that losing streak tonight. She was getting ready to deploy in less than two months with the brigade. She didn't need a one-night stand with one of the company commanders to complicate things.

Not that he didn't look like the perfect candidate for a one-night dance with the devil. If she did those sort of things. Which she didn't. But still, this man didn't look remotely the way she'd expected he would. His shoulders were wide and solid, and beneath that starched white shirt, his chest looked powerful. She could easily imagine those arms wrapped around her, holding her tight while he . . . *Down, girl.* She might not have moved from her spot on the low wall surrounding the dance floor, but her hormones had snapped to attention, that was for sure.

The way Reza had described him made her imagine a man who would show up in military uniform despite the Texas casual dress code.

He seemed out of place in this smoky, seedy bar. This guy seemed stiff and rigid, as if he'd rather be anywhere but here at this moment. The top button of his shirt exposed the strong line of his throat, revealing dark hair and a glimpse of smooth skin and carved shadows. Beneath the First Cav Stetson, his hair was black and cut close to the strong line of his neck. There was confidence in the way he moved, a raw power that wrapped around Claire like the smoke in the bar and drew her close.

Claire stuck out her hand, needing something to distract her from her deviant thoughts. Small talk ought to do the trick. "Nice to meet you. Evan, right?"

"Yeah." His hand was rough and strong as her fingers slid into his. "How did you get the last name Montoya with hair like that?"

"I have no idea." Oddly self-conscious, she tucked her red hair behind one ear. "So you're Reza's commander?"

"For the last two months."

"And your first order of business is dealing with sexually transmitted diseases?" His scowled fiercely and Claire laughed out loud, despite her best efforts not to.

"Glad you think it's funny." His voice rumbled over her skin, holding the promise of dark fantasies and primitive yearnings. It had been too long since she'd been with a man. Being around him made her want to do reckless things.

"I've never been a commander, but I hope I never have to deal with what you're dealing with right now." Evan looked so disgruntled, she smiled. She didn't know him. She shouldn't be amused by his discomfort, but the situation was ridiculous. Plus, the conversation came with the added bonus of locking down her hormones. Nothing said sexy like diseases, she thought dryly.

He leaned forward, bracing his elbows on the low wall next to her hips and dragging his hands over his face. "I can't believe that this is what I'm dealing with. Not weapons training. Not running patrols or shooting bad guys. Sexually transmitted diseases."

"Well, commander, what's your plan for dealing with the rash of diseased penises in your formation?"

Evan groaned and buried his face in his hands, then took a long pull off his own beer. Reza emerged from the crowd and clapped him on the shoulder. "I already took care of it. I sent Ramirez to the clinic to pick up a case of rubbers. They're sitting on the counter in the company ops."

"I should make them an inspectable item and have every soldier keep one in their wallet," Evan grumbled. Claire laughed so hard, she almost fell from her seat on the wall. Evan gave her a pointed look.

"I'm sorry," she said, trying to stop laughing before she permanently damaged his pride. "But you should see your face."

He took a pull off his beer. Claire watched his throat move, enthralled by the motion of sleek muscle and dark skin. "I feel like I should have a formation and make the platoon sergeants demonstrate how to put on a condom the correct way."

"As one of your platoon sergeants, I'll be the first to refuse that order," Reza said before taking another drink.

Finally Evan laughed and the sound twisted Claire's insides, teasing away the tension and the fatigue and the bone-crushing pressure of being the new girl. Something warm unfurled against her heart, like hot steam rising from a hidden vent. Something that told her she needed to stay far away from the source of the warmth.

THE FORMAL PORTION OF THE EVENING WAS ABOUT TO GET started, and Evan found himself regretting that. He was enjoying himself immensely, a feeling both surprising and unexpected. Claire Montoya was proving a sexy detour for the night, and while Evan didn't do one-night stands, he was not above taking her to a quiet corner of the bar. Her mouth drew him. She had the kind of wide, full lips that were made for kissing.

He wondered how his big platoon sergeant knew her, but couldn't drum up the energy to ask. He simply hoped he wasn't spending the evening flirting with one of Reza's castoffs. It hadn't taken him long to learn that Sergeant Iaconelli spent his free time curled up with a bottle or a woman.

"So other than unprotected sex, what do you think about being a commander?" Claire asked. Her breath kissed his skin as she leaned close enough so she didn't have to shout.

Evan leaned in, fighting the urge to lift her hair away from her ear. "I love it. It's the best job I've ever had. But it's the most stressful, too."

"You don't seem like you relax very often."

He shrugged, sipping his beer. "I don't. There's not a lot of time for relaxing when you're getting ready to take a company downrange into combat."

"Guess they're getting ready to do the introductions." Claire tipped her chin toward the stage. "Guess I need to get ready to smile and wave for the crowd."

Evan frowned. "You're a soldier?"

She smiled, and her green eyes glittered in the smoky bar. "Yeah."

There was a sinking feeling in Evan's stomach. "What rank are you?"

She frowned. "Does it matter?"

"Yes."

She grinned, and it was wicked. "What, afraid you've spent the evening flirting with an enlisted woman?"

"I don't date army women as a rule." Evan breathed out sharply. "Dirt and dust on deployments aren't exactly great conditions for love and sex."

"Pretty stiff restrictions on letting yourself relax, huh?"

"Everything in my life comes with conditions," h said softly. "Besides, you don't look like you'd be in the army." He felt a flush creep up his neck as he heard the rudeness of his own words, but Claire didn't look offended. "Sorry. I didn't mean that how it sounded."

"Relax. I'm a captain." She looked up at him, studying him quietly. "You should see your face. You were really worried, weren't you?"

Evan couldn't get the tight knot in his chest to relax. She had stunning red hair and green eyes cast in dark, smoky shadows. A body that took Evan to a dark and primal place. Her dark red hair tumbled down her back and she looked like a woman who spent more time at the mall than on the weapons range. He couldn't picture her in uniform. Thankfully, she didn't seem to care that he had been worried about her rank.

"I'm prior service. Did a stint as enlisted before I went to Officer Candidate School down at Fort Benning."

She bumped her shoulder against his, her eyes sparkling. "You really need to relax. It's mandatory fun, and you don't look like you're having any."

He turned his attention to the dais, where the brigade

commander was introducing new folks to the rest of the brigade.

Her hand on his forearm dragged his attention away from the stage. He glanced down at her fingers, long and slim against his skin, burning him. "This is a really big deal for you, isn't it?"

"No, just a surprise."

A big surprise. One that would complicate things tremendously.

"Captain Claire Montoya." The brigade commander called Claire's name, and she hopped off the wall without a backwards glance at him. "Claire hails to us from . . ."

Evan stopped listening, lost in his own thoughts, which were a hell of a lot more than unprofessional. He waited until she was up on the stage before he melted into the dark safety of the bar, putting a stop to what would have been a very big mistake.

⚜

IT WAS BETTER THIS WAY. CLAIRE HAD LEARNED A LONG time ago that work relationships—hell, any relationship that involved her—never really worked out. She palmed her car keys and walked out of *Ropers* into the intense Texas heat. The sun had gone down hours ago, but the temperature was still set to broil. Sweat trickled down her neck and her hair clung to her scalp.

She rounded the corner of the bar and clicked the key fob, her car lock chirping in the sweltering heat. But that wasn't what caught her attention.

Evan Loehr was talking to Reza. Arguing, more like. Frowning, Claire hurried over, knowing she had no authority to intervene between a company commander and his subordinate and prepared to do it anyway. But before she crossed the wide gravel parking lot, Reza snatched his keys and dropped them into some cute brunette's hands, stalking off.

Evan saw Claire approaching before she could veer off and pretend she'd been walking toward her own car.

"What was that all about?" she asked, tucking her hands into the back pocket of her jeans.

"Work." She could hear the lie as it rolled off his tongue. "You always walk up to strange men in dark parking lots?"

She raised her eyebrows. "Yes, it's a regular habit of mine. How did you think I earn extra money?"

Silence, thick and sweaty, hung between them for a long moment. Then a slow smile spread across Evan's mouth, followed by an easy laugh. "You've got one hell of a way with words."

"I try." She pointed to her car over her shoulder. "Guess I'll see you at work?"

"Probably not. I don't get up to brigade very often."

"On purpose?"

"Yeah. It isn't on my top-ten list of places to hang out."

She laughed. "Yeah, all we do at brigade is come up with good ideas to screw with you down in the companies." She studied him, the dark shadows cast beneath his eyes, the tight lines around his mouth. Tension wound its way around her, radiating from him with the same power and confidence he wore like a shield. "Well, then I won't see you around."

"No. Probably not."

Hesitant, unsure of her reception, she took a step forward. Close enough that she could see the faint shadow against his jaw. "Do you ever relax?"

His only movement was a slight flare of his nostrils. "No."

She took another step. Reached up and placed her hand on the solid wall of muscle over his heart. "Never?"

His lips parted, just a hint. "No."

His scent was dark and arousing. Making this big man go

still and quiet? Powerful. He was wound so tight, tension burned beneath her touch. "So you think this would be a mistake, don't you?"

"Yes." His voice was rough.

"Do you ever make mistakes, Evan?" she whispered, her mouth a breath from his.

"Mistakes get people killed." His words traced over her lips, sending a hot spike of arousal racing through her blood.

"Hmmm." It was nothing to brush her top lip against his. His chest stopped moving beneath her palm.

His mouth opened, until she could feel his breath mingling with hers. Her blood sang with thick and heavy sensual need. His tongue flicked against hers, an open, hot invitation.

❧

EVAN HAD NO IDEA WHAT THE HELL HE WAS THINKING, BUT this woman had struck a chord inside him, awakened a hunger that refused to be ignored. Kissing her was a mistake, a sensuous, gorgeous mistake.

He gave over to the temptation he'd fought earlier and lifted his hands to her neck, sliding his palms over her skin to thread them into her hair. It was warm silk against the back of his hands, a raw, simple pleasure.

Her mouth opened beneath his, her tongue sliding against his, signaling a salient desire that penetrated his defenses and made him no longer care that she was in his brigade. There were no rules against them doing any of this—whatever this was—but he didn't date at work. As he lost himself in her taste and touch, he seriously reconsidered that personal rule. He captured her quiet gasp against his mouth and felt the locks turning on the chains that held his restraint.

It was a long moment before Claire eased back, nibbling

on his bottom lip before she broke the tentative connection between them.

"What was that?" he asked, his voice rough and unfamiliar to his own ears.

She smiled. "A mistake." She swiped her thumb over his bottom lip. "But one I enjoyed."

She eased back until he was forced to release her. Regret settled in his belly that this would go no further. "I'll see you around, Evan."

He watched her go, the slight sway of her hips more alluring because she did not try to affect any sensuality. She simply walked, cloaked in confidence and sexual appeal.

He let her go. Because Evan Loehr knew all about mistakes, and he wasn't about to make one with Claire Montoya.

$\maltese$ I $\maltese$

Late 2008
Colorado Springs, Colorado

"So this is hell? Very scenic." Claire shivered and slouched over a steaming mug of coffee, wishing it were a bathtub she could crawl into. The lobby of the Evergreen Lodge was polished ski-lodge elegance and pretty much guaranteed to give the budget overlords coronaries. A huge stone fireplace in the middle radiated a welcoming heat from all four sides. Overstuffed chairs were intermixed with coffee tables and potted plants. Tiny white lights decorated the rafters and looked like diminutive stars against the dark oak. The dining room took up half the lobby, and dozens of windows let the wild mountain view in while keeping the cold out.

Across the white tablecloth, Claire's oldest friend and fellow army captain Sarah Anders laughed and stirred her hot cocoa. "You know, if you stopped complaining for a second, you'd realize that it's called the Garden of the Gods for a reason."

"There is not enough cold-weather gear in the entire army inventory to make me stop complaining. I've never been so cold in my life," Claire grumbled. "I can't believe I'm saying this but I'd rather be in Iraq right now. At least I'd be warm."

"It doesn't help that you get to stay in this beautiful ski lodge because the budget people screwed up?"

"Not a bit. They could have us at the swankiest place in Colorado Springs and I'd still complain about the cold."

"But you love me, which is why you're here." Sarah's flip remark belied the serious edge to her words. Claire had been friends with Sarah far too long to miss the fact that she was, in fact, deeply worried.

"I'm here because my brigade commander ordered me here," Claire said as she cradled her coffee mug. "The only good thing about it is being stuck with you. Why did you have to be the one tapped for this mission?"

Sarah shrugged and sipped her hot chocolate. "I'm the only company commander who hasn't deployed recently. It's my turn."

A shadow fell across her friend's face and Claire reached across the table to squeeze her friend's hand. "We'll get your team ready, Sarah."

In truth, nothing they did in training could prepare Sarah for the mission she was about to command. She was leading a logistics company into the tail end of the Surge, the buildup of American forces designed to stabilize Iraq. As someone who had recently returned from Iraq, Claire knew Sarah's mission intimately.

Nothing was going to help take a company of combat-inexperienced soldiers and turn them into steely-eyed killers inside of a month. But Claire said none of that. It was the dead last thing that Sarah needed to hear right now.

Sarah tucked a stray lock of hair behind one ear and slid her water to one side of the table to make room for a briefing folder. "Okay, so let's talk about the mission, because I'm in way over my head and I could use your expertise."

Claire mirrored Sarah's movement and leaned forward to look at the timeline of events Sarah had slid in front of her. "Inspections, mission briefings, ranges," Claire read. She glanced over at Sarah. "What's the problem?"

"Look at the first three days." Sarah flipped the page over. "We're shipping our equipment in exactly five weeks. We have a sixteen day training exercise to get our crap together because at the end of this exercise, we are shipping out our equipment, then we're going on leave. All told, five weeks start to finish. And the brigade commander . . . Claire, he doesn't understand our mission."

"Wow." Claire let out a low whistle. The training timeline was packed full of events that no one who'd deployed would waste time with. "Equal opportunity training? The only thing equal opportunity about this war is the roadside bombs that don't care who they kill. Whose good-idea fairy was this training plan?"

"Someone who's not paying attention to the fact that we are in no way ready for this mission. My company is full of supply clerks and the commander has us training mostly on shoot houses and hand-to-hand combat instead of convoy training. We don't do convoy training until the last two days of the exercise . . . But that decision is way over my head. My focus right now is getting my team ready for running the roads in Iraq."

"Then I'm your gal. I've got more than thirty thousand miles under my belt on the roads in combat." Three tours to Iraq, one as a young enlisted soldier, two as an officer. She was all too familiar with the threat that was buried beneath Iraq's roads. Sarah hadn't deployed in almost four years. She should be nervous. The war had changed a lot since the first troops went in back in '03. It changed every time Claire went back.

Sarah glanced over Claire's shoulder and perked up. Claire twisted in the plush leather chair and groaned.

"Who is that?" Sarah murmured.

Claire sighed. "You're just like every other female on the planet," Claire said, ignoring the flip of her stomach. Evan Loehr was giving her an ulcer. Lovely. One kiss and it would freaking haunt her forever. She regretted ever touching him. "Sarah Anders, get ready to meet Captain America himself."

"You know him?"

Oh yes, she knew him. Many a long night in the tactical operations center downrange had been spent fantasizing about those shoulders, along with other parts of his anatomy.

Stupid hormones.

"Wring out your panties, honey, he's not someone you want knocking on your door."

"I didn't say anything," Sarah said. Claire laughed quietly. It was good to see Sarah show some interest in a man—she hadn't dated much since her husband's death in Iraq four years ago. Claire wasn't sure how Evan would react to Sarah's appraisal, but she wasn't about to tell him. That man's ego did not need any stroking.

She took a deep breath, reminding herself she was not here to fight with Evan. Or pant after him. Neither would do her a damn bit of good. She was here to train her best friend for her deployment to combat. Lusting after the officer in charge was not part of the plan.

His gaze met hers across the wide-open space. He nodded once in greeting, but his mouth was set in a grim line. Obviously, Captain America wasn't happy to be here, either.

Lovely. Just what she wanted to deal with on this last-minute Hail Mary mission: a cranky superhero.

Evan winced and shifted his assault pack to the opposite shoulder as he studied the only woman in the room wearing a military uniform. Glancing at the other woman's name tag as he approached, he recognized Captain Sarah Anders, the support company commander. But Evan couldn't take his eyes off Claire. A woman who ate napalm and pissed razor wire and inspired Evan to want to throttle her every time they were in the same room together.

An officer who could not spell doctrine if it was stapled to her forehead.

A woman he could barely be in the same room with without watching her body move, without wondering if she was as wild in the bedroom as she was on the battlefield.

He stopped and looked down at her where she sat, next to the massive fireplace in the center of the lodge with the support company commander. "Why are you in uniform?" His words came out too sharp, but then again, what else was new.

Claire raised both eyebrows. "I'm working, ergo I'm in uniform," she said. "Is there a problem with that?"

"You're in a civilian ski lodge, off-post, after duty. You should be in civilian clothes."

She smiled coldly. "That's rich, coming from you. You've practically got 'Duty, Honor, Country' tattooed on your ass."

Evan sighed and shifted his pack to the other shoulder. "Fine. Sleep in your damn uniform if you want."

"What crawled up your ass?" she said. "You're not usually this charming until day four of a field problem."

"Never mind. Forget I said anything." Evan sighed hard. "I have more important things to do on this mission than argue with you."

"I would have thought you had more important things to

do in, oh, say, Iraq but you still managed to argue with me all the time over there."

He pinned Claire with a deadpan look. "Are you trying to piss me off?"

She smiled sweetly. "I don't actively have to try, now do I?"

"Okay, well, you two obviously have some catching up to do." Sarah stood and Evan shifted to let her by. "Claire, call me tomorrow?"

Evan watched as Claire stood and hugged the other woman. An odd sensation caught in his throat at the genuine emotion on Claire's face. She looked soft and appealing, in a way he had forced himself not to notice. He stared at her for a long moment before he caught himself and roughly cleared his throat.

"I need to run through the plan with you," Evan said. Claire looked like she was about to argue but she didn't say anything. "But I need some coffee first. Can we go to the restaurant?"

"Sure, I could use a refill," she said.

Wary of the sudden truce, he followed her back to a quiet corner, wishing he didn't notice the way her hips moved. There was an aching familiarity about seeing her in uniform. As though he'd been missing it—missing her, which was ridiculous. He didn't even like her, let alone miss her.

He supposed it was just part of the transition of coming home. Every single time he returned from a deployment, he went through a period during which he wanted nothing more than to be back with the team he'd been with downrange. Seeing Claire in uniform fed the need for the familiar he'd found himself longing for since he'd been back from this most recent trip to the sandbox. Being around her was comforting, even if it was Claire.

He let himself wonder if she ever wore her hair down. He

hadn't seen it down since the first night they'd met. Was it still long, or had she cut it? It was a beautiful color—dark, dark red, halfway between copper and deep cherry.

He'd long ago come to think of Claire Montoya as all hard angles and sharp edges. Prickly. But with her head tipped forward and her hair starting to come loose at the back of her neck, she looked . . . soft. Soft and—dear lord, was he about to think desirable?

Holy hell, he needed to get some sleep if he was going to keep this little obsession under control.

The waitress saved him from any further awkward thoughts. Evan ordered a coffee, and then flipped open his files. "So let me ask you this," he said, pulling out a timeline. "What's your assessment of the unit? Are they prepared?"

"They're a brand-new brigade. More than half the soldiers have never deployed and Sarah's company, sadly, is just as inexperienced as they are. Hell, Sarah hasn't deployed since '04, right before her husband died. The war has changed so much since then. So the long answer to your short question is no, they're not prepared." Claire's eyes darkened, the strain showing in the tension in her neck. He looked down at his coffee as she continued to sift through his files. "There is not enough time for all this," she said, her movements stiff and jerky, and he caught the slightest tremble of her fingers. She set the papers down, picking up a sugar packet. She sipped her coffee and set the cup down abruptly, pulling out a folded sheet of paper from her notebook and drawing his attention there. "Look at the timeline. It's filled with things we don't need to waste time on. We don't have time for this stupid bonfire tonight. We need to get these guys on the range and start training as soon as possible."

He recognized the gesture for what it was: an attempt to shift the conversation away from the worry for her friend to something she could control. He tapped the paper in front of her. "I take it we didn't manage to get out of the bonfire?" He wondered if she would be changing out of her uniform for the evening, and then mentally slapped himself for falling down that rabbit hole again.

"No, we didn't, and I resent the hell out of glad-handing and ass-kissing when we could be training."

Evan sipped his coffee silently, watching her try to rein in her emotions.

"The platoon leaders brief their mission plans to the brigade commander the day after tomorrow, and the next day we start training. They don't have enough tents, though, so they're sleeping in their motor pools to simulate small forward operating bases in the cities. We're back in the hotel every night instead of sleeping in the field like we normally would on a mission like this." Her voice lowered, dark and husky and filled with unsaid things.

"Are they ready for the inspections to start?"

"The fact that these inspections are another stupid waste of time notwithstanding, no, they're not ready. But we're starting tomorrow, regardless." She blew out a hard, frustrated breath. "If I were running this damn thing, I'd skip all the useless PowerPoint briefings and go straight to running missions. Training isn't something you talk about, it's something you do."

A spark of passion lit her eyes when she spoke about training. Her intensity sparked a latent energy inside him, twisting in his belly. His lips curled into a faint answering smile as it dawned on him—she got a charge out of training. Call it an adrenaline boost or a combat high, but Claire didn't just enjoy what she did, she loved it. Her eyes were dark and aroused, her body keyed up. It was singularly the most stunning change he'd ever seen in a woman.

"What?" she asked.

"The army. You really love it."

Claire smiled, the first real smile he'd seen on her lips since their team had arrived in Colorado. "Yeah. I do."

It wasn't her hot temper or her fierce beauty that drew him. It was something else. A barely contained fire, a spark on the edge of a pool of gasoline, waiting for a gust of wind to ignite the world around her. And the reaction it caused in him was no less intense. No less fierce.

He shifted uncomfortably, then cleared his throat. The sound pulled her attention from the agenda and made her look up. She shifted the paper, and he gripped the edge to angle it so he could see it better. His fingers slid against hers, and he froze. She looked up, their fingers still touching, her green eyes darkening. Then she swallowed and pulled her fingers free from his touch.

This was not the woman he knew—the wildfire, out-of-control officer he was used to seeing in the tactical operations center. That woman made snap judgments and spoke before engaging her brain. This woman was restrained. Tense. This was new, a side of Claire that Evan had never seen before.

Her gaze met his, hesitant.

"What are you doing?" Her voice was thick, edgy and filled with a wariness that made his heart flip in his chest.

"Listening to your brief." His voice sounded off to his own ears, harsh and rough.

"You haven't heard a word I've said." She leaned back in the booth and stared at him, a sharp, hunted expression in her eyes. "Don't look at me like that."

"Like what?"

Silence hung over them, awkward and cold. She said nothing, and he could see her searching for the right words, fighting the edge of panic. "Like you're looking to start rumors. Captain America doesn't sleep with members of his team, remember? Violates some superhero code or something."

"I wasn't planning on sleeping with anyone, let alone with you," he said dryly.

She laughed out loud and just like, that, the tension snapped and fizzled into an almost comfortable silence. "Well played, Captain America. Well played." She paused then. "Do you have any issues with this training plan?"

He studied the chart that outlined the key measures of success for the convoy operations. After a long moment, he glanced up at her. Shadows fell across her face, casting it in a soft, subtle glow. "No. The timeline sucks, but the convoy stuff is a good plan."

"All right, that does it," she snapped.

"What?"

"You've never said 'good job' to me on anything. Why are you suddenly signing off on this without an argument? What's wrong with you?"

He stared at the simmering anger reflected in her features, his body tightening at a sudden, vibrant image of Claire rising above him, her body glorious as her hips spread over his. It slid through his veins insidiously, taunting him with Claire and suddenly so much more. No more tight hair and harsh angles. Lush hips and full, heavy breasts and wild, unrestrained passion.

Claire the woman, not Claire the soldier.

"Nothing." Abruptly, Evan pushed away from the table and walked from the room. He had no idea where this massive error in judgment was coming from, but there was no way in hell he was attracted to someone like Claire.

Except that he was. And it shook him to the core of his soul to admit he had been from first time he'd first met her. He'd just spent every waking moment denying it since then.

It unnerved him to think Claire was suddenly more than a woman in uniform. He didn't date army women. He didn't bring many women into his life or his bed, and invariably, they left, and it was always the same story. He was cold. He was distant. He was too rigid, too controlled.

Maybe that was true. But it hadn't mattered to him until now.

What he saw when he looked at Claire was a dark and primitive being. It was Evan surrendering to the wild need burning inside him.

AN HOUR LATER, EVAN CLOSED THE DOOR TO HIS ROOM, wishing he could appreciate the understated luxury. High-vaulted ceilings made the room feel bigger than it was. The wide bay windows disappointed him—a gnarled old oak blocked his view of the mountains. Dead branches swayed gently in the evening wind. Snow coated the grey bark, creeping down the branches and dripping into the white mound below.

For a moment he was thrown back into a field soaked with blood, to another oak tree twisted with smoking metal and dusted with ash.

He wished he could blame the trembling disquiet inside him on Claire's distracting presence, but he couldn't. He'd be lying to himself if he tried. Giving himself a shake, he yanked the curtains closed. He needed to get another room. One where the trees didn't spark such painful memories.

It wouldn't help. The room wasn't the problem.

It was this place—too many memories and not nearly enough sleep collided with a single resurrected ghost. Turning his back on the window, he walked into the bathroom. It felt tiny compared to the high ceilings of the main room, but it beat the hell out of the tin trailers he'd called home on his last deployment to Iraq. He washed his face and brushed his teeth, then ran his wet fingers through his hair. Hell, he was just happy to have running water.

Still, he couldn't rein in the emotions churning in his gut. Panic? No, not by a long shot. But the feeling was so foreign and unsettling, he didn't know what to call it. He felt . . . like the boy he'd been once upon a time. Like the kid who'd stood in his parents' living room and listened to his mother's heart-breaking sobs.

He stretched his arms over his head, easing the tendons and focusing on what he could control. The tight pull of muscles across his damaged shoulder forced him back to the present.

Just weeks before they'd been scheduled to come home from the latest deployment—and wasn't that always the way?—their brigade tactical operations cell had been blown up and a freak piece of shrapnel had sliced across his upper back. Four months later, the wound had healed, leaving a jagged scar. It still ached if he didn't take care of it.

Taking over a brigade readiness exercise with less than two weeks' notice was going to limit his ability to take care of it. But what the hell. The entire Iraq war was run on less planning and even less preparedness.

He'd survived burning command posts, blown-up trucks, and complex attacks by an enemy they were supposed to easily subdue. His entire experience from West Point through Armor Officer Basic Course to his four tours in Iraq had instilled in him one thing: purpose. Training had readied him for the fog of battle. He knew how to react to sniper fire and how to hit the deck when the whir of a rocket blew up overhead. From the moment he'd turned seventeen, his life had had a direction. A purpose. To lead soldiers. And he was good at it. That wasn't arrogance, it was fact. But nothing had prepared him for the single act of coming home.

He was not used to feeling so unmoored and off balance.

Having Claire here didn't help matters, either. But he was a professional and he wasn't going to let Claire distract him from the reason they were here: to prepare the soldiers of Golf Forward Support Company to face that same war, that same chaos.

It was a no-fail mission, and Evan Loehr did not fail.

❦   2   ❦

An hour later, Evan stepped into the hallway and came to a grinding halt. Claire, it seemed, was staying in the room next to his.

"You've got to be kidding me," she muttered when she saw him. She sounded so disgruntled, Evan almost laughed. "My life is a cliché," she added, but then shot him a smile he recognized. "I promise not to turn the music up to eleven if you promise not have drunken orgies." She snapped her fingers and wagged her finger at him as if she'd just had an epiphany. "No, wait. That would require you have some kind of personality other than Captain America. Never mind."

"I'm not Captain America." Evan started walking, irritated by the nickname that he should be used to by now.

"What, that's it? No snappy comeback?"

"I'm not in the mood. So sue me." He couldn't even take a moment to appreciate the stunning transformation of Claire into civilian clothes. Her eyes were as deep as midnight in the shadows. Her hair tumbled down her back, reflecting the hallway lights like red star-cluster flares. He was fascinated by the change in her, a memory of another time mixing with the sight of her now. His blood stirred with latent arousal, making him want to feel her body pressed against him again.

And if he kept up this line of thinking, he was going to end up in the gym tonight or taking a cold shower. Holy crap, he was a disaster.

They rounded the corner, and Claire froze. Evan could practically see the hackles rising on the back of her neck. "Oh, perfect."

Evan stopped and frowned at the tiny woman coming out of the stairwell. Dim light made it hard to distinguish her from any other generic brunette, but he was pretty sure he recognized her. "Is that Lieutenant Engle?"

Claire breathed out heavily and kept walking, her shoulders stiff. Mildly curious about the strength of Claire's reaction, Evan followed her. He must have missed the part where the professional disagreement between them had morphed into active hatred on Claire's part. This ought to be interesting.

First Lieutenant Mallory Engle stopped in her tracks when she saw them. Engle was the kind of cute and perky that gave female lieutenants a bad reputation. Back in Iraq, Evan had barely tolerated the ditzy officer, who seemed to care only about the latest brainless celebrity scandals. Claire's patience had been significantly less than Evan's on a good day.

"So this is where she disappeared to," Evan said under his breath as they approached. He'd barely noticed her absence from the headquarters back at Fort Hood.

"God hates me. All the lieutenants in the army and I can't get away from this one." She folded her arms over her chest. "I'm going to slap the shit out of Iaconelli if he's the reason she's at the lodge."

Evan glanced sharply at her, wondering what exactly she was getting at. She didn't honestly suspect Iaconelli would violate army policy by sleeping with the lieutenant, did she?

Relationships – especially sexual ones - between officers and enlisted were forbidden.

"Why are you here, Lieutenant?" she asked Engle. Only another officer could make the rank sound like a dirty word.

Engle's eyes widened a little bit, and she stiffened, attempting a slightly more military bearing. Which was pretty difficult, considering that her cleavage was helping to prop up the box she carried. "Well, um, I was looking for Reza—I mean, Sarn't Iaconelli asked me to take him to get some food, but then he said he had some briefing, so he asked me to bring it upstairs for him and—" The words tumbled out in a rush, with absolutely no reservations whatsoever. With abrupt clarity, Evan remembered why he'd hated listening to her briefs.

Claire's words were laced with bitter cold. "I think you could better spend your energy with your current team, Lieutenant. It sends the wrong message that you're in an enlisted man's room when he's not even present. Leave the food and go home."

Engle's cheeks flamed red, and she dropped the food in front of Reza's door before she disappeared back down the stairs. He waited until they turned another corner before broaching the subject with Claire. "What's with the attitude? You'd have thought she was the Antichrist disguised as a lieutenant."

Claire was the one to keep walking this time, and Evan was certain it was to avoid his gaze. "She is."

Deeply curious now, Evan followed her. Tension radiated off her in waves, and while he was no stranger to Claire's temper, this seemed different—far beyond normal competition or rivalry—and he wanted to know why. "Are you going to tell me what that was all about?"

Claire sighed heavily. "Inquiring minds want to know, huh?"

Everyone knew she and Engle had a personality conflict. Hell, it had been perfectly obvious every time the two of them were in a room together. This was somehow more. "Try me," was all he said.

"Engle went to the brigade commander while we were still in Iraq. Told him that I was being mean to her. And while he told her to pound sand, the battalion executive officer, my boss, entertained her bullshit because she made it sound like it was a female thing instead of a senior officer correcting a junior. The XO told me to back off. And since I'm so good at obeying orders, I did. I'm not ending my career over some trashy lieutenant who can't even spell LT." Her words dripped with sarcasm and latent hostility. He'd never heard her sound more jaded or cynical.

Evan said nothing for the length of an entire hallway, unable to reconcile the Claire walking next to him with the reckless officer from Iraq. He caught himself looking at the strands of copper-red hair that had fallen across her forehead, remembering that long-ago night that he'd kissed her and nearly tumbled into a dark mistake. He cleared his throat roughly. "Well, then. That explains the hostility."

Claire's smile could have cracked glass and she walked off, leaving Evan alone with uncomfortable thoughts. And for the second time in the three years he'd known her, Evan allowed himself to be intrigued by the woman he saw behind the fractured smile.

CLAIRE WALKED THROUGH THE CAVERNOUS LOBBY OF THE ski lodge, heading out into the crisp, cold Colorado evening. Alone. She couldn't figure out what was going on with Loehr and he was freaking her out. Reza melted out of the shadows, startling her.

"So you do own clothes besides military uniforms. I'd wondered," he said by way of greeting.

"Funny. Real funny." She offered a smart-ass smirk to her friend. "You know, you have serious ninja-like qualities. How does someone your size move so quietly?"

"I'm a man of many talents. So how long do we have to stay tonight?" His smile dazzled white against the deep mahogany of his skin.

"Why? Anxious to get back to your deployment snuggle bunny?"

"Not funny," Reza said dryly. "You need to lay off Engle."

"So do you," she shot back. "We're not in Iraq any more. Things that might have been overlooked downrange will get you rung up back stateside."

They walked out into the cold night, crossing the village of ski shops and coffee nooks that made up the base of the resort. The bonfire was supposed to be at some pavilion near the edge of the running trail that Claire had been enjoying since she'd arrived. It might be cold, but that didn't mean she didn't need to work out.

"How's life with my favorite TOC roach, anyway?" Reza asked after a while.

Ever since Claire had gone over to the dark side and earned her commission, she spent more of her life in the tactical operations center, or TOC, where commanders controlled their troops on the ground. Reza harassed her incessantly about leaving enlisted life behind. From anyone else, it would have gotten old, but Reza was family in every way that counted.

"You're just as much of a TOC roach as I am these days. The master gunner spends all of his time planning ranges and gunneries instead of shooting them."

"Ha ha fuck you, ha ha" Reza stuffed his cell phone into

his pocket. "Look, Engle isn't as bad as you think she is," he said.

"I knew this was coming," she grumbled. "You're going to ruin your career over this girl. That or your drinking."

The sheer magnitude of her hypocrisy did not escape her. Her own relationship with Reza bordered on a violation of army policy, after all. Then again, she wasn't sleeping with him and while it might be splitting hairs, there was a distinct difference.

"No, I'm not, because it's not like that. But you very well could if you don't let it go and leave her alone. It's not like you don't have a track record there. Engle was looking for a friend downrange. I'd think you could understand that."

"Yeah, well, Engle is and always has been an officer. She needs to be looking for friendship in the officer ranks."

"Pot, meet kettle. Did it never occur to you that you and I are not supposed to be friends because you're an officer now?"

"Did it never occur to you that as a former enlisted soldier, I could give a shit about that rule? I'm not turning my back on my friends just because of my rank. It's different, dammit."

When they'd gone through combat together the first time back in '03, she'd developed a strong appreciation for what this man was capable of, despite his best efforts at ruining his career every single time he came back from the war.

They walked into the pavilion, where the bonfire licked the night sky with brilliant oranges and golds and reds. "Stay out of trouble tonight, will you? All the combat awards in the world won't help if you get caught with your pants down," she said lightly. But Reza was already moving off, zeroing in on a cute blonde who looked positively miniature next to him.

Personally, Claire hated these kinds of military social events. Attendance was strongly encouraged but that was just a nice way of saying mandatory. Hail and farewells. Right-arm night, where commanders typically bought their first sergeants a drink. None of those things appealed to Claire in the slightest. But she was an officer, and mandatory fun was in her duty description—or so she'd been told.

She refused to listen to the nagging voice in the back of her mind that said it wasn't so different for her to hang out with Reza than it was for Engle. In truth, being friends with him was a risk to her rank. Officers and enlisted weren't supposed to have close personal relationships. And Reza was one of her best friends—which was why she was so worried about him. Considering the sheer amount of alcohol he drank on a regular basis, she couldn't help it.

But no matter what, she could not—would not—report her friend to the army's drug and alcohol program. She knew the seductive pull of addiction and she knew she could never compete with the sweet relief at the bottom of a bottle. And it terrified her to think she might lose Reza the way she'd lost her father.

Reza would kick her ass if he knew she worried about him as much as she did. She hated the way he chased his demons away with women and alcohol. But for Reza, it was always one or the other. Tonight, she hoped it would be a woman. Because if it was alcohol, she might not be able to find him in the morning.

Claire spotted Evan near the bar at the edge of the pavilion, nursing a drink. He sat with his back to the bonfire, but every so often he'd glance in the massive oak mirror behind the bar. Who hung a mirror over a bar in an outdoor pavilion? Still, in the flickering firelight, it was beautiful. Intricate branches wove around the edge of the glass, giving it an aged, gothic look.

He caught her watching him. He studied her now, his gaze dark and haunted. For the longest instant, their eyes met, and Claire could not look away. Frozen in the moment, echoes of torment lashed out at her from those dark depths, a violent storm she had never, ever expected to see in Evan Loehr.

Loss. A deep, soul-crushing loss that he did not, for the barest flash of a moment, try to hide.

Then he blinked and looked down at his drink and just like that, the spell was broken. And Claire turned away, before she did something infinitely stupid.

Like ask him what was wrong.

EVAN HAD ALREADY DONE THE GLAD-HANDING WITH THE commanders. As the party ground on, he waited for a good time to slip out and head to his room while trying not to freeze to death.

At least the fire helped heat the frigid Colorado night. The pavilion was wide open on three sides, filled with tables that had small candles floating on gel. Everyone who wasn't huddled around the fire congregated around the bar at the far end. A flash of red caught his eye and he paused, struck by the sight of Claire in her civilian clothes. He watched her from a distance, stealing glances at that beautiful red hair.

Evan pulled his faded Patagonia jacket closed as he watched Claire. She stood at the edge, scanning the crowd of mostly unfamiliar faces. He had never considered himself a coward before, but approaching her took a different kind of strength. As he walked across the pavilion, he recognized it for what it was: a test. Facing someone who teased the edge of his control.

"You look like you'd rather be walking patrols in Fallujah right now." Claire's spine stiffened automatically at the sound of his voice, and Evan smiled. He'd snuck up behind her on purpose, remembering that first night he'd met her.

He studied her failed attempt at a poker face. The flicker

of emotion that danced in her eyes reminded him that some-times, jokes about combat were too soon. Fallujah had been bad -really bad- both times he'd been there. And Evan hated doing shoot houses to this day, because the reality was so much worse than anything they could do in training.

"Pretty much," was all she said in response. He wondered if she'd almost choked on that unusually restrained remark. She shivered and pulled the neck of her coat tighter around her throat. "Whose brilliant idea was it to have a bonfire in the middle of winter? A bonfire, period."

Evan smirked. "There is always time to rub elbows," he said dryly.

"Yeah, well I'd rather not do it while freezing to death. I can't get used to being cold all the time," she said. Her eyes danced with flames from the firelight.

"It's not just you. I grew up here, and I'm freezing my ass off." He wasn't sure why he'd shared that with her. Some part of him just wanted her to know.

"You're from around here?" Claire asked.

Evan breathed out a sigh of relief, determined to keep the tentative truce between them. Talking about home seemed to be a safe enough subject. For now. "Yeah, I grew up a few miles away."

She frowned and tipped her chin, studying him. Old memories swirled beneath his simple statement, closer to the surface than he preferred. "Huh. Never figured you from Colorado."

"What's that mean?"

"It means I figured you were hatched from an egg or carved from stone." He almost took offense, but her lips curled in a slight smile, and he realized she was teasing him.

She always put on such a façade, hiding the real woman beneath the uniform. She always kept her distance from people, and had for as long as he'd known her—which was a while now, he realized. More than three years. He hadn't seen her much that first deployment. But on the second, they'd both served operations duty after he'd left command.

They'd never been friendly during those long hours in the TOC, but every so often, in the relentless hours of day-to-day operations, a slice of personality would sneak through past the barriers of egos and spikes of adrenaline when they'd had troops in contact with the enemy. He'd just never allowed himself to pay attention before now.

"Is that what's bothering you? Being home?" Her question caught him off guard. The words were smooth, lacking the vitriol she normally reserved for him. "You've been . . . off your game since we got here. Unhappy childhood?"

You have no idea. He swallowed back the comment and searched for anything else to avoid acknowledging the riot of emotions inside him. "No. It's just . . . I don't like being bored. We haven't done jack shit since we came home from the war three months ago."

She smiled. This was a safe subject for them. "Yeah. Sometimes the only thing that feels right is being at work. Like fifteen-hour days in the tactical operations cell is what's normal now, you know?"

"Normal is relative," he said quietly. "You look nice. You should try to wear civvies more often."

Her eyes were cast in shadows as she studied him. "What do you want, Evan?" There was no acrid bite to her words. Just a simple, loaded question.

Evan said nothing. Until he'd come home to Colorado, he'd thought he had what he wanted. He loved being an officer in the army. The brothers he'd made in uniform had filled the hole in his life where his family had once belonged. He'd been satisfied with the occasional date, the occasional social outing. He'd thought the uniform completed him, filling the void inside him.

Now? Now he looked at Claire, at the firelight dancing over her skin, and everything he'd been missing in his life stood before him in aching, vibrant clarity. It wasn't as though he suddenly wanted to settle down and get married, but he couldn't ignore that he wanted more than the regimented existence he'd allowed himself. For the first time since that kiss, he wanted to act on the lush fantasies he'd entertained about her.

Claire braced one arm over her stomach, resting her other arm against it and holding a beer in front of her. He wondered briefly if she knew that standing that way plumped her cleavage, accenting the soft curves of her breasts. That, or his imagination had entirely too much time on its hands, because she was wearing a winter coat.

When had he started thinking about her like this? Why the hell couldn't he stop?

A crash at the end of the pavilion in the vicinity of the bar caught his attention, saving him from having to answer her question.

"Iaconelli is going to get arrested," Evan muttered. "He should be more professional than that."

Claire shot him an odd look. "Are you going to tell on him? He's not out wrecking his car. Let the guy relax." She took a sip of her own drink, appearing calm, but her words were laced with sarcasm. "You should try it sometime. Relaxing? Might do wonders for your personality."

She'd meant it as a joke. He knew that, but it did nothing to stop the powerful memories of twisted metal and burning leather. His beer suddenly tasted sour.

"There's a fine line between relaxing and being unprofessional," he said shortly. He threw his beer in the trash with a clink of broken glass. "You of all people should know that."

CLAIRE WAS STILL SIMMERING FROM EVAN'S CAUSTIC remark a few hours earlier. Unprofessional? Who did he think he was? She hadn't seen Evan for much of the rest of the evening, but she hadn't been able to shake the deep, seething anger that had settled over her heart when he'd stalked off. It was probably for the best that he'd left. She'd been about to tell him where he could shove his attitude, and telling off the officer in charge was never a good plan. The last thing she needed to do was get into yet another argument with Evan.

Pressure had long ago started wrapping around her lungs, squeezing the air from them along with her ability to keep her temper in check. Mandatory fun had long ago petered out for all but the most devoted ass-kissers. Or, in Claire's case, for those who were tailing the drunks while they continued to party. Reza was still chatting up the cute blonde, and he was the only reason Claire hadn't left yet. At least he'd stayed away from Engle tonight. Evan already thought Claire was a shitty officer. If he found out she was covering for Reza, it would only cement her status as a bottom-rung captain who didn't follow the rules.

Claire just wanted to get Reza home and locked safely in his room before he showed his ass and got in trouble. At least two men who Claire would have bet money were command sergeants major were currently giving him the hairy eyeball. If she could just get him out of here, she had a snowball's chance in Texas of getting him safely to bed and keeping Evan from seeing him piss drunk.

Claire sighed and tried to figure out the best way to get him out without looking like she was babysitting him—or taking him home herself. This was turning into one of those pesky times when it would have been better if she were in uniform.

"Crap," she mumbled beneath her breath. She tossed her drink into the trash and started weaving through the picnic tables toward Reza and the giggling blonde. She offered up a silent prayer that he wasn't going to make a scene. Though it wasn't really a question of if he would make a scene. Only how big.

Reza swayed on his feet as she approached, and the woman next to him laughed and leaned into him to help prop him up. Claire narrowed her eyes, wondering if the cute young thing even realized he probably didn't know her name.

Reza chose that exact moment to stagger into the tiny blonde, and the two of them went crashing to the floor. Claire rushed across the rest of the space and pulled the big man off the squirming female, who appeared to be enjoying herself a little too much. She bit back a horrified laugh as Reza mumbled, "Stop wiggling," while Claire struggled to heave him to his feet.

After she finally managed to get him upright, she jerked her chin at the small blonde, who was brushing off her white pants. "You okay?"

"Yes, Ma'am." She stiffened and looked at Claire as if she were stealing her date. Not in this lifetime, sister, Claire thought darkly.

Trying not to look like she was staggering beneath his weight, Claire maneuvered Reza out of the pavilion. Silence hung around them as she struggled to get him outside without tripping over his feet or her own. She shivered, and it had nothing to do with the cold. No, the chill was laced with a slithering fear that Reza was closer to the edge of a breakdown than she'd ever wanted to admit.

The full moon hung heavy and pregnant over the mountain, casting the snow-covered path in soft silver light. They were making steady progress when Reza shifted too quickly and Claire barely got out a "damn it, Reza" before the big man stumbled and went down, dragging her with him. Reza landed with an elbow in her ribs, knocking the air from her lungs. She barely managed to keep her head from smacking against the wall as they landed in a pile of limbs and muffled curses.

"Get off me." She struggled to keep the panic from her voice as the air fled her lungs and rational thought flittered for an escape route. A memories rushed in. "Reza, get off!"

3

Evan was moving before the last panicked words left Claire's mouth. Not once in three years had he ever heard panic from Claire Montoya. He'd been watching with interest from a distance as she tried to maneuver the big platoon sergeant home but when they'd fallen, it was the panic in her voice that had his feet moving before he'd given it conscious thought. He shoved Reza off her, not caring where the big man landed on the frozen earth so long as he no longer held Claire down.

Her eyes were wide, her lips parted just a fraction of an inch. Her throat worked convulsively as she swallowed, staring at memories only she could see. Her breath came in short, quick huffs. His heart ached for her. He knew the reaction to trauma all too well. There was too much adrenaline spiking through her system for her to process it all at once.

A dark and powerful emotion rose from a deeply buried place inside him. She was not his to worry about. Not his to protect. She complicated everything. Evan didn't like complicated things.

He stood for the longest moment, unable to move.

Unable to offer comfort. Unable to break free from the torment of his own demons. Still, his hands hung clenched and useless. Just like always. Just like before, with his sister. Until her panic overwhelmed him and he pushed aside the bleeding memories to kneel by her side. He forced his voice to work. "Claire?"

All at once, she came back to herself with a single, sharp inhaled breath. A pink flush crept up her neck and she sat for a moment, visibly adjusting her clothing and pulling herself back together. She pushed abruptly to her feet, ignoring his outstretched hand. "I'm so done with this. Let's get him to bed so I can go back to my room."

Her voice was sharp, but for once, he recognized it for what it was. Defensiveness. And sheer stubbornness. And behind all of that, he saw Claire's sheer determination to put Reza to bed and nothing Evan was going to do would stop that. He might as well help out.

Shifting, he stepped under Reza's other side, ignoring Claire's surprised expression. Hell, *she* surprised *him* when she didn't argue.

Sighing, she started fishing around in Reza's pockets for his wallet. "A little to the left," he mumbled.

She slapped Reza's back. "Knock it off, pervert. Where's your room key?"

"Wallet. Front pocket," Reza mumbled. He frowned and leaned up, squinting at her. "Aw shit, Claire. You went and cock blocked me, didn't you?"

After much swearing, banged extremities and dropping Reza at least once, they managed to get him into bed.

Claire stepped back and folded her arms over her chest, looking down at her prone friend. Evan watched her carefully, looking for any trace of the panic he'd seen earlier. Instead, there was fierce determination. *Stubborn*, he thought and almost smiled. Yes, Claire was certainly stubborn.

She rubbed her hands down her arms as she scanned the room, then pulled the plastic liner from the trash can. "I feel like we're in some weird alternate reality where we're a couple of privates instead of a pair of captains."

"What are you doing?"

"Saving him some money on hotel damage fees. Help me get this under his ass."

"Maybe he needs to pay for some damages. Does Iaconelli drink like this all the time?"

Claire froze. "So what if he does?"

"Do you do this all the time? Put drunk NCOs to bed?"

Claire visibly flinched at his words. She might have been cracking morbid jokes but it was all an act, a valiant attempt to hide the wounded creature he'd just caught a glimpse of. She shifted then and caught him watching her. The war—specifically the Surge—had etched its way into Evan's soul. Maybe permanently. What had it done to Claire? Who had she been before she'd gone to war and come home again?

"I'm sorry. That was uncalled for."

She smirked, and he saw a trace of the familiar smart-ass starting to surface. "Did you choke on that apology?" he asked, keeping his voice light.

She breathed deeply, and Evan braced for whatever she was about to say. Instead she turned and left Reza's room silently, placing his room key on the dresser near the television where he could easily find it in the morning. Evan followed her.

They stood in the hallway outside Reza's room and Evan finally could take a full, deep breath. In the soft light, Claire looked vulnerable and tired. But not weak. Never weak.

"I'm worried about him."

"I can see that," he said quietly, wishing he had more to offer. Wishing he knew how to do this, whatever this was.

At that moment, the vulnerability he'd seen in her eyes

overrode any thoughts of self-preservation and he reached for her. A light touch, her shoulder beneath his palm. Evan felt her tension in the space between his gesture and her surprise. Her mouth opened, just a bit, and she didn't move for a long moment. His blood bolted through his body like a razor, slicing any trace of his composure to shreds. He'd never before had the joint desire to throttle someone and hold that person close. But Claire tended to bring out the strangest reactions in him. He should be used to the dichotomy by now. He'd never been very smart when it came to Claire Montoya.

Touching her after all those years was stupid. Yet there was nothing else he could do, nothing else he desired more than to simply touch her, to find some way to offer comfort.

"What happened back there?" he said. "When you fell."

They stood in silence for several moments, and Evan was certain that she'd turn away from him—that she wouldn't answer his question.

Then there was a subtle shift as Claire leaned into him. She didn't turn. She didn't look up. She simply leaned against him. And Evan, fool that he was, held her up.

"I don't like being pinned down," she finally admitted.

Evan frowned, leaning away from her to peer down at her face. "But you do combatives. Several of those fighting positions involve being laid on. Crushed, even."

She lifted one shoulder in an absent shrug, an infinitesimal move away from his space. "That's different. I'm fighting back against a fully conscious opponent." She sighed quietly.

"That's not really an answer." He stepped closer and for once, she didn't dance away in retreat. She stood her ground, lifting her chin and meeting his gaze.

"When the TOC got blown up at the end of our last deployment, I was pinned down. I don't know for how long, but I panicked." Her voice cracked. "While the building burned around me, I did nothing but lie there and scream." She swallowed and looked away. "I couldn't do anything but scream," she whispered.

❧

"Combat brings everyone low, Claire," he murmured.

He was close enough that she could see the shadow of a beard along his jaw. She had the intense urge to see if it was soft or rough. His scent wrapped around her, whispering for her to do something incredibly stupid like stand there and breathe in the spicy heat from his body. His words were a caress, a subtle sweep of emotion over her skin.

They were alone in the late-night hallway. For once they weren't ripping each other's heads off. She expected him to chew her out for her hasty decision to rush into the blown-up building. To echo the harsh criticisms she'd levied against herself since the day she'd gotten blown up. Claire waited, searching his eyes for a trace of the stoic arrogance she'd come to expect from him. But she saw nothing she expected.

"I didn't know you were hurt when the TOC blew up," he said quietly. And with those simple words, he challenged everything she'd thought she'd known about Evan Loehr.

She frowned at a not-so-distant memory and at the unexpectedness of his words. "I walked away. More or less. You got hurt though, right?"

"Yeah. Just a flesh wound."

She swallowed and glanced at him then. She opened her mouth to speak but he shocked her when he lifted his hand, tracing his thumb over her bottom lip. A violent shiver wracked her body, stunning her with the force of her reaction to this man's touch.

"I'm sorry you were scared," he murmured. "But that's nothing to be ashamed of."

Right before he kissed her.

❦

IT WAS A GENTLE KISS. HESITANT AND SOFT AND unexpected. Her lips were parted the barest of fractions before his mouth even moved against hers. Her breath huffed against his mouth as he tasted her, an easy, light caress of lips. He nudged her top lip with his and she opened for him. His breath caught in his throat as his tongue flicked out, stroking hers, coaxing past the barrier of her teeth. Shields crumbled as he deepened the kiss, overcome by the honeyed taste of this woman. Of Claire.

Her body was soft where she brushed against him. He could have crushed her to him, but he didn't. Conscious of her earlier panic, he skimmed his hands up her arms to cradle her shoulders gently between his palms. When she shifted and sighed against him, when her fingers curled into his chest, only then did Evan dare slide one hand into the soft mass of her hair and angle her mouth so he could take all of her.

Need, raw and powerful, slammed into him, overpowering the cold control he'd maintained from years of practice. Nothing, not even the first time he'd kissed her, had ever struck him with such naked force. Need made him want to wrap her in his arms and drag her into the crisp, cool darkness.

Her gasp collided with his a moment before he traced the seam of her mouth with his tongue. Her skin was slick and hot beneath his touch, her mouth offering a warm, wet feast of texture and taste. He drank from her, taking everything she had to give. It was a gentle, unending battle for supremacy that neither of them could hope to win.

CLAIRE WAS NOT PREPARED FOR THE STRENGTH OF HER reaction to Evan's sensual assault. She raised her hands to block him, but instead her palms collided with the soft, warm cotton beneath his steel-grey jacket. She almost smiled, but that would have required that she do something other than hold on for dear life.

She didn't want this. Not with him. Not with anyone. Sooner or later, everyone let her down. Years at war had only reinforced the lessons she'd learned far too young. But with Evan, every stolen look dragged her closer to the edge of the abyss. And kissing him was a dangerous gamble, threatening far more than casual, mindless sex.

Because what Evan offered was the promise of something so rare, so fleeting, she was certain that the moment she allowed herself to crave it, he would vanish. Or worse, let her down.

Right now, none of those things mattered as she lost herself in Evan's taste. Her palms ached to touch his bare skin, to feel the raw power of his body beneath her touch.

This was a bad idea. A disaster.

And Claire no longer cared.

EVAN WAS LOST IN HER. HER TONGUE DANCED WITH HIS, smooth strokes that mimicked the movement he craved with her body. His hunger built until he was aching and hard, desire lashing inside him like a war drum. Touching her, molding her feminine strength with his palms, was by far the stupidest thing he'd done in a long, long time. The temptation to strip bare her defenses along with her body demanded relief. He had no ability to resist this woman. She was a rare, fierce creature, one that yielded beneath the onslaught of his mouth even as she held her own against his desire.

What had begun as a reaction to something powerful was now sweet torment, a relentless downpour of ragged desire that branded them both. Arousal ripped through him, a pure, unadulterated lust. Where this woman was concerned, there was no restraint. No half measures.

For the life of him, he couldn't figure out what it was about this woman that drove him to distraction. But as he pressed against her, he wished with everything he was that they were alone and naked where he could do this right.

He cradled her cheek in his palm as he eased back, nibbling on her bottom lip. He didn't want to give up the taste of her but he wasn't an idiot. Even if he managed to get her to bed tonight, they had to work together for the next few weeks. Kissing her might be the sweetest mistake, but taking her to bed would be worse. It would ruin the only chance Evan had ever had at getting to know this fierce, vibrant woman who hid so much vulnerability behind a warrior's façade.

And he wasn't willing to give that up.

❦

CLAIRE STOOD IN THE WARMTH OF EVAN'S EMBRACE, unwilling and unable to pull away. "Who are you and what have you done with Captain America?" she whispered.

"I'm not Captain America." An awkward, familiar hush settled over them like a shroud. She smiled.

"Thank you," she said quietly, holding his gaze. "For helping me look after Reza tonight."

"Did he really pass out while he was walking?"

Claire swallowed and eased a little more space between them. "He tripped."

The lingering warmth between them cooled a little bit more.

"Why are you making excuses for him? He's so drunk he couldn't even keep himself upright."

"He had a few too many tonight. So what? It happens." A harsh memory rose inside her, squeezing her heart and pressing against her lungs. She'd had this argument before, when she was too young to fight her way out of it. "Besides, I'm fine. Nothing wounded but my pride."

Even pushed out an exasperated sigh. "You've got to be kidding me. You're really defending him?"

"I'd take a bullet for that man," she said, pulling clear of his personal space, the silence between them a familiar cold. "Putting him to bed after he had a few too many drinks is nothing."

"Wow, that's a hell of a lot of loyalty you've got going on there, Claire."

She bristled at his tone. "What is that supposed to mean?"

"It means you're an officer. You're not supposed to be that close to an enlisted soldier. Your relationship crosses a lot of barriers."

"Don't you dare." Her voice was hushed. "Don't you dare stand there and tell me that to be an officer, I have to turn my back on someone who has been family to me since the day I joined the army. You might be a shiny army brass, but you don't know jack shit about loyalty." She never raised her voice. She simply turned and walked away and left him standing in the hallway, refusing to be judged by him for a moment longer.

$\maltese$ 4 $\maltese$

The next morning, Claire woke up with the sheets twisted and soaked around her body, her blood slamming through her veins in the aftermath of a powerful fantasy featuring her own personal superhero. Her own body was betraying her over Captain America. Damn it. She didn't need someone like Evan distracting her.

Dawn was still at least two hours away but Claire knew she wouldn't get back to sleep, so she headed down to the gym to work off some serious sexual frustration.

One the padded mats normally used for combatives, the army's version of mixed martial arts, she raised her arms over her head, focusing on the feel of the warm material beneath her feet. She let her concentration glide through the ether, attempting to release the tension in her shoulders as the noise from the other rooms in the gym echoed against the edge of her skull. Nothing drowned out the incessant ache between her thighs that had tormented her since last night.

Physical activity normally left in its wake a sort of calming buzz, but this morning she was anything but calm and centered after her workout. A mix of endorphins and spent energy pulsed through her veins, slamming through her and keeping her edgy. She shivered violently, as arousal and vulnerability mixed in her blood.

What was it Gunny Highway always said in the movie Heartbreak Ridge? Improvise, adapt and overcome?

Yeah, Claire was an expert at improvising new and exciting ways out of complicated relationships. Especially when it came to avoiding intimacy in her life. And Evan had only complicated things more when he'd kissed her.

She'd kissed Evan Loehr. Again. The army's poster child for the perfect soldier. He was all-American West Point while she was a working-class mustang, an officer who'd come up through the ranks. Evan judged her for cherishing the first real friend she'd made, not just in the army but in life, more than the rank on her chest. A man like Evan didn't kiss a woman like her.

And yet, he'd been the one to cross the boundaries between them. He'd been the one who leaned in and brushed his lips against hers, who'd kissed her like his life depended on it. And she'd been all for it. Her hormones had stood up and taken notice and practically shouted hooray for penis.

Good thing her brain had veto power over her hormones. As a former enlisted officer and a soldier herself, she'd never fit into Evan Loehr's polished world of chic officer's wives and monthly teas with the ladies. So why the hell had she crossed that line and tasted the luxurious sin of forbidden fruit? The first time she'd kissed him, she'd been trying to win a bet with herself, wondering whether he'd really stay stiff and rigid or relax. Now? Now she'd crossed the line into stupid. Was she just into self-torture? Was that it? She reached her arms over her head again, hoping to banish the chaos churning in her belly.

Who was she kidding? She'd kissed him back, the sharp bite of human contact a potent compulsion. She could not remember a time when a man's kiss had rocked her world so completely. No wonder she'd woken up aroused and frustrated this morning. Her body ached. And it wasn't just yearning for some random male.

No. She wanted Evan. And that simply was not allowed to happen. He'd gone too far. They both had.

She couldn't sleep with Evan. Even if they weren't on the same team, she couldn't face that kind of scrutiny. The idea that the soldiers around her would see her as a woman first and a soldier second burned in her belly. She always, always chose the mission first.

She fell to her knees and slammed her palm against the mat, still unable to concentrate. She lowered her head onto her forearms, giving up on the tai chi and transitioning to yoga as she moved into child's pose, seeking an elusive quiet inside her.

She'd made a mistake last night—and while she couldn't erase it, she could certainly learn from it. She had to push away the memory of his touch and focus on work. She'd been doing it for years, ignoring the aching loneliness that sometimes crept up on her. She'd settled for being one of the guys, on trying to be a good soldier, ignoring the emptiness of her life.

A poignant regret slipped in and took hold, whispering that she was walking away from something good. Something powerful and seductive. There was more to Evan than she'd ever imagined. Still, she shoved away the memory of Evan's taste and touch and focused her energy on the one thing that mattered: getting Sarah and her team ready to deploy.

There was no time for self-pity.

She was a soldier, damn it. And that meant lacing up her boots and accomplishing the mission. Because that's what good soldiers did.

Her lips were parted just a hint. A whisper of space, teasing him with thoughts of that warm, wet mouth. A mouth that for once wasn't cursing or ripping someone's head off.

A mouth that Evan was finally able to admit fascinated him.

Arousal spiked through his veins and whipped his blood to a frenzy as he spanned the distance between them and pressed his lips to hers. Claire's taste encircled him, ensnared him and urged him deeper.

She did not simply open her mouth and let him kiss her. Not Claire. Never Claire. They sparred, their tongues twisting and twining and sliding against each other in a battle for more than victory.

Claire rubbed her hips against his and he felt himself stepping backwards. "Take your pants off," she said, her voice husky.

He threaded one hand in her braided hair and kissed her, hard and fierce. "I feel so cheap. You won't even offer to cuddle afterwards?" Where the hell had that come from? It was a playfulness that Evan had not allowed himself in . . . years. And then she slid down the length of his body, her nails scraping against his sides and . . . digging into his forearms until they drew blood.

The screech of tires against asphalt ripped through the darkness. The stench of burning oil seared his nose. He tried to open his eyes. Casey. Where was she? Where was his sister?

Evan bolted awake, arousal wrestling with absolute grief. Grief won, crushing the lingering power of the dream beneath its heel, leaving only a sad emptiness inside him. He sat up, breathing deeply until his heart rate slowed and his mind no longer sped along that dark curving road.

He glanced at the phone on the bed stand. He couldn't remember the last time he'd called his parents. Months? Had it been since before he'd deployed? The phone calls never lasted long and he always ended up filled with more regret and bitterness.

It was easier not to call.

He pushed himself out of bed before the familiar melancholy dragged him under. He'd learned a long time ago that wallowing only produced more wallowing, so he pulled on workout clothes and headed downstairs to the gym, offering a silent thank-you prayer to the budget people who'd screwed up and sent them to the lodge instead of the barracks on main post Fort Carson.

He should have gotten some coffee before he'd headed to the gym, but it was too late now. He glanced inside the racquetball courts as he walked past, then stopped and backed up. The nightmare, the grief and the aching loneliness fell away as he stood and watched Claire writhe and twist in a graceful dance of hands and feet.

She moved in a way that was elegant and confident and sharply arousing. There was no hint of the trembling fear he'd seen last night. No trace of the wounded woman who'd leaned against him as she'd reined her panic back under control.

He lost himself in the mesmerizing dance of her body with the air, remembering with poignant clarity the way that body had molded to his. Funny, he'd never thought of her as controlled before but watching her now, knowing the panic that lay dormant within her, he realized she had much more control than he'd ever given her credit for. Her body was fluid, her arms and legs stretching and twisting in a graceful dance. It was such a far cry from how he was used to seeing her, he almost doubted what he saw. Her brow furrowed as she twisted into a new pose, as though she were battling demons only she could see.

Except that now he'd caught a glimpse of those demons.

Her trim, athletic frame belied the strength she kept concealed beneath uniforms that were too big. He wondered if she knew how much the physical fitness uniform T-shirt she wore accented the swell of her breasts.

Claire opened her eyes. One moment she was moving, fluid and graceful. The next, she'd frozen, her eyes colliding with Evan's in the mirror. Arousal slammed into him hard and fierce as she shifted and slouched, in effect shielding herself from his gaze. In that instant, he realized that she hid herself on purpose.

She'd put away anything that was soft and feminine and oh so vulnerable when they'd been downrange, and she was doing the same thing here at Fort Carson.

Claire Montoya was afraid to face the world without the rank on her chest.

He didn't move for a long moment as he wrestled with the fractured emotions raging out of his tight control. Claire had always known which buttons to push with him—the perfect ways to drive him crazy with frustration. Now? Now there was more between them. Something they shared beyond the scars they both carried from combat.

He cleared his throat roughly, trying to push past the block of thick arousal gripping him. When he finally spoke, he chose the most innocuous words possible.

"Good morning."

❧

"Good morning," Claire said, her light words belying the powerful crush of energy that had pulsed through her veins the moment he stepped into the room. His cheeks cut sharply against the shadows beneath his dark, dark eyes.

He hadn't slept well and she wondered why. She couldn't see the almighty Evan Loehr succumbing to nightmares. That would be too common of him. But she wondered if he dreamed. And in those dreams, did he let himself go or did he retain the tight control she saw now, pulsing through his clenched jaw and the tight muscles in his neck?

The hard contours of his chest stood out in stark relief against the grey cotton T-shirt. She smiled faintly. He wore his dog tags even in civilian clothes to work out. Always a soldier.

She pulled her rampant thoughts roughly in line, then dug her nails into her palms to keep herself grounded in the moment. A deep, primitive hunger clawed at her and made her want what she could not have. "So, ah, about last night . . ." Claire really didn't have the words to put what she needed to say into anything resembling coherent conversation. Too bad her brain was somewhere between her thighs at the moment.

He said nothing for the longest moment. Then he exhaled sharply. "There's a storm coming in tomorrow."

That was it? A kiss that rocked her entire way of looking at Evan Loehr and he wanted to talk about a snowstorm. Wow, how was that for a confidence boost? She narrowed her eyes. He wanted to avoid the subject. Fine. She damn sure wasn't about to beg him to talk about it.

"I just got off the phone with the brigade ops officer. Colonel Danvers is talking about cancelling training because of the snowstorm."

Claire swore beneath her breath, pissed about Evan's brush-off and fully irritated at the thought of the snowstorm interrupting the training timeline. "Damn it, first we waste half a day with that stupid bonfire. Now a storm? Are we ever going to get any training done?"

"If the roads are too dangerous, they need to shut them down. Otherwise, people do stupid things like try to drive on them." He shrugged and a shadow crossed his face, a hint of old memories. Something in his eyes pulled at her and she stomped it down, uncomfortable with the direction of her thoughts. This. This was why she didn't fool around with people she worked with.

"Yeah, well, there's such a thing as being too risk averse. We're not getting anything done."

"I can't believe you're complaining about this," he snapped. "You can't control the weather, Claire."

Her mouth worked but nothing came out for a long moment. This was an old, familiar path between them. The tension of that awkward-as-hell kiss was gone, melted into the floor like a pool of melted snow. "Really? Well, on the bright side, if they close the post, maybe they'll cut out a day of death by PowerPoint and we can get out to the range and start blowing things up instead of just *talking* about blowing things up."

Anger flashed across Evan's face. "You honestly think they're going to cancel the briefings? If anything, they'll tack on extra hours to each day to fit them in."

"Heaven forbid we don't teach a lieutenant how to brief." Claire let the irritation rip, glad for the cover it offered from the lingering distraction of his kiss. She didn't want to remember the feel of his lips moving over hers or the thread of his fingers through her hair. She felt needy. Claire hated feeling needy. "You could recommend it," she said suddenly.

"Recommend what, exactly?"

"Recommend to Colonel Danvers that he change the focus to ranges and weapons training instead of insisting on all these stupid meetings." A faint wisp of hope uncurled in the vicinity of her chest.

Evan shook his head. "Do you have any idea what it's like with some of these guys? I'm a captain. Captains don't recommend that a full bird colonel change his training plan just because someone on my team thinks it's stupid."

"What part of combat operations leads you to think that a PowerPoint slide on the proper storage of gasoline in Iraq is important? What war have you been fighting? Because the one I've gone to? The check-the-block stuff isn't what saves lives. We need warriors teaching these kids how to survive."

"Warriors like Iaconelli?"

"Yes, warriors like Reza," Claire snapped. "Don't start again."

"He's got a big problem if last night's bender was anything close to routine for him."

"So what are you going to do, Evan? Call up our brigade commander and tell Colonel Richter the Wonder Twins are screwing up again? 'Cause that's what you want to do, right? Just like with the range fire?"

"You burned down fifteen acres of Fort Hood," he said, his words harsh. "It's not like I could hide that little fact from the boss."

She smiled thinly. "You're right, Evan. There was always only one option, right? Notify the commander. Not let Reza and me get things under control first. Make sure you brief that shit went to hell in a handbasket and we were the ones carrying it." She sniffed and pulled on her sneakers. "You'd never guess that Reza used to work for you. You wouldn't piss on him if he was on fire if it wasn't in accordance with the regulations."

"Claire, you're being unreasonable."

"No, Evan, I'm being completely reasonable. Because you've never once broken the rules in your entire life. I shouldn't expect you to start now."

AN HOUR LATER, EVAN WALKED OUT OF THE GYM, NEARLY

plowing into Iaconelli. Irritation reached up and grabbed him by the throat. "Surprised to see you upright."

"Nice to see you, too, Sir." Iaconelli straightened and held Evan's gaze for a long time. "Is there something you need to say?"

Evan opened his mouth, then snapped it shut. To hell with it. "Yeah, there is. You acted like an ass last night. You ever feel like trying to be a little more responsible? You damn near crushed Claire when you fell on her."

A dark emotion flickered across Iaconelli's face, the muscles in his jaw pulsed, hostility abruptly replaced with deep concern. "Did I hurt her?"

"You honestly don't remember?"

"It's . . . fuzzy." Iaconelli swallowed hard. "She okay?"

"You've got a funny way of showing you care about someone," Evan said, watching the big man's reaction with keen interest. He couldn't ask about their relationship. Couldn't face the possibility that there was more than just loyalty and friendship between Claire and Iaconelli. Not after he'd kissed her last night. Not without revealing the true depth of the complicated feelings he had for her. Just admitting that there were feelings at all was a major step for him.

"It's not like that." Iaconelli shifted his gym bag over his other shoulder. "Sir, that would be like fucking my little sister. If I had one. Which I don't."

For some reason, the thought of Claire having Reza looking out for her calmed the sharp bite of emotion swiping at his insides. Little sisters needed watching over. That's why they were issued big brothers. Or at least it should be. "Why's that?"

"Why's what?"

"Why would it be like fucking your fictional sister?"

Iaconelli scowled, finally noticing the edge in Evan's voice. "I've known Claire for years. We served together when she was enlisted and again after she was a lieutenant in my brigade combat team on the initial invasion of Iraq."

It was Evan's turn to frown. He hadn't known she'd been on the initial invasion. In the year following the September 11th attacks, the march to war with Iraq had been steady and constant, starting almost before the dust had settled in Afghanistan. When the war had started violently with the Shock and Awe bombing campaign, everyone had thought it would be over before it started.

But all of that changed when the U.S. troops got to Baghdad.

The Thunder Run had been engraved in army legend. A single army division—hell it had really been one army brigade —had started and finished the fight against Saddam's elite Republican Guard forces before the rest of the invasion force had even caught up with them. There were few if any modern parallels on the battlefield. Evan had watched the war unfold on the television monitors in the hallways of Armor Captains Career Course, anticipation mixing with a potent dose of adrenaline that combat was no longer talked to death in PowerPoint classes.

The slice-and-dice operation through the center of Baghdad had been violent, and it had ended any rumors that the Iraqi Army wasn't going to resist the U.S. invasion.

And Claire had been a part of that violent battle. So had Sarn't Ike.

Evan looked at his former platoon sergeant with renewed respect. "Third Infantry Division?" The Third ID had pushed north, cutting through Iraq's defenses like there was nothing there at all.

"Yeah." Reza shifted his gym bag as they walked down the sterile hallway toward the locker room. "We lovingly refer to it as the You're Fucking Kidding mission."

"Why's that?" Evan glanced inside the racquetball court

where he'd spoken with Claire earlier. It was empty now. A vague and unexplainable disappointment settled in his stomach.

"Because that's exactly what my battalion commander told his brigade commander when he was briefed on the plan. The Thunder Run was nuts, sir, totally nuts. We outran our supply lines." Reza hooked his thumbs into the strap of his bag. "Claire took charge of the logistics resupply convoy trying to get us ammo and water."

"You really ran out?"

Reza scowled. "Don't look at me like I rolled out without my full load. We got pinned down and damn near used everything we had to keep ourselves alive. Got a piece of shrapnel in the ass to show for it, too."

Evan pictured Claire running hell-bent for leather through the center of Baghdad, swearing the whole way. A fierce Valkyrie, leading her soldiers to victory. A twisted, grudging respect formed in his belly. She'd make a fierce opponent on the battlefield. Unpredictable and unrestrained.

Reza swiped his palm across his forehead. "By the way, if the briefing is delayed, I'm heading over to The Greasy Tube."

Evan didn't laugh. "And what the hell is The Greasy Tube?"

"A bar. I've got a potential date tonight."

"Did the last five minutes of conversation actually happen? You need to cool it on the drinking and the catting around, Ike."

Reza started to argue but instead shut his mouth, grinding out a harsh "Roger. Sir," before he stalked off, irritation lining the hard set of his shoulders.

Evan let him go, distracted by thoughts of Claire, her body moving as she attempted to ease her mind. There was a new tension between them, and it had nothing to do with their different approaches to being an officer. No matter how much he might want to pretend otherwise, he wanted to taste her again. Wanted to touch the fire that was Claire Montoya.

He wanted her. He could at least admit that to himself now.

He just had no idea what to do about it.

⁂

THE SUN HAD NOT SET. NO, IT WAS TOO COLD FOR THAT. Instead it froze behind the cold, grey clouds, sending the world into darkness. Claire threw her battle book onto the table and stripped off her wet uniform and boots. She'd spent the entire day freezing her ass off in the snow, trying to inspect a company that didn't even know the meaning of the word inspection. She pulled on a dry sweater and jeans along with her boots and stepped out onto the balcony, needing the cold air to calm the burning anger in her lungs. Sarah had been embarrassed that Claire had seen her unit so jacked up, but that wasn't the worst of it.

No, Lieutenant Engle had decided to take a particularly bad moment to argue with Claire. She'd made a dozen excuses why they weren't ready to deploy and she'd actually had the gall to raise her voice. Claire had locked her heels, putting Engle at the position of attention, and had proceeded to go up one side of her and down the other. Claire might have received quite a few ass-chewings in her day but she also knew how to give them, and Engle had struck a nerve. Not because the inspection had gone so poorly, but for whining about it instead of pulling herself up by her bootstraps and fixing it.

Engle was an officer, damn it. Officers were not supposed to make excuses. They were supposed to get results.

The sky was gunmetal grey, casting shadows across the

suite.

The overcast sky reflected Claire's mood, and she stood for a long moment and just watched the snow fall. Tugging the sleeves of her light-blue ski sweater down, she leaned against the railing. The cold wrapped around her, penetrating her layers of clothing, and she shivered even as she took a deep, cleansing breath of crisp, biting air.

Everything about this mission was a disaster. Colonel Danvers, the brigade commander here at Fort Carson, was focused on the wrong things. He wanted his lieutenants to learn how to brief, how to do inspections, instead of training for combat. Not only that, but the inspections had not even gone well. The officers here might be able to brief well, but Claire doubted they could lead their way out of a paper bag. Not a single weapon had been touched yet. Not one piece of ammo fired. Their commander back at Fort Hood, Colonel Richter would never have focused on checking the block. No, he was a warrior, focused on training. Real training. The kind that saved lives.

At least she didn't have to worry about burning down Fort Carson. No, that thought wasn't sarcastic. Not at all.

The thought did nothing to cheer her up. Idly, she piled some snow into a small mountain on the rail, then started forming it into a snowball, needing to do something with her hands as her mind tumbled over the problems with the evaluation.

It was killing her that one of her only friends was going into combat unprepared, untrained. And there was nothing she could do about it.

From the information she had, the brigade commander wanted to go into all of the exercises, from the shoot house to the mock-up of the city, without any ammo at all. He wanted the noise and the chaos more than he wanted people to actually get shot at with dummy rounds. And instead of tailoring each evaluation for the mission each company was doing, he was making everyone do everything.

So while Sarah's company would spend the bulk of their time running convoys in Iraq, they were going to waste their precious training time doing shoot houses and inspections, instead of doing convoys with simunitions and pyro, which was probably the best way to get soldiers prepped for actual combat.

It was a waste of precious training time. Troops had a hell of a lot less bravery when there were actual rounds shooting at them from the end of a weapon instead of someone shouting bang-bang-bang.

She chafed under the restrictions. They limited the value of training and made it harder to recreate the realism of actual combat. The more realistic it was, the better prepared the soldiers would be. She set the first snowball down and started forming another one, ignoring the biting cold in her hands.

Lost in thought, she didn't hear Evan's door open on the balcony next door. Or the incoming projectile, until it landed with a splat against the side of her neck. Frigid snow slipped down the neck of her sweater and she shrieked, swatting at the cold wet stuff. She looked in the direction the missile had come from and glared as Evan melted from the shadows on the deck outside his own room.

"Not funny," she said, rubbing the cold from her neck.

"Yeah, actually it was." His laugh was warm and unfamiliar. Claire paused, unable to remember the last time she'd heard him laugh. It sounded foreign and reserved, but it was a laugh nonetheless. Something warm unfurled inside her at the sound, and she watched him walk across the snow-covered balcony to the barrier that separated their two rooms. Snow dusted the top of his head and he brushed it off.

"I take it you're not mad at me anymore?" she asked him,

brushing the snow from her neck.

"I'm too cold to be pissed at anyone. I just want to be warm," he said, leaning on the rail in a move that dredged up old memories of the first time she'd met him. "What has you so distracted?"

"The entire day was wasted. They need at least a week to unscrew the inspections. It's ridiculous that they're trying to run an entire operation like this." Her voice broke and she looked away as the fear finally slid through the cracks in her control. "They're not ready for this. Sarah's company . . . their lack of training scares me."

"Are we ever really ready for stuff like this?" His voice was steady and low, but not warm enough to chase the creeping cold away. She shivered, and his gaze slid down her body. The gesture alone was enough to send heat running through her veins. "We should go inside," he said. "I prefer to have my training doctrine conversations when I'm not freezing my balls off."

"Have you been drinking?" She narrowed her eyes, studying him, looking for signs of imbibing.

"No, why?"

"Because you just made a joke." She slid the door to her suite open. "I'm going to make some coffee. Do you want any?" She didn't trust this unspoken truce between them, but she was too cold and too tired to argue with it. Or him, for that matter.

"Yeah. I'll be over in a sec."

He wasn't lying. He climbed over the rail, and Claire took a step back to give him space. "Seriously? Climbing over railings and snowball fights? Who are you and what have you done with Captain America?"

Lines of fatigue attempted to pass for a smile. His day had not gone well, either. "You've always said I needed to relax. Guess I'm taking your advice to heart."

"Since when?"

"Since now," he said roughly, and she caught the dark edge of strain in his voice.

"Being home is really doing a number on you," she murmured, opening the door and leading him through.

"Doesn't going home throw you off balance?" he asked. The door closed behind him with a muffled click, shutting out the cold. But the warmth in the room wasn't nearly enough to chase away the chill that had penetrated down to her very bones.

"Yeah, well that would imply that I had a home to go back to. Home is where the army sends me." She dug into the small fridge for a bottle of water, avoiding the scrutiny of his gaze.

"Really? No family?"

Setting the bottle down, she started making the coffee. "Not really. The army is the only thing I've got going for me."

Evan's eyes were warm and speculative as he studied her for a long, silent moment, and she tried not to flinch beneath his scrutiny. "Kind of makes it a bigger deal when your career is on the line, doesn't it?"

She swallowed the lingering resentment that he'd played a role in that. In truth, she only had herself to blame. "Yeah." She took a long pull from the water bottle, then finished dumping the grounds into the filter. "I'll manage, though."

"You always do. So what's got you so worked up that you're not sleeping?"

She frowned. "How do you know I'm not sleeping?"

"Your lights reflect on the snow when you turn them on," he said softly. He came around the large table that sat in the center of the living area, leaning on it. He was entirely too close. Close enough that she could feel the heat radiating off his body.

She took a step back, uncomfortable with the warmth his

nearness sparked. It felt too much like need, too much like a want that went beyond pure sexual attraction. Lust she could do. Need?

Need was not something she could control.

"Yeah, well, that only means you're not sleeping either."

"I don't. Much. Maybe four, five hours at a stretch."

"That's a whole lot of free time. What do you do with it?" Oh, but she didn't want to know. Knowing what he did with his downtime made him less cold and calculating and significantly more human. More appealing. More desirable.

"This and that. Makes it easy to get work done when you don't have to sleep." He watched her move, and Claire felt the weight of his scrutiny. "You're really upset."

Claire finally stopped, clenching her hands on the counter in front of her. "Yeah. Sarah's my friend. And it's killing me that her team isn't trained. I mean, none of us are ever ready to go, but . . . this feels worse than normal."

"They're still going. Nothing we do here is going to change that," he said quietly.

Claire ground her teeth. "Colonel Danvers is taking a brigade downrange to the middle of the nastiest fight in Baghdad and he's training all of his people the same instead of giving them the flexibility to train for their actual mission."

"He's the commander. Just because it may or may not be stupid doesn't mean we get to disobey." He stiffened, and the easy, relaxed Evan instantly shifted into work mode. "Claire, you don't know this guy. Changing the training plan is admitting he's a shitty commander to his boss. He won't do it."

She set the water bottle down. "They need to be more prepared. The fight is entirely different now."

"And we're not going to be able to get them a full-blown Training Center rotation here. We've got all the time we're going to get."

"That's your answer? Follow the rules? Evan, these guys

have such limited experience. The only people who've deployed with them are, God help me for saying this, folks like Engle."

Evan pushed away from the table. "Commanders look at timelines. We've crossed the red line. There is. No. More. Time."

"Did they teach you that at West Point?" He flinched, and she felt almost guilty for swiping at him about his pedigreed background. Almost, but not quite. "Commanders are supposed to set priorities. Not everything can be a priority. We could skip the briefings and the endless meetings, redo the inspections, then go to the weapons ranges. Tailor the training for the mission they're going to do. They're going to war, Evan."

Finally his temper snapped and his voice rose. Just a hair, but it was enough for his frustration to seep through. "That's right, they're going to war. Whether or not we change the timeline, or train for twenty-four hours a day or cancel Christmas, they're going to war. So we'll do what we can with what we have. Nothing we do or don't do is going to change that."

Claire lifted her chin, folding her arms over her chest. She said nothing for a long moment. Then she murmured, "I think you should go now."

"What, you're not going to argue with me?"

She smiled thinly. "You're the officer in charge. I'm just a lowly training officer."

"Claire . . ."

"No, Evan. Don't. You made your point."

He said nothing, letting the silence hang between them. A silence that felt normal in its frigid chill. Unwelcome, but at least it was familiar.

Evan shut the door quietly behind him. And Claire? Claire cursed the officer corps that was failing her.

❦ 5 ❦

The snow gods hated her. The white stuff was falling slow and steady, and it had taken every effort by the brigade staff to get Colonel Danvers not to cancel the briefings. The next day, Claire stood in the Pale-horse Brigade headquarters, getting ready to watch a bunch of lieutenants get their collective asses handed to them, because they were toast if their mission briefings went anything like their inspections. They were supposed to brief their understanding of the plan to their brigade commander in order to demonstrate that they actually understood the plan. There was not enough caffeine to get her through this morning.

The army spent too much time training its officers how to give presentations and use PowerPoint and not enough time with them in the trenches, learning how to lead their soldiers. Taking a bunch of lieutenants and training them on how to brief their mission instead of training them to lead said mission was a colossal waste of time.

But she was not in charge, and Evan had effectively told

her to shut up and color. All she really needed to ask was what hue of crayon she was supposed to use.

The Palehorse Brigade headquarters was obviously a new building. Or at least a recently renovated building. While the floor of the brigade headquarters back at Fort Hood was caked with fifty years of wax buffed to a greasy-looking shine, the Palehorse floor was buffed to a mirror-gloss shine. Even though the headquarters were temporary, the Palehorse staff had certainly taken over their battle space and made it their own. Claire wondered briefly if renovations had recently been done or if there were just a whole lot of sergeants major who had individuals in need of corrective training.

She suspected it was a little bit of both. Then again, some command sergeants major were known for their ability to make floors shine through sheer meanness. Claire had learned long ago that someone who was shiny and polished probably lacked substance. She suspected the same about the brigade to which Sarah now belonged.

"Nice place," Reza mumbled next to Claire as he followed her into the conference room already filled with lieutenants colonel and sergeants major along with far too many captains and junior lieutenants. Claire sighed, releasing frustration and irritation in that single breath, then glanced at her longtime friend. At that moment, looking at his lined, weather-worn face and tired eyes, Claire felt far older than her thirty-two years. Reza was a warrior but his time at war was wearing on him, carving dark lines into his soul.

Shaking off the errant thoughts, she gravitated toward the coffeepot. It was a thing of beauty. A stainless-steel monument to caffeinated goodness. A double-decker machine where one carafe could warm on the top while a second pot brewed. Endless coffee.

"I might have to ask this coffeepot to have my children," Claire said, topping off her mug, trying to lighten the nervous tension twisting in her guts. She breathed deeply and let the aroma of coffee soothe her ragged nerves.

Reza glanced at her as though she'd lost her mind. "That's sick and wrong on so many levels."

"If loving coffee is wrong, I don't want to be right." Claire laughed quietly at Reza's disgruntled expression. Claire smiled and pointed at his Rip It energy drink. "How did you get a Rip It in the middle of Colorado?"

"Amazon.com. Turns out, UPS will deliver in a snowstorm. On snowmobiles." He took a long pull. "And don't be jealous. My superpower is an indestructible liver."

"Yeah, well, I'm just amazed you never smell like you just crawled out of a bottle," she mumbled.

He flashed a quick grin. "I eat a lot of pineapple," he said with a shrug.

"Pineapple?"

"Yep. Makes, ah, other stuff taste better, too."

Claire rolled her eyes and wished he weren't making her laugh about something so serious. "Have you had many compliments?"

"No complaints. Does that count?"

"Ugh, okay, I'm officially sorry I asked," she said, giving in to the urge and laughing. "Really, Iaconelli? We really just had this conversation?"

He shifted then, and tucked his hands into his back pockets. She couldn't see herself relaxing like this with Evan. Granted, she didn't want to sleep with Reza, and that always helped. There was also the small matter of trust.

The conference room door opened and several of the company commanders walked in. Sarah offered a quick nod of greeting in Claire's direction but said nothing. A gaggle of the day's sacrificial offering—a.k.a. platoon leaders—gathered to one side. They looked so . . . young.

Claire scanned the crowd for Evan, still worrying silently

about Reza. He'd sobered the moment they'd entered the conference room. Despite the jokes, his smile was tight, the lines on his face tense. She let it go for now, but when Reza was being quiet it meant one of two things: either he was hung over or he was plotting.

Claire glanced at her watch, wondering what was taking so long. Shifting her stance, she held her coffee cup like it contained liquid gold. "You've worked with Colonel Danvers before, right?" she asked, eyeing the coffeepot and wondering if she had enough time to refill before the commander walked in. She doubted it.

Reza nodded. "Yeah. He's well known in the combat arms world."

A dark edge in his voice made Claire stand up and take notice. "Any pointers?"

"Don't interrupt him," Reza said, swirling the drink in his hand. "Don't even move your lips like you're about to, or you'll see the devil."

Claire smirked. "Seriously? You're acting like we're briefing the President."

"The President is easier to brief. If you're a fan of public floggings, interrupt him. I'll pick your corpse up off the floor when the smoke clears."

The conversation ground to a screeching halt and everyone stood or straightened to attention when the brigade commander walked into the room, Evan close on his heels. Claire was instantly on guard. Evan's eyes glittered coldly in the sterile conference room. Why had he been with Danvers?

Colonel Danvers was a sour-faced man who looked like he spent more time bench-pressing Fiats than commanding the brigade. He had a reputation as a pit bull and the tense, harsh lines around his mouth were a dead giveaway that he didn't spend much time smiling.

"Take your seats," he said, pulling his chair in behind him.

Evan sat parallel to him as the first sacrifice—Lieutenant Engle—moved to the podium. She looked confident and calm, which if her past performance was an indicator told Claire she had not done her homework in the slightest. Claire sipped her coffee. What else was new?

"What the hell is that?" Danvers demanded as the screen lit up.

"Sir, it's a recommended change to the training plan." Engle's voice wavered. Just a little, but enough for Danvers to sense weakness.

He rocked back in his chair, resting his hands on the top of his head. His cold gaze fell on Claire and she straightened her shoulders slightly. Why the hell was he looking at her? Colonel Danvers smiled thinly. "Exactly when would you like to rework this plan? The first round goes downrange tomorrow morning, Lieutenant." He shifted and gripped his coffee mug, studying her over the rim. Claire noticed the shining white stallion against the glossy black finish. She could have sworn the horse had devil eyes, but they didn't begin to measure up to Danvers' cold blue gaze.

"Sir, my platoon is going to be running logistics convoys through Baghdad. We should be focusing on convoy operations, using realistic pyro. The shoot house, while valuable, isn't what a bunch of supply clerks need to be training on." Engle spoke, clear and strong, hiding her nerves with sheer will and volume. Holy cow, she'd learned to brief. "Sir, I recommend we focus on a few critical tasks that directly relate to our mission instead of trying to do everything."

Colonel Danvers' jaw pulsed but he said nothing. Engle took that as a sign to continue, and Claire mentally flinched. Engle might have improved her briefing skills, but she damn sure hadn't learned to read body language yet.

"Sir, by focusing our efforts on convoy training, we'll be ahead of schedule and we'll allow valuable time in the shoot houses to go toward training troops that will actually be kicking in doors." She clicked to the next slide. "Sir, I've coordinated for pyrotechnic support from the contractors at division headquarters. They're prepared to meet the revised commander's intent . . ."

Colonel Danvers cut her off as soon as the word intent left her lips. "So you're telling me that you failed to train your people for all situations, Lieutenant?"

Engle's mouth opened, but Sarah interjected before she could insert her foot. "Sir, we've had less than three months to get a year's worth of training done. We're doing the best we can, but right now, we're trying to do everything instead of preparing for the most likely scenarios and the most dangerous scenarios."

A vein in the middle of Danvers' forehead visibly pulsed against his skin. "Captain Anders, I don't know what kind of operation you're used to at Fort Hood, but here at Fort Carson, we accomplish our mission. Either you're capable of commanding your company or I will find someone else who is."

Across the table, Claire saw Sarah's first sergeant give a quick shake of his head. Sarah would only make things worse by trying to save her lieutenant. Claire saw her grit her teeth, but she remained silent except for a harsh, "Roger, Sir."

Colonel Danvers scanned the room, pinning the now squirming officers with a hard look. "Who decided that changing the approved plan would be a good idea?"

Something cold and slick slithered over Claire's skin. She straightened and leaned forward. "Sir, I've recommended we tailor the training plan to several people but not to Lieutenant Engle." She kept her voice neutral and lifted her chin with a quick glance at Engle. "But I agree with her assessment."

Colonel Danvers looked up at her with a dispassionate

apathy that made her feel two inches tall. "And tell me, young captain, in your vast experience, what should I cut off the timeline? The inspections to make sure they have all of their proper equipment? Training on the laws of war? Or maybe weapons ranges? What in your esteemed opinion should I cut from the timeline?"

The question was rhetorical. These questions always were.

"I am not going to division to request additional pyrotechnics. I am not going to brief my division commander that we're going to throw out the plan that took three months of eighteen hour days to develop just because some captain," and he spat the word, "thinks she knows more about training soldiers for combat than I do." Colonel Danvers leaned forward in his chair, his hands gnarled from too much sun over too many years. He stood, jerking his cup off the table. Coffee splashed onto the polished glass. "I am not a patient man. If any of you deviate from the approved timeline of events to so much as take a shit out of order, I will crucify you. Do I make myself clear?"

Claire did her best to ignore the stone that had settled in her stomach. The officers around her murmured assent.

"We'll do these briefings again at nineteen hundred when you've all unscrewed yourselves and gotten back in line with the approved training guidelines." He glanced at his watch and stood abruptly. "You're dismissed."

EVAN STALKED DOWN THE HALL AND LIFTED HIS HAND, prepared to beat Claire's door off the hinges until she opened the damn thing. It could not be a coincidence that Engle had briefed the exact changes Claire had mentioned. But she ripped open the door before his fist had fallen once. Claire rocked back on the heels of her running shoes, her eyes filled with unspent fury.

"I'm not in the mood right now, Evan." She shoved past him, heading for the stairs. As she disappeared down the hall, he took in that she was prepared for a run. Just what he felt like doing, going for a jog through the woods in full army combat uniform, complete with boots. And of course, Claire made it look like she was up for a marathon, not a quick jog.

"Too bad." He tried to grab her arm to slow her down. "I need to talk to you."

The vinyl of her jacket slipped through his fingers as she yanked free. "What part of 'I'm not in the mood' don't you get?"

Stunned by her ferocity, he let her go, unable to reach her past the fury that radiated from her every movement. She slammed into the stairwell, heaving the door shut behind her.

He swore quietly, pissed that he wasn't dressed for running in the cold. But, hell, he'd gone through Ranger school and Airborne school running in boots. He took off after her, bolting down the same stairwell where she'd disappeared.

Afternoon had fallen and with it, light fluffy snowflakes drifted down, dusting the world in deceptively peaceful quiet. A snow machine rumbled somewhere in the distance. Evan caught a flash of white and blue as Claire disappeared down a snow-packed trail.

The frigid air seared his lungs, ripping the breath from his body. He followed her at a distance, hoping some of her fury would abate by the time he caught up to her.

She plunged headlong into a narrow copse of trees, their branches hanging heavy and pregnant with ice. If she heard him following her, she showed no sign of it. He heard nothing now but the huff of his own breath. The hair on the inside of his nose froze, his fingers following quickly. He might have grown up here, but his blood had thinned in the years since he'd left.

Finally she slowed, and he caught her before she rounded the next bend in the trail. "Damn it, Claire, will you stop?"

"Why, Evan? So you can tell me that you threw me under the bus today? What the hell did you tell Colonel Danvers before that brief?"

He grabbed her arm before when she tried to take off again. "I was trying to find out if he was even open to the suggestion of changing the plan. Then Engle got up there and ruined the whole thing. Did you put her up to it?"

She yanked away from him. "You think I tried to set her up for failure? I haven't even talked to her since we saw her in the hallway."

"You mean to tell me she came up with that all on her own?"

"Well, I damn sure didn't tell her to do it. And screw you for thinking I would." She squared her shoulders and lifted her chin. "I'm supposed to be obeying orders, remember?"

Evan stopped suddenly, caught off guard by the defeat that settled around her like a shroud, despite the defiance in her eyes. She thought he'd turned on her today. That he'd sold her out to the brigade commander. That she thought so little of him hurt, even if their track record was less than perfect. But it was the expectation that people would let her down—that he would let her down—that stung the most.

This was a woman who was used to being on her own. Used to being let down by the people she was supposed to count on. What had shaped her into this creature who distrusted the people around her? Whoever had let her down had done it so often and so hard, she didn't see him when she looked at him, she saw only the echoes of the people who'd failed her in the past.

"You're right, you are supposed to be obeying orders and

accomplishing the mission." He took a deep breath, knowing his next words were going to shatter any hope of a truce between them. "But this isn't about the mission, Claire," he said quietly. "This is about you. You want to do this mission your way. You've always got to win by any means possible. I don't. I have to do things the right way."

She balled her fists up at her sides, her mouth drawn into a tight, hard line. "Why, Evan? Why is the commander's way the only way with you?"

"Because this is the commander's mission. They're going downrange and as much as I wish it were otherwise, not everyone is coming back. There's no time to change things up this late in the game. If this is how the commander wants things, then that's what we do."

"That was very much an officer thing to say," she said quietly, an odd note in her voice.

"What does that even mean?"

"Never mind." She squared her jaw and straightened before she started walking past him. Maybe it was the sinking realization that she would never, ever open up to him. But something snapped and he grabbed her arm, yanking her to a halt.

"Let go."

"Talk to me, Claire." He released her but only to circle her, a predator. She lifted her chin, a beautiful defiance of his failed attempt at intimidation. A bolt of desire shot through him. She was edgy and nervous, but she refused to be cowed, and her defiance ignited a hard arousal deep in his blood.

"About what, Evan? You want to plan, I want to train, and therein lies the simple difference between us. Maybe it's the fact that you've been an officer your entire adult life and I spent a good chunk of time in the trenches as enlisted. No matter how long we argue about it, we don't see this problem the same way."

Evan took a step back, searching for a way out of the argument they were headed toward. He was so tired of fighting with her. "How can you be an officer and be that emotionally attached to everything you do?"

"Because at least I give a shit about what I do. I may be loud and I may speak my mind, but no one will ever say I don't care." She took a single step backwards, crossing her arms over her chest. "How can you call yourself a leader when you don't care about anything but doing what the commander wants? Those are people, not means to an end, Evan. You get the right people in the job and the rest will take care of itself."

"That's part of your problem, Claire. You might be good, but you're not good enough to succeed on talent alone. You're reckless. And you don't believe in the rules. But they exist for a reason." The cold moonlight shifted on the breeze, dancing over the frozen, snow-covered trail. Her eyes glittered in the pale luminescence as he skirted closer, his body skimming against hers. He did it on purpose. He wanted to see if she would stand and fight or keep running away when things got too rough. He wanted to push her past her comfort zone.

He wanted to get closer to the fire she kindled inside him.

HER LUNGS SUDDENLY REFUSED TO COOPERATE. BUT SHE held her ground, refusing to retreat. Refusing to expose the twisted, trembling weakness that hunted her, threatening to reveal just how useless she really was.

"Rules?" She forced the words over her tongue, forced her voice to relive a memory that tore at the fabric of who she was. "Rules get people killed. Rules leave people on the battlefield a few miles from help because they're not the main effort. Don't talk to me about the rules, Evan because the only thing you know about rules is that you never break them."

"You know what pisses me off about you, Claire?" He stepped closer, until his breath lingered against her skin, his mouth the barest span of distance from hers. "It bugs the ever-loving shit out of me that you truly think I don't care about anything but doing what the commander wants." The fierce anger in his eyes held her, pinned her to the spot. Panic slithered up her spine, cold and grasping. He was standing too close to her. "You're not the only one who cares about the people around you, Claire. But there are more important things than the army according to Claire." His words were a harsh caress against her jaw.

"This mission is about the people. You're not going to convince me otherwise." Her pulse jumped against her skin, a scattered staccato.

His smile was cold as steel and just as biting. It fit the man she knew. This was Captain America that stood before her. The ruthless training officer, relentless in his drive for perfect timelines. What the hell had she been thinking? They were too different, from two completely opposite worlds. No amount of desire could change the fact that they saw the world through opposite ends of the spectrum: she looking up at things she could never attain, he looking down on a world he never had to experience.

Evan's laugh was filled with frustration. Claire bristled and would have lashed out, but his expression stopped her.

He shook his head slowly, and then he lifted his hand, his fingers a breath from her cheek. "No matter how hard you try, you can't will their training to be a success."

Her breath caught in her throat as his fingers held, just above her skin. "I know that." Her words came out a harsh whisper, unconvinced.

They were alone in the woods. Silence pulsed around

them filled with a hundred unsaid things glittering on their frozen breath.

"What are you so afraid of?" he whispered.

Claire swallowed hard and tried to moisten her lips without licking them. "You have no idea what it's like to go to sleep at night, wondering if you could have done more if only people would have listened to you," she admitted.

"People listen to you, Claire."

"You don't." She swallowed and looked away, her words slapping at him like a cold, wet towel. "The only thing I'm good at is being a soldier, and it kills me to know that I can do more to help Sarah and her team but I can't because my hands are tied. Because a commander says no."

"That's not true." He studied her for a long moment and she lifted her chin, uncomfortable at the depth of his scrutiny. "You're more than just a soldier."

"You don't even know me, Evan," she said gently. "Being a soldier is the only thing I've ever been good at and no matter how hard I try, I'm always screwing things up." She breathed deeply, releasing her breath slowly. "None of this changes anything. Nothing we do matters."

"That's not true. You matter."

He had no idea when she'd made the transition from being a pain in the ass to someone he found himself following into the frozen night. Her green eyes were dark and wary, ringed with disappointment and a lingering hesitation. She turned and tried to head off down the trail again. A dark frustration lashed out in him, refusing to acquiesce to her desire to be alone. She'd been alone too much.

So had he.

"Damn it, stop walking away from me." He grabbed at her

arm and the sudden movement threw them both off balance. She stumbled and slipped, grasping at him to keep from plunging to the ground. Her sudden weight made him misjudge his step and his boot slipped on a patch of hard frozen snow. He stumbled backwards. Trying to keep her from crashing, he pulled her toward him and took the brunt of the fall on his back. Her weight and the bad angle knocked the frozen air from his lungs.

Panic clutched at his heart when his diaphragm refused to work. Clenching his arms around her when she tried to rise, he clung to her until he could breathe, taking a frozen hit of oxygen that had never felt so good.

It was only after he started breathing normally again that he realized that Claire had stopped fighting him.

Her eyes widened in a flash and her mouth opened, but no sound came out. She was close enough that in the low light, he could see the frost on her eyelashes, the strands of hair clinging to her cheek beneath the knit cap she was wearing.

Beneath the surface of her eyes, a dark and powerful emotion flashed briefly and was gone. A twisted torment that writhed in the depths of her soul.

And then she met his gaze and Evan was lost in her.

He'd meant for it to be a gentle kiss. A tentative request for forgiveness for not believing in her. For being one of the people who let her down. He gave over to it, straining to get closer to her despite everything that separated them. Right now, he didn't care where they were or who might find them.

He'd never thought that sex in the winter woods could be a good idea but at this precise moment, he wanted nothing more than to lay her down in the middle of the moonlit trail and strip away every barrier, every defense. He wanted to see her body gleaming in the moonlight, watch her shatter in his arms.

The thought of the moonlight painting her skin sent desire spiraling wide inside him and he dragged her against him. She rubbed against his erection and he almost lost his mind in a harsh wave of pleasure.

Arousal pounded through his body like the fire of an artillery battery, pulsing over his skin like a blast wave.

The utter loss of control terrified him, licking at the edge of a chaos he'd buried so long ago, it felt as if it belonged to another person. When she nipped his earlobe, tracing the sensitive skin with her tongue, he forgot everything except for this moment, this wild, unbound sensation.

A distant rumbling moved closer. Claire tensed, her breath gentle huffs against his skin. Evan eased back, pressing his lips against her jaw, wanting so much more but afraid to move and chase her away.

Because if there was one thing he'd learned about Claire Montoya, it was that she was a hell of a lot more skittish than he'd ever imagined. The overwhelming urge he had to protect her would only make her angry and drive her farther away.

And while the thought of her eyes flashing with anger turned him on, he wanted her desire, not her fury. It stunned him, how fiercely he wanted this woman. Wanted her in a way he hadn't allowed himself to want a woman in . . . ever.

He held her for another moment. Held on to something more powerful than the storm he saw still broiling in her eyes.

Another moment and he helped her to her feet.

And for once, she did not pull away.

❦ 6 ❧

They walked back to the lodge, the heat between them chilling the closer they got to warmth, to reality. They stepped into a puddle of artificial light from the overhead lights. Claire looked up at Evan, seeing him, the man, not the officer. "Did you really try to change Danvers' mind?"

"I was leading up to it," he admitted quietly.

It was such a simple declaration, but there was so much more running beneath it. Something Claire had never seen before: a crack in the cold steel façade of Captain America.

A slithering thing traced down her spine, a fierce whisper that she did not know this man at all. The man she thought she knew? She did not like that man. The polished army brass who was never faced with the choices that those at the bottom of the heap had to make every single day. But this man, standing before her? This man who admitted that he'd tried to help her change a commander's mind? This man was complicated and conflicted. He disagreed with her but he'd gone to Colonel Danvers to try and change his plan. It was an act of faith.

Of trust.

And it spoke of something new between them: a revelation and a declaration not of war but of dark and sensual promise.

Tempting her to break the one rule she'd relied upon since learning a brutal lesson about trusting the wrong people.

They walked in silence through the foyer and down the hallway, Claire's thoughts racing about the choice she was about to make. She wanted to turn away, to shield herself from the dark emotions he inspired in her but instead, she opened the door to her room, terrified of what she was about to do. He followed her in and the quiet sound of the door closing behind them might as well have been the clang of a vault.

She smiled as a warmth slid through her as they both stripped off their wet jackets. He stood a little too close, the heat from his body penetrating her workout clothing. She shivered and his eyes swept down her body, then back up to collide with hers. A hot bolt of desire sparked through her blood, chasing away the chill.

Evan moved in front of her, his chest skimming against hers. It was the expectation in his eyes that destroyed the last of her barriers. "What is this, Claire? Between us?"

"A mistake?" she said honestly, looking up into his eyes. "I don't know." She pressed her lips together, struggling not to say the wrong thing.

His gaze dropped to her mouth, then caressed its way back up to her eyes. He lifted his hands, gently resting them at the base of her throat. A light touch. Hesitant. "I want . . ."

His eyes went from brown to black in an instant, his big body stilling. His throat moved as he swallowed roughly. He cupped her cheek with one hand. His palm was solid and strong, the thumb he stroked over her bottom lip was callused and rough. She flicked her tongue out, tracing the lines of his fingerprint, and she heard his quick hiss of breath.

"What?" she whispered. "What do you want?"

She licked her bottom lip, wondering just how far she could push him. Wondering if she herself dared to step off the edge of sanity and into the depths of pleasure that his gaze promised.

"You." His fingers twitched against her throat, caressing the line of her neck. "I—"

She smiled then, her fingers resting on his sides. Lightly. Unsure whether to tease or tempt. She brushed her lips over his. "Say the words, Evan. Say 'I want you.'"

Neither of them moved for the longest moment. They stood, Evan's palm cupping her cheek, his thumb stroking her lip and a slow burn building in the seat of her soul. His nostrils flared and she felt rather than heard his breathing grow rough.

"Do you always have to be in control?" she whispered. Her breath failed to fill her starved lungs. Anticipation bloomed inside of her.

"Claire—" Her name, a barely restrained desire.

It was enough.

She closed the space between them. His thumb caressed her lips as she opened herself to him, her tongue slipping inside his mouth. All the tastes and textures were him and she didn't realize until this moment just how much she'd wanted this.

How much she'd wanted him. His arms wrapped around her, his palm stroking the space between her shoulder blades as she kissed him. Here was power and strength. Desire and sensual heat all mixed together with the lingering pain of old wounds.

She slipped her hands beneath his shirt, her palms flat

against the smooth muscles of his back. He stiffened beneath her touch and in that moment, realization dawned on her.

He didn't have nearly as much control as he wanted her to think.

She lifted the hem of his shirt, just a little, dragging one nail along the edge of his pants. Across the small of his back. He shivered but didn't move. His hands clenched at his sides, a fierce restraint, his breath shallow and quick. She flattened her palms against his back, sliding them up against the raw silk of his skin, dragging his shirt higher and leaning back to take in the pure masculine beauty of his body.

She froze at what she had revealed. Holding her breath, she pushed the shirt over his shoulders until he finally reached down and tugged it the final distance over his head.

He stood stiff and straight for her inspection. His eyes were closed, his shoulders rigid, his head bowed, his breath harsh and ragged.

"You're just full of surprises, aren't you, Captain America?" she murmured.

Tentatively, she reached out, tracing the gnarled roots of an old oak tree, tattooed in black at the base of his rib cage. It curled and twisted over his left deltoid, the black, gothic branches spreading over his shoulder and halfway down his bicep and the left side of his chest.

This was not a tattoo that someone did for fun. This was a memorial. This was pain. A wicked, vicious inscription carved into his flesh.

In the middle of the tree, a faded pink scar ripped through indecipherable writing. "What is this?" she whispered, tracing the lines over his back with the tip of her index finger.

"My sister. It's a tribute to my sister." His throat moved as he swallowed hard.

"What about the scar?" she whispered.

"When the TOC got blown up, a ricochet from the mortar blast tore off her name. I've been waiting for it to heal enough to get it fixed."

Claire couldn't speak past the block in her throat. This was more than just a flesh wound.

She'd never dreamed that Captain America—that Evan—had experienced such a loss. The depth of his pain was written all over his body. She stood near his shoulder and met his gaze, looking past the constrained façade to the torment beneath. Then slowly, slowly, she traced the black branch twisting over his biceps with the tip of her tongue.

His lips parted, the only visible reaction to the intense sensation of her mouth on him. He held his breath as she tasted the black branches covering his shoulder.

A tribute. She pressed her lips to the scar at the center of his shoulder. She wanted to ask about his sister, wanted to know more about a man who would mark his body permanently for someone else. It was the kind of thing she would have done when she was young and stupid. She pressed her lips to his shoulder, felt his muscles jump beneath her kiss. For a brief moment, she wrapped her arms around his waist from behind, pressing her cheek to the black lines covering his back, wondering at the boy he had been. At the pain that carved that boy into the man before her.

For once, the silence between them was empty of blame and hurt. Claire was moored to the spot, filled with a warmth that nearly overwhelmed her. Desire burned low and deep in her belly, but now there was more—the connection of shared loss.

He'd shared at least part of the loss that had shaped him into the man she held in her arms. But would he accept the losses that had shaped her?

She didn't know. And her inability to trust in this fragile connection between them nearly broke her heart.

THERE WAS NO REASON FOR HIM TO BE STANDING IN THE middle of her room. He could have turned out the lights, hiding the tattoo. There was no reason for him to have shown her the ragged memory he'd carved into his body as both penance and tribute.

He wrapped his hands around hers, which were folded against his abdomen. He couldn't see her face, couldn't see the questions or the judgment there. Would she look at him and know he was a killer long before the army had pinned a rank on his chest and placed a weapon in his hand?

She called him Captain America. Claire looked at him and saw the man he'd forced himself to become after a single reckless night had driven him away from the home he'd once loved.

It terrified him how easily he'd handed her the power to crush him. A hundred thousand things tumbled through him, twisting and writhing, refusing to be locked down again. Never had a lover taken the time to do something so incredibly erotic and so touching all at once.

Claire shifted until she stood in front of him. She pressed her lips to his collarbone, at the edge of a single, twisted black branch. "How did she die?" Claire's whispered question pierced the silence. The thin veil of Evan's control vibrated like a wall of heat rising from the pavement in August.

He shifted then, lifting one arm over her shoulder to cradle the back of her neck, struggling to find the words that were not a lie. "Car accident." He released a shuddering breath. In the thirteen years since his sister had died, he'd never told anyone the full truth of what had happened. "She was sixteen."

Her palm flattened over the scar where his sister's name had been, her arms a warm and comforting embrace. Even thinking about it caused the ache in his soul to pound against his veins. "How old were you?" she whispered.

He tipped her head back until he could look into her eyes. They stood, their bodies separated by clothing and heat, the scar on his back a brand. He'd never had a lover ask about him. About his tattoo? Yes. About his little sister? That too.

Maybe it said something about the partners he'd chosen. But before this moment, he'd never wanted to explain about the sister he'd killed, the parents he'd let drift away because it was easier to ignore his pain than face it every time he looked into their eyes, eyes that reminded him so much of Casey. It was easier to turn away from their crushing blame.

"Seventeen." His breath shuddered from his body. Her fingers curled against the scar, her nails a light pressure on his skin.

Claire said nothing, but Evan met her searching gaze. He stood beneath her scrutiny, his soul open and bared, and he waited. For pity. For some pithy comment. For anything to shatter the moment, giving him a reason to leave. Claire was not the only one running from what she'd been, he thought ruefully.

Instead, she simply leaned into him and kissed him. Her tongue slid against his, a warm, welcome caress, saying so much without words. He surrendered to her touch, to the sweet taste of her mouth, and for the first time in his life, he dared to want something without the overwhelming need to control it.

She pulled away for a moment and looked him in the eyes. Her palms gently cupped his face. "I'm sorry that you lost her," she whispered.

He lowered his face to her neck and said nothing. He couldn't speak. His throat closed off, his voice crushed beneath a wave of grief that was so strong it threatened to cut off his air supply. "Me, too."

It was all he could manage.

Somehow, it was enough.

EVAN'S ARMS WERE TIGHT AND STRONG AROUND HER. Claire simply stood in his embrace, resting her cheek against the solid muscle of his chest, the lines of his tattoo burning into her skin.

She had not felt a man's arms around her in . . . forever. The simplicity of the embrace unnerved her and unlocked a craving for so much more than she'd ever allowed herself to feel. It terrified her, the depth of the want inside her.

An eternity passed, but the weight of the silence between them felt warm for once, a comfort instead of a frigid chill.

Their breathing was the only sound, pulsing with the solid, steady beating of Evan's heart beneath her cheek. The tenderness, the quiet connection with a man who held so much loss inside him. She knew loss. She'd simply never thought that someone as polished and rigid as Evan had lived through something so soul-crushingly sad.

In the silence, a quiet beeping interrupted their requiem. He shifted then and lifted his head as she pulled her wrist around to glance at her watch. "We've got to go soon," she whispered.

"Yeah." He stepped away from her then and she watched his body twist and flex as he pulled his shirt back on. He tucked it into his belt, his eyes dark and watchful. "Claire?"

"Hmm?" She could find no other words.

He stepped close, tracing his fingers over her cheek. "This would have been a mistake."

She flinched, pulling away from his touch, the unexpected bite of his words. His fingers snapped to the back of her neck, halting her retreat. "It would have been mistake I would have enjoyed making," he finished.

Her mouth went dry, her heart beating in time with the echo of his words as they penetrated the shields around her soul. She let him go, because anything else would have shattered the remnants of self-preservation to which she was so valiantly clinging. The door closed softly behind him. Too late for him to hear her whispered response.

"Me, too."

$\maltese$ 7 $\maltese$

Late that night, long after the briefings had finally been completed and Colonel Danvers had released them from PowerPoint hell, Claire sat in the crowded restaurant, utterly alone in a sea of eating, swearing, laughing humanity recovering from a day on the mountain. A deep, unsettling disquiet danced in the shadows of her heart, stealing her focus.

Evan had gotten under her skin, and she couldn't shake the image of his tattoo from her memory.

His revelation had been a powerful trust, a trust she did not deserve. And yet, he'd given it to her. She shook her head and tried to push away the panicky sensation in her belly. She didn't do trust. Not this kind of trust. Trust to guard her six on the battlefield? Hell, yes. This? The kind of trust that made a man put his heart in her hands? This was not her area of expertise. Not by a long shot.

She didn't usually think of herself as a coward, but then again, she didn't usually make out with a coworker because she'd had a bad day at work. She pushed the chicken on her plate around with her fork.

"You look like you're going to puke."

She glanced up as Reza set a heaping plate of food down across from hers, and took a seat in front of it. She hadn't seen him come in. "Hey," was her only reply.

"Who pissed on your leg?"

"Colonel Danvers, for starters," she grumbled. In truth, there were more important things for Claire to worry about. Like the man sitting across from her. The man who'd missed the makeup briefing tonight. Claire wished she didn't suspect where he'd been.

Reza frowned and opened his mouth to speak but snapped it closed, leaving her with her nagging sense of worry. He pointed at her with his fork. "Ass-chewings are good for you. They build character." He smeared butter on his broccoli. "How can I help?"

"I wish I knew," she said, chasing a French fry around her plate. "If I was heading back downrange, I'd want them to learn how to react to chaos, and who better to provide that than someone who knows weapons and explosives? But I don't get a vote." She sighed. "We can't deviate from the plan, even though it kills me to say so."

He swiped a roll from the basket in front of Claire and tore it open. She could have taken that moment to talk to him about his drinking but she didn't. She couldn't. And it made her a coward.

The trust she had with Reza was not the same as the trust that was building, slowly, between her and Evan.

"So are you going tell me what's eating at you," Reza said, "or am I going to have to drag you to the gym and beat it out of you?"

She cracked a smile. "I don't feel much like fighting at the moment." She felt like she had a massive scarlet letter tattooed on her forehead.

"It's Loehr, isn't it?"

"That apparent?"

"Hello, Captain Obvious. You two have been swiping at each other for so long, I figured it was only a matter of time before you realized that you're just two sides of the same coin."

"How long have you known him?" she asked suddenly, hoping it wasn't glaringly transparent why she was asking.

"A few years," Reza said, spearing a broccoli tree.

She cleared her throat. "He helped me bring you home the other night."

"Glad he felt compelled to help out." Reza stiffened slightly, avoiding her gaze.

"I didn't expect him to." She studied him quietly before asking a simple, loaded question. "Why, Reza?"

He cleared his throat, a deep flush creeping up his dark skin. "What's the big deal? Shit happens in combat. It's not like he's my hetero life mate or anything."

"Rules, Reza. Evan doesn't break the rules. Any of them."

Reza set his fork and spoon down and folded his arms over his chest. "Have you ever been faced with two choices? And neither of them are good?"

"Yeah." She'd learned about hard choices long before she'd ever donned a uniform. Decisions you could never take back. Her chest tightened as she thought again about her father. Reza cleared his throat, then wiped his mouth with a napkin.

"Choices suck sometimes. And they're permanent. For the rest of your life, you have to live with them. No do-overs. No instant replay or living with regrets. Loehr is a hard man to work for, but when you need him to make a hard choice, he'll do it."

Claire retreated into silence for a moment, heading away from awkward territory. She knew about hard choices. About weighing the loss of her career over the loss of a friend's life. "So what's your point?"

"My point is that it's not about the rules so much as it's about choices. You just think it's about the rules with Loehr." Reza shifted uncomfortably. "So, ah, speaking of bad choices, sorry about the other night."

"About what?"

"Falling on you and shit."

She gave Reza a hard stare and said nothing. He had been a heavy drinker since they'd first met. There was nothing new in his getting drunk. But an old, familiar fear made her want to protect Reza in a way she hadn't been able to protect her dad.

The problem was that the demons at the bottom of the bottle always got a vote. Sometimes more than one. It hurt Claire every single time she watched those demons tear at Reza's soul, slapping at her with the knowledge that no matter how good she was at her job, she wasn't good enough to figure out how to say the words "stop drinking" to him.

Such a simple thing. But sometimes the simple things were the most difficult. The girl she'd been hadn't been able to say those words to her father. The woman she was now could not say them to her friend.

⁂

EVAN TURNED DOWN OLD HOLMAN ROAD BEFORE HE KNEW where he was going. He'd been driving aimlessly in the snow, the wipers working harder and harder to keep the windshield of his rental car cleared. He drove past Purchase Farm, past the trailer park where his best friend from high school had grown up.

He hadn't spoken to Billy Meir since the accident. He'd barely spoken to anyone for the remainder of his senior year. He'd been lucky to graduate and if he hadn't already been accepted into West Point before the accident, he might never have gone to college. He rounded the corner, driving past the small pond where he and Casey and Billy had learned to skate.

And then there it was. The old farmhouse where he'd grown up. He'd taken his first steps there, but he hadn't been back since his high school graduation. The first steps of his adult life had been to walk out the front door. He didn't recognize the cars in the driveway anymore. He wondered when his parents had bought them.

He could stop. He could ask. Make small talk. But Casey's ghost would stand in the middle of the room until the awkward silence twisted with regret and everyone was desperate to escape.

He ground his teeth, remembering the day they'd buried Casey. Evan's arm had been bound in a sling, strung across his chest. No one had helped him get the suit on. He hadn't been able to knot his tie with one hand.

The snow blanketed the road as he rolled past the place that would never again be his home. Crushing loneliness pressed in on him from all sides. He'd always been on his own. Ever since he'd come to in the twisted metal of the car wreck, he'd been alone.

He drove past his parents' home and headed back to the lodge and the one person who'd touched the frozen core of his soul since his sister had died. And as the walls around his heart melted, he craved the thing he wasn't sure he could hold on to.

Claire Montoya's heart.

Claire dragged her hands through her hair and stared at her computer screen as the snowstorm continued to rage at the mountains outside. The whole team had made it back to the lodge from the last of the late-night inspections just before the storm hit and it showed no sign of letting up. Claire was taking the extra time to figure out how she could layer in more actual training during the events that were already planned. Trying to get the most bang for her buck, so to speak. She'd give anything for more time.

Someone rapped on the door and she frowned, glancing at her watch. It wasn't unheard of for someone to swing by this late. They worked long into the night in Iraq. Still, she was surprised someone was at her door at this hour. People had to sleep sometime. Tying her hair up into a quick loop, she padded to the door, curious.

She opened the door to find Evan. Standing in the hallway, holding two cups of coffee. Clean-shaven and freshly showered and looking like he had just run a marathon instead of listening to mission briefings for a bunch of lieutenants getting ready to go to war.

He stood framed in the door, his shoulders stiff and straight, a casual tension emanating from him. Evan was not a man who was used admitting to his vulnerabilities, and it showed.

He was unsure of himself, she realized. He'd shown her something dark and deeply personal, something she doubted he revealed very often. It filled her heart with a tender warmth to see this side of him.

Evan shifted and handed her one of the mugs. As he moved, she noticed the tiniest hint of black branches peeking beneath the sleeve of his white T-shirt.

She opened the door a fraction wider and took a single step backwards, inviting him into the suite.

"You look dead on your feet," he said, sliding into a chair next to her at the dining table, his coffee mug in his hands.

"It's close to one a.m. and I've been on my feet all day. Not exactly my prime energy time," she said, breathing in the hot, moist aroma wafting up from her mug. "This smells like Dunkin' Donuts." She took a sip and the warm liquid burned her nerve endings awake on its way down to her stomach.

"It is."

"Where did you find Dunkin' Donuts coffee in a blizzard in Colorado? Do they even have Dunkin' Donuts here?"

Evan grinned, and Claire looked away before she did something stupid. "I brought my own."

"Seriously?" She raised both eyebrows and gratefully sipped the steaming coffee. There was something deeply sensual about the smell of coffee and freshly showered man. And the way his dog tags were outlined beneath his shirt sent her imagination down a dirty, gritty path filled with dark temptation. "I never would have thought of you as a coffee fanatic."

"There's a lot you don't know about me," he said quietly. "Any chance your inspections went any better than mine earlier today?" Evan asked.

She raised her eyebrows again. "You have to ask? They had the wrong markings on their ammo and their trucks haven't been serviced in lord only knows how long. It's a train wreck, and no one seems interested in trying to redirect the oncoming disaster."

He looked away, down at the map she'd been studying. Red and green pushpins made small clusters around Baghdad and the Triangle of Death, the center of mass for the majority of U.S. deaths in Iraq. "What are you doing?"

"Looking for a pattern in the recent attacks so we can try to duplicate them during training." She frowned and leaned back, cradling the mug in both hands. "I'm not breaking any rules. I just want to maximize the training time we do have."

Mere hours had passed since they'd touched. Since he'd burned his taste into her soul, affecting her more than any man had in a decade, maybe more. Maybe ever.

She'd missed him. And the thought terrified her. They'd sparred when they'd been assigned to the brigade operations cell together, but despite the arguing, he'd become a part of her normal. A piece she'd been missing since she'd come back from Iraq.

A piece that had clicked back into place during this mission.

"Not that I don't love your company, but what are you doing stalking the hallways, anyway?"

"I saw the light reflected on the snow from your window again. I wondered why you were up."

She frowned slightly, shifting until there was space between them. "Why were you up?"

He shrugged. "Like I said, I don't sleep much."

She glanced at his shoulder, then met his eyes. "Why?"

⁂

"AFTER MY SISTER DIED, I STARTED TO HAVE TROUBLE sleeping." It was a confession, one that wasn't easy for him to admit. "I'd already been accepted to West Point before the accident. I stayed busy enough there that I was too exhausted not to sleep." He shrugged and stared into his coffee. "Staying busy seems to be the best way to keep the insomnia demon at bay. But it's hard to stay busy enough when I'm not deployed," he murmured, his voice thick.

She offered a wry smile, leaning back to look up at him. "It's too quiet. The quiet really gets to me. Who knew that would be what I noticed most about coming home?"

"How many times have you deployed?" he asked, shifting his stance as she rose from her chair. The movement shifted the air and it brushed against his skin. He wanted to feel the fire in his blood from her body against his.

He loved watching her body move. There was strength

beneath the beauty, a strength that called to him in dark, seductive whispers. "Last tour made three. You?"

"This last one was my fourth," he said.

She glanced at the map, releasing a quiet sigh. "Do you honestly think we've got a snowball's chance in hell of getting them ready to deploy?" she asked.

He watched as she transitioned in one instant from the Claire who was soft and feminine and relaxed to the Claire he was used to at work: tough and no bullshit. It was an almost physical change, one that he could see in the renewed tension in her shoulders, the slight widening of her stance.

What did it say about him that both versions of her appealed to him equally?

"I was talking with Sarah after the briefing this evening and she said that Colonel Danvers is up for his first star soon. His battalion commanders are under a ton of pressure to perform." Claire took a long sip of her coffee. "Apparently the pressure has already made one company commander quit and a first sergeant is being court-martialed for disrespect, among other things."

"I didn't realize things were that bad here," Evan murmured, watching her as she turned back to the map. For a brief moment, his mind flittered back to Iraq and to another Claire, one who was driven to protect her soldiers first and accomplish the mission second. But looking at her now, Evan felt a tug, a tug that was respect mixed with desire. A potent combination.

"I don't think any of us did, honestly. Sarah's my friend and I'm terrified for her."

He shifted, leaning against her shoulder to look at the map. Heat radiated off her body, wrapping around him and sliding through his clothes to caress his skin.

"We're so limited on time. I feel like we're cutting too

many corners," she mumbled, moving a pushpin to another area outside a town on the map.

He laughed, low and deep in his throat. Scowling, she glanced up at him and he realized how close he'd managed to get to her. "Now that's funny, coming from you."

Claire looked at him sharply, the quick retort dying on her lips as Evan rotated his shoulder, the motion slipping the T-shirt up his biceps, revealing more of the tattoo. Warmth flooded between her thighs as she remembered licking the edges of that hidden tribute.

She wanted to ask him more about it. About the sister he'd loved so much he'd permanently marked his body for her. But the way he'd stood, head bowed, as she explored the branches etched into his skin told her he wasn't ready to talk about that. He rotated his shoulder and she frowned. "Sore?"

"It stiffens up if I don't work out regularly."

"You skipped the gym today?"

"Yeah."

She wasn't used to being uneasy around a man and everything about Evan made her uneasy. She needed to put it away, needed to get things back to what they had been. Her Super Woman to his Captain America. It was much easier that way.

He looked at her then and she saw just how serious he was. Very, very serious. Something was eating at him, more weighty than their argument or their kiss. He looked at her sharply, the torment in his soul etched into the lines beneath his eyes. Maybe it was the storm that had kept him up. Maybe it was something else.

Whatever it was, he did not want to be alone right now.

And neither did she.

❧ 8 ❧

The storm pounded against the walls of the lodge. Wind whistled through the spaces between the buildings, howling like a banshee.

The T-shirt Evan wore clung to his chest like a second skin, revealing hard angles and sharp planes that disappeared into the belt around his jeans. Claire breathed in and caught the scent of . . . laundry soap?

Never in three combat tours had she figured out how to get her laundry to smell like something other than the sterile, pungent odor of dirty water and cheap detergent. One thing she missed when she was traveling was the smell of warm clothes fresh from the dryer. Tonight that smell mixed with the scent of Evan's skin and it sent warmth spiraling through her.

She shifted so that she could look up at him.

He sat too close, close enough that she could see a smudge of shaving cream below the line of his jaw. She reached for it before thinking about it, swiping her thumb over his pulse. He swallowed, his dark gaze capturing hers. "Do that again," he said, his voice rough.

The temptation to touch him, to feel his hot skin beneath her fingertips, was too strong to resist. She traced her index finger beneath his ear, down the strong line of his jaw to the sensitive skin covering his pulse.

He slid one hand into the hair at the base of her neck, his fingers strong and hard against her skin. She tipped her neck, tacit permission for him to touch her. Hot sexual tension ripped through her, slicing any hint of restraint to shreds. Heat pooled between her thighs and she was suddenly, achingly aware that they were alone.

He nuzzled the sensitive skin beneath her ear before cupping her face and urging her to turn to him. She smiled against his mouth, flicking the tip of her tongue over the full edge of his bottom lip, acutely aware that she was doing more than just teasing him. She was crossing a line she'd set for herself years ago. She was lowering barriers that had been guarding her heart for what felt like a lifetime. And it felt good.

She opened her mouth and kissed him. His surprise was a burst against her tongue, his taste a potent, raw hunger. He moaned low in his throat, his fingers clenching the back of her neck.

Her fingers curled into his chest of their own accord, the chain of his dog tags biting into her skin through his T-shirt.

❧

He couldn't resist the urge to push the boundaries of this new aspect of their relationship. A sensation rose inside him, a longing so fierce and primal it nearly dropped him to his knees.

He craved Claire, but more, he respected her strength, her determination. And he wanted her complete and total surrender.

The boundaries of appropriate conduct had long ago fallen away between them and damn the consequences, he wanted more. There were no rules against what he wanted with her, at least no formal rules. They were unwritten, impossible to navigate but he no longer cared. He wanted to be reckless for the first time in his adult life and do something completely unplanned.

He wanted . . . he wanted no barriers. No hiding behind uniforms or rank or customs. He wanted her to look at him, just him, and still want what she saw. It was a needful thing in him, growing and demanding more than, perhaps, either of them was willing or able to give.

Claire said nothing for a long moment, and Evan felt the silence pressing against his soul. Her palm slid against the back of his hand, a gentle, firm touch that said so much more than any words could hope to convey.

"Do you ever cut loose? Ever truly let go?" she asked, tracing her tongue over his bottom lip.

He swallowed. "Not really. I don't like to do things if they're not going to be done right."

"A perfectionist," she murmured. "I knew it." She shifted so that she was standing between his thighs. Her fingers skimmed over his forearm, a touch of silk.

"I don't want to be perfect," he admitted.

She smiled gently. "No, you just want to be in control," she murmured against his mouth. Her breath traced across his lips but they did not touch.

"Bad things happen when I lose control," he said.

"Bad things happen regardless. You can't control everything." Her fingers traced up the sides of his neck, a light, teasing touch.

"I've been fairly good at it so far." He was strung out and tight, afraid that she would destroy the fragile remnants of his restraint.

She licked her lips, her eyes dark with promise. "If we were to get naked, would you lose control? Or would you stay wound too tight?"

She rubbed the tip of her index finger along the seam of his lips.

"There's only one right answer, Evan."

SHE SIGHED SOFTLY AS HIS PALMS SKIMMED THE SWELL OF her breasts, an electric, erotic shock to her system. She slipped from his embrace, circling him. Raw power surged through her—whatever this was, he would let her set the pace.

His stomach tightened beneath her touch as she raked her nails down his sides, sliding her fingers beneath his shirt to claw gently at his skin.

"Claire—"

She met his gaze, her green eyes glittering darkly. Not once in a decade had she done this. Not like this. Not when she would have to face the man the next morning.

This was more than just sex. There would be consequences. Evan would not be a reckless lover, she thought, shifting against him slowly.

His arousal was hard and thick between them, rigid against her belly. A temptation. A seductive pressure. Her hand moved then, sliding from his hips to the bulge in his pants.

HER MOUTH WAS WARM AND WET AND SO INCREDIBLY SOFT as she sucked his tongue, even as her palm stroked him. He struggled not to thread his fingers into her hair and tear control from her.

"I'm going to die if you keep that up." A ragged moan ripped from his throat as she squeezed him.

She flicked her tongue against the seam of his mouth. "That would be a disappointing end to the evening."

The laugh tore from somewhere deep inside him, unexpected and . . . welcome. And then he was done thinking. She took his mouth again, circling her tongue with his and driving him closer to the edge.

His stomach flexed beneath her touch, and his cock tensed and tightened beneath her wandering touch. With a gentle kiss, she stood, her mouth a whisper from his. "Tell me. Does Captain America carry condoms?" she whispered.

He kissed her then—fierce and hard and deep—his tongue sparring with hers in a wild release of wicked tension. His fingers dug into her hips and he tried to guide her to the bed, but Claire slipped from his grip.

Someone was pounding on the door as if the lodge were on fire. Evan dropped his forehead to hers. "Someone needs to die," he murmured.

Arousal faded from his blood, leaving him aching and hard. But Claire was already gone, answering the door in the middle of the night.

Because that's what good soldiers did.

CLAIRE WASN'T EXACTLY SURE WHEN HER ROOM BECAME Grand Central, but at some point in the last hour, Sarah, Engle, Reza, and of course Evan had all ended up in the living area of her suite. It was a testament to how worried Sarah was about the training that she'd dragged her lieutenant out in the dead of night in the snow. Sure, it was late and they'd been working all day, but apparently none of them could sleep. Irritation ran thick through the group and the consensus was that they were wasting their time.

The briefing slides were displayed on Sarah's computer and there were half a dozen empty bottles of alcohol sitting around the suite. For once, Reza wasn't pounding the hard stuff, sticking to beer, and thankfully, he was staying away from Engle, too.

Engle swore and threw her pen down. "This is stupid, Ma'am," she said to Sarah. "Maybe I'm just not cut out for the army, because doing what the colonel says is dumb if he's got a bad plan. We need to be on the ranges, practicing driving in convoys, not talking about safe traveling distances between vehicles in the convoy."

Sarah studied her lieutenant for a long moment, and Claire waited with interest to see how she would handle Engle's snit fit. Granted, she agreed with this particular fit, but still.

Sarah's words were a quiet dose of reality over the group of malcontents. "You know, I might have disagreed with him when he said it, but when the Secretary of Defense said you go to war with the army you have, not the army you wish you had, he was right. We're going to war with Colonel Danvers, LT. We can piss and moan about it or we can figure out how to deal with it and keep our soldiers alive."

Engle opened her mouth to speak, but Evan held up a hand, silencing her.

"Your commander is right," Evan said. "You have to make do with what you have."

Engle frowned and glared at the slides, as though the answer to the problem was going to magically appear from the PowerPoint gods. "This is bullshit," she mumbled.

Evan continued easily but there was tension in his voice, a deep disquiet that he probably didn't know was there. Claire watched him closely, wondering what demons he wrestled. "We've got to focus more on what we can do and less on what we can't," he glanced at his watch, "otherwise, we're wasting what little time we do have."

"Can I ask a stupid question?" Engle asked, glancing between Claire, Evan and Sarah. Claire noticed she deliberately did not look at Reza. "Why are you so hung up on doing this the way the brigade commander wants? I mean, if no plan survives first contact, why are we so hung up on doing it his way instead of improvising and making the mission happen? Doesn't it matter more that it gets done?"

A shadow crossed Evan's face and Claire felt a punch of shared emotion in that single look. She cleared her throat.

"When we were getting ready for the initial invasion—" Claire said quietly. All eyes turned to her. "—we spent days developing the commander's plan. Mission analysis about routes and tribal identities and enemy capabilities. All of it went to shit about thirty minutes after the first troops rolled into Baghdad."

Engle latched on to the wrong point. "Right. So why spend so much time on it?"

Claire's voice was quiet, hoping she got the words right. "There comes a point when the commander's plan becomes the be-all and end-all. An eighty percent solution now is better than a ninety-nine percent solution an hour too late. And when you're going to knowingly disobey orders, you'd better know why you're doing it and what the consequences are."

"When you break the rules," Reza said, finally adding to the discussion, "you better have a really good reason for doing it. Just disagreeing with your commander doesn't qualify as a good reason."

Sarah shook her head. "That doesn't help me figure out how to get everything done. You heard Colonel Danvers: if I can't accomplish the mission, he'll find someone else who can. And I'm not leaving my team."

Claire pulled her knees up to her chest. "Sarah, I don't know how to help you," she said, fear tainting her words. "Because, honestly, I think the focus of this plan is all wrong. It would almost be worth it to check the block on the unimportant stuff so we could focus on the important things."

"So you'd falsify training reports?" Engle asked.

Claire started to speak, but Evan cut her off. "No, LT, no one's going to falsify training reports. There has to be a reason why the brigade commander wants things done this way. We have to figure out how to get it done."

Claire stood, fed up with Evan, the whole mission and the helplessness of knowing there was little she could do to make a difference. "Look, Sarah, go home. You too, Engle, get some sleep. The first day of field training is tomorrow. You all need to be on your game."

It wouldn't do any good to keep this conversation going in front of Evan. He'd simply shut it down. She hugged her friend and for once, was sociable to LT Engle as they left the room. She didn't bother to look and see if Reza followed Engle or simply went to bed. At the moment, she didn't care what he did or with whom he did it. Too many sleepless nights were finally catching up to her.

THE DOOR CLOSED BEHIND IACONELLI, LEAVING THEM alone in the silence. Evan turned back to see Claire picking up the papers and stacking them neatly in piles. Busy work.

"What's wrong?" Evan asked.

They were alone in her suite again and he could see the conflicted emotions written all over Claire's face. She looked exhausted but more, she looked like a ghost had risen from the dead and was howling on the wind outside.

"Nothing, Evan." She turned away, looking out the wide bay window, which was white with snow.

"Talk to me, Claire," he whispered, wanting so badly to approach but the relentless barriers between them were back, higher than ever.

"Not everything requires psychoanalysis."

"I was just asking a question," he said quietly. "Forgive me for confusing you with someone capable of rational conversation."

Anger flashed in her eyes. "Do we really need to do this tonight? I don't have any energy left to fight with you."

Evan stepped in front of her, frustration clawing at him that she continued to shut him out. "You know what I'm not in the mood for? For you encouraging young officers like Engle to play fast and loose with the rules. You're teaching them to be reckless and reckless gets people killed."

Claire held up both hands, fatigue written across her features. "Look, I'm just tired of having to kiss the boss's ass just because he's the commander. Commanders aren't God, Evan. They make mistakes. Danvers is making a mistake, and I think you know it but you're too much of a play-by-the-rules guy to argue with him. I just want out of this ski lodge and I want to go blow something up. Is that reckless enough for you?"

"You know what's reckless, Claire?"

She released a sigh, heavy with resignation. "Yeah, I do. And I'm asking reckless to leave my room right now so I can be a true daredevil and go to sleep. There's no point in arguing about this any more. I can't win. Not with you. Not with Colonel Danvers."

"You're giving up?" It was such a simple question, but her

unwillingness to fight sparked a deep, unsettled concern in him.

⁂

"I'm going to bed. Alone, if you don't mind." She folded her arms over her chest, keenly aware of his closeness. But the sensual connection between them was gone, replaced with a long-standing familiar argument about how an officer was supposed to lead, supposed to act. Supposed to genuflect before the will of the commander, regardless of whether that commander was right or wrong.

Evan refused to back down. "I can't believe you're giving up. Just because it's not going your way?"

"It's got nothing to do with my way, Evan." Fear gripped her, denying her the escape she so desperately needed. She knew what she'd do if Captain America wasn't there. She'd do exactly what she suggested to Engle: check the block on the stupid stuff and spend time doing the important training. But she couldn't do that with Captain America looking over her shoulder. He'd never let her lie, even if it would save lives. "I just don't know what else to do. We're wasting time on bullshit training and these guys are leaving unprepared. And I can't keep fighting with you or Colonel Danvers. I'll do my job and I'll do my best. But I can't keep going through these mental gymnastics because it hurts too much." The admission pained her but he needed to hear it.

"And sometimes, you need to find a way to get the best out of a shitty situation." He approached her then, stepping too close, and traced the tip of one finger down the side her neck. "I never took you for a coward, Claire."

"I'm not a coward. I just don't see the point in fighting a losing battle." She didn't flinch away from his touch, but it was a close thing. "I'll do my job. Isn't that what you wanted? No more arguing? No more fighting about how to train?"

But her words were filled with defeat. Maybe it was time to admit that there was nothing she could do to help her friend's team. The helplessness galled her, but it was the fear that she would be standing at Sarah's memorial that threatened to drown her.

"Sometimes, the only battle worth fighting is the one that lets you keep your integrity."

"Integrity doesn't mean anything when you're dead." She shook her head, sadness threatening to spill down her cheeks. "I've seen that movie, Evan. The correct answer is that we die honorably. The right answer is that we cheat." She lifted her chin. "I'll choose to cheat every time if that means someone comes home alive."

He took a single step backwards. "That says more about you than anything else you've ever done," he murmured.

She said nothing for a long moment and then the door closed quietly behind him, his words cutting her deeply. They shouldn't have hurt the way they did. She'd given him what he wanted: an officer who would do her job. So why did he disapprove of her decision.

And worse, why did it matter?

❧ 9 ❧

It was still snowing lightly the next morning as Claire and Reza drove up to the edge of the training area and pulled to a stop.

Evan was at another training area, which was good. She was pretty sure he'd knocked on her door this morning. She'd ignored him. He was going to accuse her of being childish, but she wasn't. She was pissed, and it wasn't just because of their disagreement the night before.

He'd hurt her. And she was pissed at herself for letting him get close enough to want what she could never have. She sucked at relationships. No amount of wishful thinking would change that. At least she knew where she stood with him now. It was better to cauterize the wound before it did any permanent damage.

Funny how the road to hell was paved with all those unkept resolutions.

As she was pulling her body armor out of the back of the truck, Reza approached. "Don't you love wearing body armor?"

Claire smiled. "We train how we fight," she said dryly. "Wouldn't want to break the rules and train out of uniform, now would we?"

Reza snorted, then pointed toward the small group of soldiers near the edge of the training area. "We have a problem."

She sighed as she hitched her helmet up, tightening the chin strap. "What's the problem?"

"You're looking at it."

Claire followed his gaze away from the SUV, and her eyes widened with disbelief as she took in the small formation. "This is it?"

A single platoon stood in front of them, no more than thirty soldiers, and other than Lieutenant Engle the highest-ranking person was a sergeant.

"Where the hell is the rest of the company?" she snapped, letting her frustration show. This was either deliberate incompetence or worse, a game of one-upmanship that was going to get someone killed. And where was Sarah? She pulled her phone out and shot her friend a text. No response. What was going on?

Lieutenant Engle, her face flushed and pink from the cold, walked up, saluting sharply. "Ma'am, half the formation was pulled over to the weapons qualification range."

"Nice of the brigade ops officer to tell us they decided to change things up. What a waste of time." She glanced at Reza, a frustrated resignation settling in her belly.

"Go to war with the army you have, not the army you wish you had, right?" he said dryly, repeating Sarah's words from the previous night.

She scanned the group of soldiers in front of them as Engle walked off to inspect her soldiers. A couple of privates were busy inspecting one another's gear. The tallest one, who looked like he belonged in high school, fumbled his fingers over the smaller one's chin strap. When he jerked it too tight, his friend protested loudly, then glanced around to make sure they weren't going to be caught screwing around.

"God, were we ever that young?"

"You might have been," he said easily. "When I was eighteen, I'd just graduated from Basic Training at Fort Benning. Let me tell you, nothing we're about to put these guys through has anything on Sand Hill."

"Sand Hill?"

"The basic training side of Fort Benning. It's separate from the main post." His gaze shifted to some distant memory. "I was a drill sergeant there six years later."

She sighed and rubbed her gloved hands together. "When I was seventeen, I'd just moved from the grill to the register at McDonald's."

"Fast tracking to management, huh?"

"Nah. Just marking time until I figured out what I wanted to be when I grew up." The sergeant called their group to attention and Claire frowned, hooking her thumbs into the shoulders of her body armor. "What's your plan for today's simulated chaos, Master Gunner?"

He grinned wickedly. "We got the sim rounds."

"Really? How did you manage that?"

"I gave the budget guy a hand job."

Claire choked on a laugh. "Say no more. Just tell me we didn't break any rules."

"Nary a one." Reza pulled on his gloves, a small smile playing across his face. "We're going to shoot at them a couple times and blow some shit up, then bless them off as ready to deploy to combat."

"Is the shoot house about ready?"

"Yeah. I'll text you when we're set."

They'd gotten the sim rounds. She couldn't believe it. And they hadn't broken a single rule to do it. Claire smiled. She might disagree with sending Sarah's company through a shoot house but it would be a good experience for them. And the sim rounds would make it a little more real. Might as well make the best of the day.

A day on the range beat the hell out of a day at the office anytime.

Other than knowing there were sim rounds, Claire didn't want to know what else Reza was planning for Engle's platoon because she didn't want to tip off the troops who were running through the exercise. It was common practice to watch the evaluators for cues on when the attacks were coming. If she didn't know, she couldn't tip them off, either accidently or on purpose. She had the basics of the plan and that was all she needed.

The enemy didn't give warnings in combat. So neither would the trainers.

She felt a teeny twinge of guilt for not telling Evan about the sim rounds. But he was off running a different exercise.

He'd probably put a stop to it. He'd be dead wrong, but he'd do it because he hadn't checked with the commander first. And Claire? Claire believed too strongly in training for chaos to let him overrule her. He'd be pissed but he'd get over it, and he couldn't get angry because she hadn't done anything to deviate from the plan or break the rules.

Ask forgiveness, not permission. Life had been simpler when she'd hated Evan. Now everything involving him was twisted up inside her, far too distracting to be good for her.

Claire pushed her ballistic eyeglasses up higher on her nose and scanned the staging area. Time to focus on the mission. These troops needed her to help train and evaluate them, and damn it, that's what she was going to do.

CLAIRE LIFTED ENGLE'S WEAPON. HOLDING IT TO HER shoulder, she looked down the sight as she demonstrated the proper technique for entering a building and clearing a room. A room-clearing operation was one of the most dangerous missions troops ever had to execute, but this team was butchering the maneuvers worse than any she'd ever seen.

LT Engle was frustrated and so was her team. Claire could understand that. She hated thinking that Engle's platoon could be training on tasks more relevant than kicking in doors, but she was going with the plan. She just needed Engle to see that any training that focused on working as a team was valuable.

She regretted ever hinting that they should check the block. Engle's heart wasn't in this training and it showed. Claire wasn't going to let her quit, though. That was for damn sure.

"You're going in with your weapon down. That means if you have to engage your enemy, you've got to raise your weapon first." Claire demonstrated how to hold the weapon so that she could fire the instant she had positive target identification. "Keep it high as you come in so that all you have to do is pull the trigger once you ID the target. It may seem like a small thing, but a few seconds can make a difference."

LT Engle nodded, her jaw set tight beneath the band of her helmet chin strap. "Roger, Ma'am. I didn't train for this, so—"

Claire thrust her weapon back at her and cut off her words. "Don't give me excuses. Excuses will get someone killed. I got it you didn't train for this, but you've deployed before so you, more than anyone, should know better than this. Learn it now, because that team is counting on you to get it right."

"I sat in the command cell reading weather reports on my first deployment, damn it, I didn't train for this shit!" LT Engle slammed her weapon onto the ground. "If we're doing this, the war has gone horribly, horribly wrong. We should be running convoys right now, not kicking in doors! We're wasting time."

It took everything Claire had not to completely lose her mind. But that would have been a waste of taxpayer dollars for all that time she'd spent in anger management counseling. Evan would be proud, she thought bitterly.

"You never left the base when we were downrange last deployment. You have no idea what to expect." She kept her voice low and quiet as she stepped close enough so that only Engle could hear her words. "Never, ever, say that you won't do this in real life, Lieutenant. You have no idea what's around the next corner. You don't know if you're going to be running the roads or not. You're going to war. Plan for the unexpected. Now get your head in the goddamn game and get your platoon through this mission like the army officer you're supposed to be."

She didn't soften her words with a smile or worry that the young lieutenant was going to think she was a bitch. She fully expected LT Engle to go running back to her battalion commander to tell her that Claire was picking on her. Claire didn't really care either way, but she'd be derelict in her own duty if she let Engle keep making excuses.

"Roger, Ma'am."

Claire ignored the faint spark of pride in her own heart when Engle lifted her chin and squared her shoulders. Claire offered a slight nod of approval. "Okay. Do it one more time."

Her phone vibrated in her pocket and she frowned as she pulled it out and read the text message. Evan was on his way to her training area. She turned, just in time to see him pulling up in his truck. He pulled his body armor on quickly and a bolt of desire shot straight through her. Damn, the man looked good in body armor. She supposed that meant she'd spent way too much time in the sandbox if she thought men in body armor was sexier than in civilian clothes.

"What's going on?" he asked by way of greeting. There was no friendliness on his face; his body language was all business.

Good. It was easier that way.

"We're running Engle's platoon through the shoot house. We have a limited quantity of simunitions to use, but the request for pyrotechnics was denied." She kept her tone short and to the point. This was business.

He looked down at her, one brow lifting above his sunglasses. "So you didn't try to do anything illegal to get pyro?"

She cocked her chin at him and smirked. "No, Evan. I'm obeying the rules, remember?" The radio on her body armor chirped. "They're getting ready to start again. I'm watching from the roof."

Evan followed her as she climbed the stairs to watch the training from the scaffolding on top of the shoot house that allowed her to observe the team's movements. He took up a position on the opposite end of the building, leaning down against the wall with an easiness she envied. A man Evan's size could easily carry the extra fifty pounds of body armor. Claire could handle the load, too; it just took more effort.

The exercise started again and the sound of ricocheting simunition rounds removed any ability to talk. At least the training wasn't a total loss because they had the dummy rounds. The opposing force walked through the sim rounds as if the troops were shooting blanks, and Reza was having far too much fun. Claire smiled as he led the assault through the building, teaching the young soldiers how to position themselves to control a hallway. She shivered as Reza took two rounds to one arm. She knew for a fact that those tiny simulated bullets shaped like lipstick hurt like a bastard and they were going to leave a hell of a mark.

Significantly less so than the real thing, but still. They stung. It was good training.

Then Reza turned and started shooting the people on his team. It was utter and complete chaos as Engle and her team tried to figure out what was going on. It took forever for Engle to realize Reza was pretending to be an insurgent.

Claire flinched when Reza went down under a barrage of sim rounds. She almost interrupted the exercise, but then Engle stepped up, surprising her. She directed two young soldiers, a specialist and a private first class, to do a proper search. Then they tried to secure Reza quickly, moving him out of the line of fire and into a room they held for their prisoners.

At least, that's what they were trying to do. She glanced at Evan, who was watching the training with a pale, drawn face.

Then everything went to hell below her. Reza did not go quietly. He wasn't supposed to. The two troopers struggled to get him under control and the scuffle attracted the attention of the sergeant, who left his position to help secure the prisoner. Engle followed him, trying to help shore up the hole in their defenses. The opposing force, three sergeants and two privates, picked off Engle's platoon one by one as they struggled to secure the prisoner and hold their defense. It was like watching a bad movie in slow motion. One by one, the platoon was taken out of the fight, forced to sit in a corner once they were defeated and taken out of the fight.

A tight knot of frustration rose inside Claire as she watched the platoon, bereft of any experienced combat leaders except for LT Engle, struggle to hold their positions and call for additional support.

It was a slaughter. A full-blown clusterfuck that, if it were real, it would have ended with a dozen letters home. Frustration burned in Claire's chest as she called a halt to the training.

She didn't give a shit if they were here all night. They were doing this over.

CLAIRE WAS ALREADY MOVING DOWN THE STAIRS BY THE time everyone finally realized that the exercise was over. Reza had Engle pinned in a corner, going off about how she was irresponsible for not holding her position. Engle struggled with tears of frustration and for once, Claire actually felt bad for her.

"At ease!" she shouted over the top of the chaos. Instant silence settled over the chaos. "Sarn't Iaconelli, take them outside and run through a play-by-play on ground and capture every single thing they did wrong. Then we're running this mission again until they get it right. I don't really give a rat's ass if we're here all damn night."

"What the hell is going on, Claire?" Evan rounded on her once they were alone, his face white with fury. It was all Claire could do not to step back from the raw emotion that slammed into her. Evan was pissed. Evan Loehr did not lose his temper, not like this. This? This was barely restrained fury, not the calm, rational response of a man who never lost control. "Why was Iaconelli acting like an insurgent?"

"Because it's realistic. Do you know how many casualties we've had from people supposedly on our side?"

"That's not part of the training plan."

"No one got hurt, damn it, and Engle was learning. Her whole platoon learned a good lesson today," Claire said.

"There isn't time for this. We've got a close-out briefing with the brigade commander in an hour." His voice was filled with ragged frustration and a hundred tormented memories. "They need to pack it up and head in."

"We're not ending training on a bad note," she said quietly. "Half-assed or not, they're getting it right before they walk off this assembly area."

"You think adding in some dummy rounds is enough to teach supply clerks how to do this?" He unhooked his chin strap and yanked his helmet off. "Hell, there are trained infantry squads that can barely do this battle drill and you're trying to teach Combat Barbie how to lead an assault? You can redo it all night long and she's not going to get it."

"And you can be as insulting as you want, but they're going to get it right before we leave tonight." She did not raise her voice, but that didn't stop the latent anger from seeping out. "And the brigade commander specifically said he wanted every team going in to know how to clear a room and secure a position on top of all the other stupid shit he's got everyone doing. I don't care if we miss the next three briefings—they're going to repeat it until they get it right." She lifted her chin defiantly. "Don't tell me you're going to go against what the commander wants?"

"Now isn't the time or the place for that argument," he snapped.

"I never deviated from the training plan, Evan. I can't help that everyone isn't here. But I'm going to train the folks I do have." Claire shook her head, refusing to budge. This was far bigger than whatever was eating at him. "What would you rather they take with them downrange? The fact that they all just died in the shoot house? Or the fact that they took a victory home with them tonight?"

Evan threw his Kevlar against the wall. "Claire, you know as well as I do that Engle can't lead a fucking assault. She can barely make it to work on time."

"And that doesn't change the fact that she's still got to run missions with this team downrange," Claire shouted, finally matching his anger with her own.

Out of the corner of her eye, she saw Reza close the door, effectively preventing anyone else from seeing them. It didn't matter. Their voices carried over the walls of the shoot house.

"Aren't you always telling me that we've got to meet the commander's intent? He wants them to know how to do this." She deliberately did not rise to the bait. There was something more important at stake than her ego or her wounded pride. "So instead of picking a fight with me, let's fix it and get it right. By the numbers, if that's what it takes. If it's the only thing we do today, let's do that," she said quietly.

The door opened. Lieutenant Engle stepped through. "Sir, I know we're not off to a good start. But we need to learn this. Captain Montoya is right. We need to be prepared for anything." Engle swallowed, her skin pale. "We'll stay until we get it right."

Silence settled over the training area. Engle paused for a moment, then stepped back outside, closing the door behind her.

Claire stepped close enough that she could see the tight lines in Evan's neck. She rested her hand on the heavy body armor protecting his chest. Right above his heart. "You can't argue with that."

She expected him to argue. To lash out.

Instead, he just turned away.

door. No answer. She supposed it was for the best, given the backlash from today's training and all the memories it had stirred up inside her. Shoving her hands into her jacket pockets, she headed down the hall toward the stairs, needing a run to burn off the leftover emotional energy.

Claire stepped outside into the pitch-black night, sinking into the thick, viscous slush outside the lodge. The only sound came from the humming of the lodge's overhead lights. Noise was a normal part of life in Iraq and she was long since used to it, so sometimes she had a hard time getting used to the quiet back home here in the States. Real quiet, not the kind brought on by noise-canceling headphones or drug-induced sleep.

The kind of quiet she found walking through a snow-covered trail in the woods. The further she walked from the lodge, the deeper the quiet became. Soon, the only sound was the crunch of her boots on hard packed snow, the huff of her breath freezing on the air. Feeling edgy and too tightly wound, she dug her thumb and forefinger into her eyes, trying to push aside the frustrated memories that lashed at her all day.

Except that she could still hear the screams as the operations center burned around her in Iraq. She could feel the weight of the broken conference room table pressing on her lungs. The smell of burning flesh and sulfur. The smell that had stolen the joy of Fourth of July fireworks from her ever since she'd laid there helpless and screaming. She hadn't counted on the training exercise to resurrect so much of her experience downrange.

She stopped, realization prickling over her skin. "Oh, Evan," she whispered into the dark.

That was what must have set Evan off. The shoot house. It had to be memories. Otherwise, his reaction just seemed . . . insane.

She walked past a few folks hanging in a smoking area, noticing that most were drinking rather than smoking, ignoring the laws on public alcohol. Living up the moment as though tomorrow were just any other day. Funny how war could make you appreciate the time you had. But the longer she spent at home, the more she slipped back into the day-to-day rush of things.

She walked because she was too tired to go running. She walked to try and find a place to stuff the resurrected memories. Her cheeks burned as she closed her eyes, fighting to keep the sobs from tearing out of her throat. Her arms shook and she rocked silently, digging her fingers into her biceps hard enough to bruise. She frowned, fighting the violent shaking as the adrenaline and the emotion attempted to escape.

There was no single event that had scarred her. No one tragic death that had created some shell-shocked, burned-out GI. There was simply the war. The constant stress of combat. The strain of not letting herself fail. The thought that tonight could be the night her trailer was bombed and she would die in her sleep.

No, there was no single event that marked her soul. It was a lifetime of fighting. Her father. Her wars. All of it shaped the person that she showed the world.

But alone in the dark, on a cold wooded trail, Claire let herself fall apart.

And wondered where she would find the strength to put herself back together.

To put her boots back on and do it all again tomorrow.

EVAN TOOK A SIP OF HIS BEER, STARING INTO THE DARKNESS at the edge of his room.

He rubbed his thumb idly on the sweating neck of the bottle and listened as the door to Claire's room closed. He was shocked by the strength of his reactions today. Old memories, never forgotten, long ignored, had risen like demons. Striking out at him, reminding him of the biting failure, the aching loss. The endless frustration that he should have done more. He'd made mistakes in battle that were almost as bad as the choices Engle had made today. It wasn't disdain that had made him react the way he did.

He'd been that platoon leader that lost half his platoon because he'd made a bad call. It hadn't been bad training that made him stop the exercise. It was the memories of death and dying that had overwhelmed him. The chaos erupting in the shoot house had made him lose his bearings, his sense of time. It had been impossible to distinguish between his bloody memories and what was going on around him and he'd lashed out at the only thing solid in the world at that moment: Claire.

He slammed back the rest of his beer, then dragged on some clothes to head to the bar. It should still be open for a couple more hours if he was lucky. He needed to drink, to try and forget the burning, twisting pain that Claire's quiet words had carved into his soul. He paused just outside her door, tempted, so tempted to knock. Just to check on her.

That was an excuse and he knew it. He didn't want to be alone. Didn't want to fight the god-awful memories by himself tonight. Claire, whatever else she might be, had her own demons. And as foolish as it was, the desire to peel back her layers drove him closer when he should have been going the other way.

He was a fool. Claire Montoya was convinced she didn't need anyone. That her way was the only way.

He kept walking.

Because only a fool would want a woman who would never let him in. He could touch her skin, touch her body, but she'd never trust him enough to let him touch her heart. Not the way he wanted. And he couldn't do that. Not with her.

Her terms were unacceptable, her barriers too high.

❧ 10 ☙

T he phone. Please, sweet baby Jesus, tell her the phone wasn't ringing. Claire rolled over, groping for the buzzing object. Vibrating steadily on the floor next to her bed, it paused, only to start up again a moment later. The only reason she'd heard it at all was because it had fallen on top of her uniform belt. The hard plastic vibrating against the metal was obnoxious enough to wake the dead.

She squinted, then closed one eye until the number came into view. She didn't recognize it. "Yeah?"

"Claire?"

She scowled and blinked, struggling to see the digits on the readout more clearly. She couldn't have heard that voice right. "Evan?"

"Wake up, Montoya, I need a ride."

Claire dropped her head down onto her forearm and groaned. It wasn't even two a.m. and they had to be back on the range in less than six hours. She tried to look on the bright side. At least Evan was talking to her again. She remembered what time it was. No, that was not a bright side. It was borderline criminal. "Is someone dying?"

"Nice." She heard water running in the background before it abruptly stopped. She had the strongest suspicion that he'd just finished in the bathroom. Honestly, she didn't know how she felt about that. "I need a ride. Before Iaconelli and I spend the rest of this little boondoggle in jail."

What exactly was Evan doing out with Reza anyway? And where were they that they needed her to come and get them? "Are you drunk?"

Evan sighed hard. "Look, you don't honestly think I'd call you if it wasn't important? I'm half-cocked and Iaconelli, ah, Ike's had a hell of a night. I can't drive and if I don't get him out of here in the next hour, the bartender is going to call the cops, which means all of Fort Carson is going to know about this by tomorrow. Later today. Hell, whatever day it is."

Claire sat up, rubbing the sleep out of her eyes, concern motivating her to actually move. She rested her forehead in her hands. "Captain America went out drinking. How 'bout that."

"Are you coming or what?"

"Yeah, I'm coming," she grumbled, and disconnected the call.

Iaconelli could have been in hell and she would have gone in after him. She'd done it plenty of times before. But Evan? Evan was another story.

But the fact that Captain America had not only gone out with the resident bad boy and had gotten too drunk to drive roused her curiosity. The firefight at the shoot house must have screwed him up more than she'd guessed

She swallowed and dragged her hand through her hair, then started digging through her clothes for a bra. Iaconelli was family, damn it. And while she didn't know what Evan was to her, she knew couldn't leave him.

That much she did know.

✦

HALF AN HOUR LATER, CLAIRE WALKED INTO THE OLD railway car that had been converted into a bar by some enterprising soul. She wasn't entirely sure what she expected from a bar called The Greasy Tube, but it definitely looked greasy and tubelike. The air was cold and thin, the kind of thin that made her lungs hurt from having to work too hard to pull oxygen from it. Even the thick smell of cigarette smoke was thin here, slinking into her hair and lungs like a sneaking thing.

She peered around the darkness, scanning faces that looked far too old and run down to be in a place that Reza would frequent. He liked energy this kind of seedy energy. Craved it. This place felt like a funeral. Or a wake.

The bar, such as it was, crouched at one end of the railway car. A couch that Claire suspected had a good chance of having fleas and several bodily fluids she'd rather not think about sat against one wall beneath barred windows. A stack of what looked like broken chairs and the tattered remnants of a table filled the space between the bar and the couch.

Reza was passed out, slumped over the arm of the couch, covering his eyes with one hand and snoring quietly. Impressive. It took a lot to drink Reza under the table. Claire flinched as the stench of old beer assaulted her nose and resurrected ancient memories.

The bartender was a tiny woman who looked like she was every bit of sixty, the kind of sixty that suggested hard drinking and even harder drugs. She was busy reading someone the riot act at the bar.

Evan. Slumped over the bar and leaning hard on his elbows to stay upright, he looked unsteady on his wobbly stool. She made her way over to him, squeezing past a couple who were swapping heavy doses of spit in a corner. Claire felt scuzzy just from being in this place. She approached Evan carefully and tapped him on the shoulder, careful to step back in case he was too drunk to realize it was her. She'd never been around a truly intoxicated Evan, and she didn't know what to expect.

"Hey." His smile was warm and welcoming. No, Evan wasn't a violent drunk. Apparently, he was an extra-relaxed, charming drunk. Wasn't that interesting?

He shifted and leaned his head on his hand, bracing his elbow against the bar. The movement stretched his T-shirt over his chest. Claire forced herself to look away. She didn't do drunk sex, even with an charming, slightly intoxicated Evan.

"You have some serious explaining to do," she said lightly. There was no judgment in her tone. She was more relieved than anything. She'd been worried when she hadn't been able to find him after the shoot house. Maybe Evan hadn't come through the war unscathed, but she hadn't expected to find him drunk at the bar. Not when he'd been giving her hell about Reza's drinking. She could not—no, she would not—judge either of them. Something had snapped in Evan today, and she of all people could understand that.

❧

"I think we need to get Iaconelli home." His voice was thick and harsh, as if he'd spent the night shouting over loud music or mortar fire. He always lost his voice when he spent time on the range. He studied Claire carefully in the smoky light.

She had come. He was surprised. Maybe he shouldn't have been. She sat down next to him on a crappy bar stool, looking every inch a warrior goddess. A chair scraped against the beer-soaked wood floor and Claire's eyes snapped toward the sound, instantly on guard.

"What happened?" she asked. He was surprised at what he didn't hear in her voice. Anger. Blame. No, it was more mild curiosity, tinged with . . . resignation? As though she'd done this a time or two.

"Some of the local boys decided they didn't like the way Iaconelli looked. Then they heard me use his name and they were sure he was a terrorist who was here to bomb this shithole bar halfway to Wyoming."

He watched a myriad of emotions flicker across her face as he spoke. She would be an avenging angel to those who wronged her friends, and there was no doubt that the flagrant racism of the local rednecks pissed her off.

"So did someone at least end up in the hospital?" she asked. He could see her choosing her words carefully.

"Hell no," the bartender rasped through a gap in her front teeth. "That would require Jenkins to talk to the cops. And he's not really what you might call a fan of the authorities." She set a glass down on a towel to dry. "But if you don't get your buddy out of here soon, I'm not going to be able to stop the cops from dragging him off to jail."

Evan glanced at Claire, who was scanning the bar for any signs of trouble. Her hair fell forward, dusting along her temple. He reached for it, stroking it behind her ear before she could stop him. She tensed but didn't pull away. He smiled. Progress, he thought. Maybe she wasn't still mad at him. He could hope.

He shifted again and angled his body toward the woman behind the bar. "Thanks for not calling the cops," he said simply. "I'll make sure he takes care of the damages."

"Well, thanks for your service." The woman sniffed and focused on wiping down the glass in her hand. Her smile looked like a tear in cracked leather. "Get your friend some help before you bury him. A man shouldn't be able to drink like that."

He fisted one hand on the bar, bracing the other against the worn oak as he prepared to stand. Ignoring the burning questions in Claire's eyes, he pulled a twenty out of his pocket and dropped it on the counter.

"Sure." He pushed the stool closer to the bar and stood. "Ready?"

The silence between Claire and Evan was awkward and heavy, the kind of silence that sucked the air from his lungs. He hadn't wanted to call her, but there hadn't really been a lot of options. He wasn't even entirely sure how they'd ended up here. He'd gone downstairs to the bar in the lobby. Of course Iaconelli had been there. And Evan had been too wound up to care that he was drinking with his former platoon sergeant. The next thing he knew, he and Iaconelli were pounding shots at The Greasy Tube. Then the local dickheads had succeeded in ruining a perfectly good time. Evan had already started sobering up by the time he called Claire. He wasn't nearly as drunk as Iaconelli, but he'd never get behind the wheel of a car after drinking. Never again, anyway. He drank because it was a way to deaden the pain, to stop the bleeding. But he'd never drink and drive.

He was glad she had come. The last thing he wanted to do was try to drag Iaconelli out of here by himself. And regardless of whatever this was between them, she'd never leave Iaconelli. That much, he knew with absolute certainty.

He tried not to be jealous. He failed. He was jealous of their trust, their easy friendship. The way she relaxed around Iaconelli but not with him.

They managed to get Iaconelli strapped in the backseat of the rented SUV without any significant injuries. He had no idea how much Steel Reserve Reza had pounded before blacking out, but it had been a hell of a ride prior to that.

"How much was the damage?" Claire asked softly as she started the truck and pulled out onto the main road.

He slammed the door shut and buckled his seat belt automatically. "Close to a thousand bucks," he mumbled, dragging a hand over his face.

"Lovely." Beside him, Claire maneuvered the big truck out of the parking spot. "Hope he has some deployment money saved up."

Evan snorted and slammed his head back against the headrest. "Tell me about it."

They rode in silence for a long time. Evan wished he could find some pleasure in the moment—in being with Claire, even under these circumstances—but all he felt was a rising sense of doom that the person he'd worked his ass off to become was one thread away from unraveling. It had nothing to do with Iaconelli sleeping off his latest bender in the backseat. It was much more subtle, like a nagging sense of foreboding tickling at the base of his skull that his control was slipping away.

"So you're not going to ask what prompted my drunken escapade?"

"I don't think you're nearly as drunk as you want me to think you are." Claire glanced over at him, then turned her attention back to the road. Her fingers tensed on the steering wheel. "Want to talk about it?" she asked after a long moment.

He sniffed and stared out the window, scrubbing his hand over his jaw and trying to figure out what to say next. They drove in silence for a few minutes, the neon signs occasionally lighting up the inside of the car as they passed tiny hamlets of civilization. Iaconelli mumbled in the backseat and then promptly began snoring again.

"Stop the car up here," he said quietly.

"We're in the middle of nowhere. There's no place to pull off the road."

"There's a turnoff." One he knew all too well.

He hadn't planned this. Hadn't left the lodge with this in mind. But as much as he'd tried to avoid the pain of coming home, part of him needed this tonight.

He glanced at her as she pulled into the barely plowed turnoff. The tires crunched through the snow. A hundred feet from the road, bathed in the soft glow of the headlights, stood a gnarled, twisted oak. He heard Claire's hiss of breath the moment she made the connection.

Grinding his teeth, he stepped into the bitter cold of his memories.

⊗

EVAN STOOD IN FRONT OF THE OLD OAK, HANDS STUFFED IN the pockets of his faded jacket. His cheeks were red from the cold but Claire doubted he could feel it.

The old tree was more misshapen than the tattoo on his back. More bent and twisted with time. She thought she saw a glint of metal gleaming from the bark, but she couldn't be sure.

"Casey was always a bit wild." He sniffed, rubbing his jaw briefly before stuffing his hand back in his pocket. "My dad worked a lot. Which left me to look after her. Mom didn't really know what to do with her. I guess Mom's answer was to do nothing at all."

He released a shuddering breath. It froze, glittering on the night air. "Is it weird that I don't hate her for that?"

Claire could barely speak past the knot in her throat. She shook her head, mute. Listening. Just listening.

"I'd snuck out to a party a week before Halloween. I

thought Casey was at home. She wasn't. She," his voice wavered and broke and he sucked in a long, hard breath, "she'd gone out with a couple of seniors from another high school."

"Oh, Evan." Her words were a whisper, a caress of sympathy.

"I got to her before anything happened." He smiled, but the smile was carved with sadness, raw and uncut. "I thought I was some kind of badass, and that I was going to get my little sister home safe." His breath caught again and he bowed his head. "Except that I'd had a couple of beers."

Claire placed her hand on his shoulder, right over the scar that had ripped Casey Loehr's name from his skin.

"I thought I was sober enough to drive. We were hit by a tractor trailer. He drifted into my lane and I jerked the wheel into his lane to try and avoid him." The muscles on his back clenched and knotted beneath her touch. "Casey died before the airlift helo could get her to the hospital."

She heard the recrimination, the self-loathing in those whispered words. The memories twisting into him. "I killed my little sister."

He bowed his head, looking away from the tree. Avoiding her gaze until she stepped in front of him, cupping his face gently in her palms, his skin frigid cold beneath her touch. Waiting until he met her gaze. "Evan," she whispered, knowing her words were useless.

There was nothing she could say that would erase the thirteen years of guilt he'd carried with him. She traced her fingers across his forehead, brushing a strand of hair from his eyes.

It terrified her, seeing this side of a man she thought of as a rock. Steadfast. Reliable.

But tonight he was shaken, his grief so real and raw, he

might have been standing at the scene of the accident after it just happened instead of in a field of snow-covered memories.

"Look at me," she said. He turned to her with dark eyes filled with sadness. She brushed her lips against his. "Evan. You can't keep punishing yourself."

His breath froze against her skin. Slowly, so slowly, the memories retreated.

"Evan," she repeated, her breath mingling with his. She brushed her lips against his again, hoping to chase away the demons that danced at the edge of his soul.

A ragged breath rushed from him and he buried his face against her neck. She wrapped her arms around him. "I can't go home. My parents can't even look at me." He lifted his face from her neck, stroking her hair from her face. He smiled weakly. "So much for Captain America, huh?"

Claire cupped his face in her hands. "I call you Captain America because you're such an honorable man. But now I know why you work so hard to be perfect." She stroked her thumb over his cheek.

He was lost. Adrift in a field of memories. And he might have been looking at Claire, but he was speaking to the memory of his dead sister, who hadn't lived long enough for him to make his apology.

"You can't change what happened," she whispered. "You're a good man, Evan."

He closed his eyes, lowering his forehead to hers. "How can you look at me and say that knowing what I did?"

She shifted, pressing her lips to his closed eyes. "Because I know all about making mistakes that will haunt you for a lifetime."

"Iaconelli is going to ruin his career with his drinking." Evan's voice was rough as Claire pulled into the parking lot of the lodge a short while later. It was close to four a.m. Dawn was not far off, but he doubted they'd be able to sleep. It would not be the first time that either of them had pulled more than a twenty-four-hour shift. The war was funny that way. Got you so used to working such long hours that when you came home, you felt like you were slacking off if you worked only ten- or twelve-hour days.

"He's getting worse." It hurt Claire to say the words—she'd tried to keep them inside of her for so long. "And I don't think he can stop."

"If he doesn't get himself under control, someone's going to get hurt," Evan said. He stared out into the darkness. "Before we came up here, I found out the sergeant major caught him with Everclear downrange." Claire said nothing, and Evan turned his face to peer at her in the darkness. "I don't know why he didn't report him, but he didn't."

Claire met his gaze, a warm sadness filling her eyes in the unlit cab of the truck. "I can guess," she said quietly. "He needed Reza in the fight more than he needed to make an example of him for drinking downrange. It might not have been the right trade-off, but it's one that anyone who has served in combat can understand."

Evan sighed quietly. "He doesn't talk about it. About anything, for that matter. He just drinks and screws and drinks and screws. Only good thing I can say is that at least he loads up on condoms, so there hopefully aren't dozens of little Iaconellis running around."

Evan caught the edge of her smile in the dark and he frowned. "What?"

"It's funny. Reza is passed out in the backseat and oh, by the way, you're breaking all kinds of rules to keep him off any police reports, and the only thing you're concerned about is his ability to put a condom on when he's shit-faced drunk?"

Evan laughed quietly. "Well, that is actually heroic, if you think about it."

"Only in your world," she said with a wry grin. "In the rest of the world, it's kind of tragic."

Silence hung over them once more, and Claire killed the ignition.

"I'll help you get him upstairs," Evan said softly.

She glanced over her shoulder, then back at him, an odd smile on her lips. "You don't have to. I'll deal with him. I've done it a hundred times before." Iaconelli shifted behind them and threw his arm over his eyes with a rough sigh. Claire was the type of woman who would come through for her friends no matter what. It hurt, knowing that no matter what happened between them, he could never garner that kind of loyalty from her.

He slid his hand over hers, her skin cold and soft beneath his palm. "Maybe it's time we both stopped trying to deal with everything alone."

THEY PUT REZA TO BED. GETTING REZA OUT OF THE CAR was no easier than getting him into the backseat of the car, but it was accomplished in much the same way. With much swearing and grunting.

Evan paused outside Reza's door. Claire stood with him for a moment, then threaded her fingers through his, guiding him past his door and into her own. The door closed with a quiet click behind them and a hush fell over the suite. The snow covered the outside world in a heavy white blanket, obscuring the dark.

Kneeling next to the fireplace, Claire stacked a few pieces of kindling on top of newspaper and waited until they were crackling and snapping before she added a small log. All the while, she felt Evan's gaze on her back. The warmth of it slid beneath her skin, sidling up to her heart and nestling close.

She shifted and sighed, settling on the floor near the fire and wrapping her arms around her knees. The awkwardness between them had to balance out sometime. They could not go the rest of this mission alternating between fighting and not speaking to each other and kissing at really awkward moments.

Evan moved to sit on the floor in front of the fire and said nothing for a long moment. The space between them was warmer now, heated by more than the flames in front of them.

"What's going on in that brain of yours?" she asked quietly.

It was tempting, so tempting, to inch across the floor and sit near him. Such a simple gesture, but one that would hold too much significance. She watched as he searched for a way to put whatever was eating at him into words.

He'd long ago convinced her that he was nowhere near as

intoxicated as she'd originally thought. Either he hadn't had as much to drink as Reza or he'd processed it out of his system faster. One thing was clear: the man sitting on the floor of her suite was sober.

His next words, much more so.

"Today when we were at the shoot house, I started thinking about our mission out in Hamamiyat." He looked up at her, his eyes glittering darkly.

"You mean the mission where you pissed your pants?" she said, dancing around a memory. It was one of the few times they'd actually worked together without ripping each other's heads off.

"I have it on good authority that I was not the only one who pissed my pants that day." Some of the tension went out of his shoulders then. His mouth relaxed. Just a little, but it was enough to take the edge off.

Not enough to keep Claire from being drawn to him, inexplicably, by a force she could not explain. He was everything that was tormented, sensual, male.

"I never figured that training for combat would never be the same again after doing it for real," she said quietly. She turned away from the want pounding inside her, ignoring the sensual warmth from the man sitting so close to her. Heat engulfed her, wrapped around her.

Made her blood sing with arousal and unsatisfied desire.

"Yeah. It makes a difference when you know that someday, the fake blood will be real." Evan scoffed quietly. He paused. "I think the only one who didn't nearly shit himself after that house blew up was Reza."

The memory of that town, of that battle stirred a maelstrom of emotions inside her. Twisted and tormented. "I think he got drunk when we got back to base after that mission," she admitted softly. "I couldn't find him for half a day, and when I did . . ."

Evan studied her quietly for a moment. "You didn't turn him in."

"Why would I?" A shadow fell across her heart. A memory of having her life uprooted and destroyed all because she'd finally told someone about the extent of her father's drinking. She pinned him with a thoughtful look and a wry smile. "I look after people I care about." She stared into the fire, lost in a maze of tangled memories.

Evan inched closer to her. He boxed her in between the wall and the fire and the heat from his body, and she fought the brief panic that gripped her heart. "What were you thinking about just then?" he whispered, sitting far too close.

Panic edged up, cloying and grasping and making it difficult for her to breathe. Cool air kissed her skin as his fingers gathered the weight of her hair from her neck.

She tipped her chin, arching her neck in subtle invitation. "This is a bad idea," she whispered.

"Probably." He nipped her ear hard enough that pleasure spiked with pain shot through her body to the vee between her thighs. "Do you want me to stop?"

"Only if you want to die," she murmured. He shifted, and in a single moment pulled her against him, so that she was cradled between his thighs. His chest pressed to her back, his arousal grazing her backside.

His breath was hot on her neck, his deep voice rumbling through his body and into hers. "I have a confession."

"Hmm?" Sensation slithered through her body, twisting and writhing with the lingering strain from the day.

He traced the edge of her ear with the tip of his tongue, sending fire sparking through her veins. "It's been a really long time for me."

She smiled, resting her head back against his shoulder. He slipped his hands over her belly, stroking her gently. "A warrior monk. I knew it."

His laugh rumbled through his body, shaking her gently. "Not exactly." He pressed his lips to her temple. "But I want to do this right."

"I was right. A perfectionist." She smiled and shifted closer. "I don't think you've got anything to worry about. You don't exactly have a lot of competition."

Behind her, he stiffened and she winced—she'd revealed far too much. "Bad lovers, or not enough lovers?"

The warmth of his body drew her closer, urging her into the promise of his embrace. She played her palms over his thighs, feeling the hard muscles beneath the soft fabric of his jeans. "Does it matter?" she whispered.

"Not really." His breath was hot on her cheek, his mouth nibbling over the tiny curve of her jaw. "But . . ."

Her breath caught in her throat as he sucked gently on the skin beneath her ear, his big body wrapping around her. Too close. She inched away slightly.

"Answer me something?" he asked, his voice soft. "Why do you always back away when I touch you?"

"Evan, this isn't a good time to go all amateur psychiatrist on me," she whispered, losing some of the fight to maintain control.

She felt his lips curl against her ear and an unexpected laugh rumbled deep in his chest. "Ever tried naked psychiatry?"

Her blood warmed, burning through the bad memories to the good that she did not deserve and could not hold on to, no matter how tightly she squeezed. The lingering edge of arousal pumped through her veins, slower now, but still potent.

Evan was here. And tonight, she understood him a little better. Understood that losing his sister when he was little more than a child had shaped the man he was. He'd shown her the scarred, damaged man beneath his uniform. She admired the hell out of that man.

He would not see the same thing if he looked closely at her jaded past. No matter how much her blood pumped in her ears, no matter how much the heat pooled between her thighs, she wanted her own past to stay buried.

HE CRAVED CLAIRE, BUT MORE, HE CRAVED HER TRUST, THIS woman who was so convinced that she needed no one. Gently, so gently, he traced a single finger down the line of her neck.

He wanted. Oh God how he wanted this woman. And with a single touch, he had shattered her barriers. He knew it when she tilted her neck to one side, the barest hint of movement. He knew it when her throat moved against his finger as she swallowed and did not pull away.

"Can I kiss you?" he asked, lowering his mouth to hover just above her pulse.

He traced his finger along the gentle slope of her jaw, their bodies separated by the barest hint of space. "Claire?" He blew on her skin, savoring the shiver that ran through her body and crossed the space into his. "Say yes, Claire."

❧ 12 ☙

A whimper tore from her throat. Pleasure surged through his veins, his cock hard and aching. He caressed the sensitive skin of her neck, but he would not give her what she wanted until she said it. "Say yes, Claire," he murmured. With infinite slowness, he traced the line of her jaw with the tip of his tongue, cradling her body against his.

She moaned low in her throat, refusing to answer. Everything about her was a challenge. To his sanity. To his livelihood. To the wholeness of his very soul. A maddening, frustrating challenge that burned in his belly. He pressed his lips to that sensitive skin then, allowing her the first round, even as he wrapped his arms tight around her, pulling her hard against him. He suckled her throat, felt her pulse racing beneath his lips as she molded herself against him, a shiver ripping through them both.

She arched against him, rubbing her cheeks against his erection, and it was Evan's turn to groan as his cock chafed against the zipper of his pants. He rocked his hips against her, feeding on the sensation of her body against his. He wanted her naked. He wanted her stripped and vulnerable.

He curled his lips against her neck, then nipped at her earlobe before he yanked her shirt over her head in a single jerk.

She shivered violently at the sudden snap of cold against her skin, but he pulled her against him again before she could register what he'd done. "That's mean," she hissed.

"You're the one who's not cooperating."

He held her close, loving the feeling of her body against his. He stroked his hands over her belly, her ribs, memorizing the shape of her before he eased her back. He'd meant to press his lips to the back of her neck.

Dozens of tiny scars crisscrossed her back, white lines against pale skin.

His gasp was a sharp, biting hiss in the silence. Her body went tense beneath his touch. He closed his eyes, his vision crossed with the razor-thin lines that threaded the skin on her back. He wanted to push, to demand the answers that would ease his burning desire to hurt the person who'd done this to her.

CLAIRE COULD HAVE SWORN SHE FELT THE HEAT OF HIS GAZE sweep over the damaged flesh. She could not force herself to relax as she waited for him to speak.

"This is not a combat injury," he murmured, his voice shaking with barely restrained rage. "Is it?"

"No. It's not." Claire felt exposed and vulnerable. Her heart trembled in her chest, skittering against her breast. She tried to pull away then, needing to stop the bloodletting before it began. "Just another piece of history."

Neither of them moved. Neither of them made a sound in

the ragged silence. Then he slowly pulled her against him, kissing her cheek, her jaw, her throat. And Claire could have wept for the relief that crashed through her.

WITH A GENTLENESS HE DID NOT FEEL, EVAN CRADLED HER body against his. He'd never guessed that the scars she carried would be physical. She hid so much beneath the rank on her chest, the grey uniforms she wore everywhere. She was filled with shame, he realized, when she had nothing to be ashamed of. He cradled her against him and pressed his lips to the scars crisscrossing her back. Had anyone ever loved her, just for her? "You're beautiful," he murmured. Her fingers tightened against his forearms.

And he started again. Slow strokes down her arms. Skimming her belly. Teasing the heavy weight of her breasts without fully cupping her and then gently removing her bra. Lying against her side, he angled his body until he could nip the side of her breast. He smiled at her tiny, surprised cry as she relaxed with his touch, her tension turning lithe and sensual.

"Patience isn't my strong point, Loehr," she growled, sounding like a fierce, wounded kitten, rotating her hips against his. They were still on the floor in front of the fire, their bodies covered in the warm, flickering heat from the live flames.

"Hmm." He held her gaze then as he traced the slope of her breast, moaning deep in his throat when her nipple puckered to a hard point beneath his touch. Her mouth parted, her lips swollen and glistening and pink, her breath a quiet gasp when he moved up her body gently, so gently, scraping her throat with his teeth.

He toyed with her breasts, careful not to cover her and

box her in, remembering her panic about being boxed in. His fingers journeyed lower, tracing faint lines over the soft curve of her belly. She shifted, parting her knees in silent offering.

She hissed in frustration as he traced a feather-light touch down the seam of her pants. She captured his wrist and pressed his hand to her sex, grinding against it. "Demanding, aren't we," he murmured.

Her warm, sexy heat penetrated the soft cotton. He freed his hand, sliding it between the cotton and her skin and into her slick, wet heat. He stroked her, slowly, slowly, skimming the length of his finger against her swollen flesh.

Pleasure burned in his belly, his cock aching and hard. He moved his hips, unconsciously seeking to release the pressure building inside of him with each stroke of his finger against her slick heat. He felt her answering tension in the rise of her hips, the sheen of sweat against her skin.

Her body bowed beneath his touch, taut and tense and ready to snap. And then he stopped. A moment before she crashed and burst against his finger, he stopped.

❧

She arched against him, her fingers digging into his forearms as she chased the release he'd denied her. Frustrated, she slapped at his arms. "I swear to all that's holy, Evan, you're going to die."

He laughed.

The bastard laughed at her.

"Now I know why Sarah doesn't date," she growled.

He flipped her onto her back again but did not attempt to lie on top of her. "Take your pants off."

"You first," she said, still sulking.

His eyes were pitch black in the low light as he shifted to do as she asked.

She propped herself up on her elbows, loving the way his throat moved when he swallowed. With deliberate slowness, he teased her with a glimpse of raw male flesh as he tugged his shirt up and over his head. His dog tags hung down the center of his chest, resting on the solid wall of muscle over his heart, right at the edge of the twisting black branches.

He shucked his boots quickly and then he stood before her, her own personal fantasy. Sculpted chest, rough with hair that tapered into a thin line disappearing beneath those damned buttons.

She attempted to swallow but her mouth went dry as he flicked open the top button of his pants. The second button revealed the glistening tip of his erection.

"You went commando?" she asked.

"Haven't had time to do laundry."

"There goes that fantasy I had of you wearing Ranger panties." She lifted her gaze to meet his eyes and collided with a fierce intensity she hadn't known he was capable of. Evan held her gaze as he dropped his pants, standing naked before her. He was perfect. "That's a hell of a salute, soldier," she murmured, taking in every detail of Evan's beautiful body.

He burst out laughing, and the movement made his cock bounce as he left his pants in a pool on the floor and came over to crouch beside her. "That's the corniest thing you could have said right now." He leaned over and kissed her fiercely. "Your turn."

Claire leaned back on the carpet, reveling in the feel of his gaze on her. She pulled down her pants first, then hooked her thumbs into the waistband of her panties and inched them down, slowly, so slowly, until she was as naked as he was.

Claire had never thought of herself as beautiful. She was fair to middling at best, and she was certain it was the simple fact that she had a vagina that had garnered her so much attention in the male-dominated world of the army. But at this exact moment she felt radiant. Evan licked his lips, his gaze sweeping down her body to the center of her. He knelt near her feet, his hands seeking out the soft, smooth skin of her calves.

She expected him to slide up her body, kissing slowly, but nothing about this was as she'd expected.

His hands were firm and strong when he parted her thighs, pushing them wide, and for once she didn't argue. Then he kissed her. A gentle kiss where she was swollen and throbbing. He teased her with a feather-light stroke of his tongue, a gentle flick across her exposed intimate flesh, and she arched beneath him, bowing her back off the floor. He repeated the gentle tap with his tongue and the pleasure was back, tighter, hotter and oh so exquisite.

He stroked her, using his tongue, teasing her until she was ready to snap. And when he finally, finally filled her with one teasing finger, her breath caught in her throat, frozen in that instance before she shattered.

✺

SHE WAS HOT AND TIGHT AND PERFECTLY WET. HIS COCK throbbed until he thought it would snap as he teased her, drawing out her pleasure until she was on the edge, ready to tumble into abandon a second time.

He wanted her overwhelmed. He wanted her panting and naked and exposed. He urged her over him but she shifted, turning away until he cradled her body against his chest. And then his finger was no longer enough. He fumbled with the condom, barely able to roll it into place, and then he stopped, unsure how to proceed with this beautiful damaged woman. She hated being pinned. How—

She crawled into his lap, spreading her thighs over his as she faced away from him. He pulled her close, her back to his chest, her entire body open to his touch. Her hips arched against him as he pushed into her tight, tight heat—tiny, sexy cries escaping her as she rocked against him. She clenched around him, drawing him deeper but not deep enough.

He surrendered control and she arched her back, pushing against him until he sank fully, deeply inside her. Reaching between her thighs, he stroked her swollen flesh as she rocked against him, taking them to a peak.

He felt her come apart in his arms, her pleasure a cry in the darkness. Only when she was shaking and spent and rocking against him in the last throes of her orgasm did he finally shatter. And in that single instant as he slid deep, deep inside her and burst into a thousand points of light, he had everything he wanted.

Except a piece of her heart.

❧ 13 ☙

Claire moved toward the coffeepot in the conference room of the lodge like a crack addict looking for a fix. Luckily, no one bothered to intercept her, which was good because she was liable to commit murder if she didn't get coffee. Soon. Holy ever-loving hell, how could she have been so stupid last night? She poured the coffee into a cheap Styrofoam cup and let the hot caffeine burn her tongue and the entire path down to her stomach.

She'd slept like shit after Evan had slipped out of her suite. She was grateful he hadn't tried to stay. Awkward didn't even begin to cover her postcoital reaction. Awkward was when you couldn't remember someone's name. This was more along the lines of epic mistake. Deeply uncomfortable. Sipping her coffee, she scanned the room. She paused for just a moment on Evan, who was sitting in the corner beneath the TV. He looked irritated and rumpled and drop-dead sexy. Her blood warmed at the mere sight of him.

Yeah, she was going to be real effective on the ranges today.

Looked like sex hadn't done either one of them any good.

She sniffed and packed away her twisted emotions. She needed to focus on work. His mood wasn't her problem.

Claire sat by the fire for a long moment, watching the flames dance as they bit into the logs. Memories danced in those flames, too. Memories of missions gone bad. She bit back the crushing sense that the dysfunction in this unit went far deeper than they could see. And she was terrified, because there were people she cared about in this formation.

Colonel Danvers seemed completely unconcerned that very few people from the support company had been out at the shoot house yesterday. They'd get people to combat practice when they could had been the response that had come through the operations officer.

Relentless frustration burned inside of her. There was little she could do to protect them. And worse, she knew that Colonel Danvers had set a command climate that placed higher value on PowerPoint skills than on combat effectiveness in their junior leaders. Bad leaders did stupid things that got people killed.

Reza walked into the dining room and made a direct assault on the coffeepot. She smiled when she saw the outdated brown sweater he had on beneath his uniform jacket. "Are those even authorized for wear anymore?"

Reza grunted as he filled his stainless-steel travel mug. "You can keep that moisture-wicking crap. I'll take my old wool sweater any day of the week."

"In my day, we had wool sweaters and we liked it," she said, making her voice sound like an old man's. "We didn't have all this fancy, shmancy gear you young pups have."

"I'm three years older than you." Reza sighed and shook his head. He looked ragged and, for the first time since she'd met him, hung over. "Only in the army would you think thirty-five is old." He breathed in the steam rising from his coffee, but his faint smile didn't reach his eyes. "I don't suppose this is any good?"

"It's better than the goat piss they used to serve in the ops office in Iraq, if that helps."

"It doesn't." He sighed and braced himself for that first bitter taste, then flinched. "This is worse than I expected. Ugh. I might do without."

"Please don't. You're not nice when you don't have caffeine and you're out of Rip Its, last I checked."

Reza smiled and said nothing, staring into his drink. Finally, he sighed. "You're not going to bitch at me about last night?"

Claire studied him carefully. Searching for the words she needed. And beneath her worry was the agonizing fear that she would lose him forever if she said what needed to be said. Just like she'd lost her dad. "Would it work?"

"Not really." He sipped the terrible coffee.

And Claire turned away from the fight. "Then I'd just be wasting my breath. I'll save it for when it will make a difference." But her voice broke, and there was nothing she could do to hide it except to turn away.

"Ah shit, Claire, don't cry."

She wheeled on him, keeping her voice low, her actions tight and controlled. She didn't want to draw any attention to them but from the corner of her eye, she caught Evan watching. Alert. Tense. "I'm not crying over you, you son of a bitch. I'll save my tears for your goddamn funeral."

She walked away before he could say anything else. Before she could see if he was angry or if maybe, just maybe, her words had made a difference.

They hadn't. She knew they hadn't.

Reza was going to die. Not from an enemy bullet, but from his own stupid choices, because whatever demons he was battling, he was losing the fight.

And she was going to lose one of the only people she could call friend.

⊙⚜⊙

THE SMALL CONTINGENT OF TRAINERS GATHERED AROUND Evan as he started to lay out the mission for the day. Finally, after days of ranges and briefings and inspections, they'd reached the important training: convoys. He glanced at LT Engle, who was blowing on her hands as though her breath were going to magically penetrate the army-issued cold-weather gloves. The kid had grown up fast in the last year. Hell, no one who went to war came back as innocent as when they'd gone in.

He glanced around, looking for Claire. She should be happy they were finally hitting the convoy portion of the training exercise but when he saw her earlier this morning, she had looked drawn and tense. He was worried about her. She hadn't spoken to him much over the last few days of the exercise and despite their having slept together, he felt the distance between them more sharply than ever.

He crouched down, pushing away his worry, and drew a quick sketch of the mock city in the snow, doing his best to ignore Claire, whom he'd finally spotted near the edge of one of the buildings, talking to Sarah. He shut down his reaction to her, focusing on LT Engle, who looked excited to finally be running convoy training. He almost smiled at her eagerness.

"Okay Engle, your platoon is going to enter the city here and you have to get the supplies to the objective here," he drew an X at a four-way intersection, "and two of the four streets will be blocked with burning tires. From there, depending on how you react to the civilians, you'll either get ambushed or make it through the rest of the city to the objective."

"Got it," Engle said. "I just wish we'd found someplace less freezing than this for the exercise."

Evan raised both eyebrows and looked up at Engle. "Unless you plan on driving the entire battalion to somewhere warm and sunny like Fort Irwin, California, no."

Reza slapped Engle on the shoulder. "Toughen up, sissy. You haven't been frozen until you've spent forty-five days in Grafenwoehr."

"What's Grafenwoehr?" Engle asked, rubbing her hands together.

"A training area in Germany. You want to talk cold, you haven't seen shit until you've spent a month at Graf in December. Takes three weeks to thaw out your balls when you get home. If you had any. Which you don't. Nevermind."

Evan glanced to his right when he heard the sound of boots crunching on the snow. Claire walked up and was looking down at the quick terrain sketch Evan had done. She stayed silent, but the bones in her jaw looked close to snapping from the sheer pressure she was putting on her teeth.

He'd wanted to catch her after breakfast but she'd disappeared after talking with Iaconelli. Now, she looked unapproachable at best. Frustration snapped at him. He'd thought last night would be the start of something new between them. Instead, she seemed terrified of the intimacy between them.

The group dispersed at once and he didn't miss how quickly Claire tried to disappear. He fell into step with her.

She was trying to put distance between them again.

Too bad for her, Evan had stubbornness issues. He caught up with her as she surveyed the frozen landscape that was standing in for an Iraqi village in today's exercise.

Evan pulled her into the shell of a building where they could have some privacy.

"What happened this morning with Iaconelli?" he asked.

She paced for a moment before answering him. Then finally she turned to him and said, "I'm tired of him drinking himself unconscious."

"You've known him a long time." It wasn't a question.

"Longer than anyone else in the army." Evan watched her for a long moment, fighting the urge to reach out, to offer her comfort.

She looked so rigid and stiff, as if she might shatter at the faintest touch. "Reza is what all the little infantry privates want to grow up and be," she said. "Any other soldier, I would have directed to the behavioral health docs long before now. I wouldn't even think twice."

Evan watched as Iaconelli worked his way through the formation. He trusted Iaconelli more than any other warrior in his formation. His skill on the battlefield was unnatural, but it kept his men alive, and Evan couldn't help but wonder at the cost of that skill. Had the descent into hell been worth it? Iaconelli was the warrior Ajax personified and more deeply flawed than any Greek hero. A nagging voice whispered in Evan's ear that Iaconelli was a grenade with the pin already pulled, simply waiting for the handle to be released to explode. "He needs help," Evan said.

Claire stood at an empty window frame, staring out at nothing as the first vehicle stopped in front of Iaconelli, focused on the battle in front of her. Claire might want to protect Reza from the consequences of his drinking but she couldn't ignore it forever.

Evan was close enough to see the tiny curls that escaped the bottom of her helmet.

Finally she turned back to him. "I can't turn him over to the army, Evan," She said. "Don't ask me to do that."

For one moment, all her shields fell away and he was looking at a woman with no barriers. No walls. Vulnerable. And damaged. So beautifully damaged.

"There isn't another way," Evan said softly. "He needs time. The only way to get him that time is if the army knows." He swallowed the next words, knowing they were going to crush her. "Otherwise, we're going to be standing at his court-martial. Or his funeral."

The last vehicle disappeared around the corner, their view blocked by an empty, graffiti-marked bell tower. The silence hung on between them and she finally looked away.

"The army isn't the answer here, Evan," she said, her words harsh and cutting.

"You don't know that."

"Really? Let's talk about what I do know. I know that when it comes right down to it, officers like you will throw someone like Reza out of the army the moment he becomes a liability. In combat? Sure, he's a god. Back here in the rear? He's a risk. He's one serious incident report too many." Claire started to stalk away, but she was stopped short by his words.

"Officers like me, Claire?"

SHE HEARD THE HURT IN HIS VOICE AND CLOSED HER EYES, clenching her fists at her sides. "That's not what I meant," she whispered.

"What did you mean, then?"

She didn't honestly think he was giving her the chance to take her words back. They'd cut him, deeply. But they were also true and came from a place that Evan would never understand.

She turned back, lifting her chin, fighting for every scrap of strength it took for her to remain upright. "You have no idea what it's like for enlisted soldiers, Evan. You've never been a private, who could be thrown out of the army for looking at someone the wrong way. You've always been an officer. You've always been protected from the arbitrary desires of whoever the current commander is."

"That's not fair."

"Maybe not. But it doesn't make it any less true." She looked up at him, saw the anger glittering darkly in his eyes. "You don't understand. If Reza goes to rehab, if he enters into the alcohol program, one wrong move will end his career." She pushed down the well of emotion. "The army is all he has. He pisses red, white and blue and if someone takes that away from him, I will cut their heart out. We need men like Reza in the formation. Flawed and all, he's still a leader that men will follow willingly."

"If he wraps himself around a tree, he'll just be another a dead hero. Can you live with that, Claire?" Evan's words were a slap. At her. At him. At everything they might have been to each other.

There was no relationship between them. There never could be. They'd been lying to themselves all along. Claire lifted her chin. It was time one of them, at least, acknowledged it.

"We have work to do," she said quietly, turning away from him. "I don't want to talk about this anymore."

"I do." He followed her, catching up to her at the top of a stairwell at the end of a dark, dusty hall littered with empty soda cans and old concertina wire. He stepped in front of her, blocking her escape.

"Damn it, Evan, this is neither the time nor the place," she said quietly. "We can't do this here."

She sniffed and took a step back, bunching her fists by her sides. Shaking her head, she looked down the hallway, toward the sound of the battle. Her bottom lip shook as she finally met his gaze. "Reza is the best friend I have. And I don't have the courage to do what it takes to get him to stop drinking." She swallowed hard, her words bitter and harsh. "And he is likely going to die because of it. Because I'm a coward and I don't want to lose one of the only friends I've got."

Shock, thick and viscous, flashed across his face. Her mouth went dry, waiting for his reaction.

"Claire—"

"Don't, Evan. Just don't. Okay? We need to get through this evaluation." Her words trembled. Her eyes filled. She tried to walk past him.

He stepped in front of her, blocking her retreat.

Again.

⁂

THEY WERE IN THE MIDDLE OF THE EMPTY FRAME OF THE building. The pretend battle popped off down the street. Duty called.

But Evan could no more break away than he could slice his own flesh. He raised his fingertips to the soft curve of her cheek, skimming her flushed skin. He lowered his mouth to hers but stopped just short of touching her. Her breath flitted across his lips and he imagined he could taste her. A thousand memories from last night rose, tormenting him with that too brief taste of perfection. He nudged her top lip gently with his own, opening his mouth just a hint more.

"You're not alone," he whispered.

The warmth of her breath teased him and with a hesitation born of desperate need, he slowly, so slowly, touched his tongue to hers. Felt her quick hiss of breath, then his own sigh as she stroked her tongue against his.

There were a million reasons why kissing her was a bad idea and only one that made him slant his mouth against hers and take everything she was willing to give him: this was Claire, a bright and brilliant spark in the center of his ragged soul.

He felt burned to the soles of his feet. There was no more cold. No more frozen fingers. The fear around his heart clenched tightly, resisting the warmth from her touch. Until there was nothing but the heat from her lips, the fire from the barest touch of his fingers on her cheeks.

He eased back, tugging on her bottom lip gently as he did. He stroked his thumb where his teeth had just been, then lowered his hand, granting her unspoken plea and letting her go.

Chaos stormed in her eyes and she looked ready for war.

And then she was gone, leaving him with too many questions, far too many regrets.

❧ 14 ❧

Claire watched as Engle's support platoon ran through their pre-combat checks for the second mission of the morning. Evan's kiss still lingered on her lips, a faint touch, a memory of the one good thing that she had done her best to destroy. Not on purpose. No, it was just how she was built.

Sarah strolled up and Claire offered a distracted smile as she watched the formation. Sarah's platoon was getting ready to run through the mission today in the mock-up of the Iraqi town in the middle of the snow-covered training area.

"Not exactly desert conditions," Sarah remarked, hooking her thumbs in the shoulders of her body armor and mirroring Claire's stance. "But miserable enough, so I guess it'll work."

Claire grinned and watched Reza take LT Engle and her platoon sergeant through checking their soldiers' gear: weapons, ammo and water, along with first-aid kits. "Engle seems like she's torn between being a cock tease and doing a good job," Claire said, toeing a dirty clump of snow.

"When she's good, she's really good. When she doesn't bring her A game, she's a disaster." Sarah sniffed and adjusted the neck of her sweater beneath her gear. "So my battalion commander is pretty pissed."

"Why?"

"Oh a little nasty-gram coming from brigade about Engle's platoon missing the close-out briefing because they stayed late at the shoot house."

Claire suppressed a smile. "Maybe Colonel Danvers was paying attention to the nightly status report, then. Glad to see it wasn't a wasted effort." Sarah stared hard at her and Claire frowned. "What?"

"The brigade commander is king here, Claire. If you don't play ball with him, you're done, and there's nothing anyone else can do about it." Sarah and Claire were silent for a moment, watching Engle fix the gear of one of her soldiers. The platoon sergeant sent another soldier to the water buffalo to fill up his CamelBak.

Claire studied her friend intently for a moment. Sarah glanced in her direction when the silence became heavy. "That is one well-put-together man," Sarah said, and the look in her eye suggested that she was mentally undressing Reza. When Claire didn't respond, Sarah cocked her head to one side. "It was a joke, Claire. I am allowed to have a sense of humor, you know."

"I know." A slow smile spread over her lips when she realized that Sarah was telling the truth. She'd lost her husband a few years ago at the Battle of First Fallujah. The fact that she was making jokes about a man, even an enlisted man, was a sign of good health. "How's Anna?"

"Growing like a weed. She's giving me fits. One of her friends has an older sister who watches TV that's waaay too old for her."

Claire raised both eyebrows, suppressing a shiver from the cold. "Define too old."

"How does *Twilight* sound?"

"What's *Twilight*?"

"You've lived in a cave, right? Teen girl. Vampire-and-werewolf love triangle. Hugely popular."

Claire shook her head and tried not to look at her friend like she was crazy. "Not ringing any bells. Sorry."

"The short version is that it's too old for my four-going-on-fourteen-year-old." Sarah shifted her body armor and tightened the Velcro around her waist.

"You're really okay." It wasn't a question.

Sarah stared out at the formation. "There are still bad days. I miss Jack." She turned and looked at Claire. "I don't think that will ever change. But that doesn't change the fact that I have to stop hurting enough to get out of bed every day." She pushed her glasses up. "Besides, I'm getting ready to deploy. Time to get my head in the game, don't you think?"

"Have I told you lately that you're amazing?"

"I am pretty awesome." Sarah laughed. "That was weak. I'm just a mom, trying to raise my little girl without her daddy. I have to find things to laugh at or she'll grow up feeling like she's living in a mortuary."

"Why did you stay? In the army, I mean."

Sarah paused for a long moment. "Because it helps me feel closer to him."

"It's just good to see you back. All the way back. I missed you." She sniffed and swallowed the sudden rise of emotion in her throat. "I didn't think you'd ever be you again after Jack died."

"Jack was a good man and I'll love him every day of my life. And can we please change the subject? I've got a damn mission to supervise and my glasses are going to fog up if you make me cry."

Claire laughed. "Some things never change."

"You've got that right. Lieutenant Engle!" Sarah moved off, her voice ringing across the snow.

EVAN APPROACHED IACONELLI AFTER THE LAST VEHICLE rumbled out of the assembly area. He didn't know what he was going to say or even how to start.

It was an uncomfortable feeling for him. His goal was always to do the right thing. To follow the rules. But with Reza, the rules were no longer clear cut. Sure, it would look like an easy choice to someone who hadn't served. Turn him in, get him sent to rehab. But that would mean disregarding the combat awards on his chest, ignoring the nearly fifty months in combat he had served and reducing the hero who stood before him to little more than an alcoholic.

The army had needed Reza and men like him. Men who would run toward the fire when everyone else hightailed it in the opposite direction. Evan had thought he was that type of a man, too. But now, approaching a man who was so much more than just a fellow soldier, Evan felt doubt. Reza was important to Claire. And that simple fact made him so much more important than just another one of Evan's soldiers.

There was no way this conversation would go well.

The wind shifted then, sending a frigid blast of tequila-scented air straight toward Evan. Already keyed up from last night's fiasco, Evan grabbed Reza and pulled him aside, forgetting he was supposed to ease into this conversation. "Are you drunk?"

Reza rubbed his hand over his mouth, a dark scowl across his forehead. "No."

Another waft of pure alcohol came off him. Evan swore beneath his breath. "You need to go sleep this shit off in the truck."

His smile fading, Reza spit into the snow, a hard look on his face. One that brokered no argument. "I'm fine. You're not my commander anymore. Sir." He spat the word.

Evan's temper snapped. "One of these days you're going to get someone hurt. You need to dial it down a notch. Especially after the other night."

"That's really rich. You're a real boy scout, aren't you? I can see why Claire calls you Captain America."

"This isn't about me and this isn't about Claire, Ike. This is about people who are worried about you."

Reza spat into the snow. "I tried to be cool with this whole babysitting thing that Claire started, but now that you're panting after her, you've picked up on—"

"Watch your mouth." Evan stepped into Reza's space, itching for a fight with the man who was causing Claire so much pain. "You have no right to drag her into this."

"I've got every fucking right. You want to dig into my life, I'm going to dig into yours."

"Do you have any idea how much watching you drink yourself to death is killing the people who care about you? Or are you too selfish to care?"

"Selfish? Are you serious? I pulled your happy ass out of a burning goddamn tank downrange and you're going to stand here and lecture me about drinking too much?" He shoved Evan, hard enough that Evan took a step back. "I spilled a drink on my uniform this morning when I was cleaning up. Kiss my ass, you sanctimonious prick."

The wind shifted again and Evan could no longer smell alcohol. He studied his former platoon sergeant, looking for any window into his soul, any way to reach the warrior he knew existed in the shell of the burned-out GI in front of him. Evan had no idea how to help him.

"You can't keep doing this." Evan straightened, looking at Reza and wondering what would finally send him over the line from needed soldier to homeless drunk.

"Don't you have training to go evaluate?" Reza asked. He

stalked off, heading to the ambush point near the objective for this mission. "Sir."

Evan had never felt so utterly useless in his entire adult life. No, the last time he'd felt this useless was at this exact moment thirteen years ago, standing in the middle of a snow-covered field as an ambulance pulled away, not bothering with the sirens because it was too late.

❧

EVAN HADN'T GOTTEN MORE THAN A GLIMPSE OF CLAIRE all afternoon. She was working closely with LT Engle, while Evan worked with the opposing force to set up a scenario that was both realistic and challenging. After all, it wasn't as if someone got to call "end of exercise" in the middle of a real-world mission.

It was the last mission of the day, and things had gone relatively well for a company that was not well prepared. Engle had done a lot to get her team all working together, a tremendous feat considering how poorly trained they'd been a few short days ago. He guessed her time in combat had served a purpose after all.

Reza had steered clear of him for the bulk of the day, for which Evan was grateful. It enabled him to shut down the emotional storm raging inside of him and lock it away. Focus on the mission. Just like always.

It was easier that way.

Evan watched Engle's convoy approach the kill zone from inside one of the empty buildings across the intersection. Colonel Danvers walked through the battlefield, talking with soldiers, making notes and observing the evaluation. It was the pivotal event for this phase of the operation, so nothing would be overlooked.

Snow glittered like diamonds in the silver daylight and his

breath froze almost as soon as he exhaled. All in all, though, the weather was milder than it had been—the wind wasn't blowing as sharply, which had taken the edge off the wicked chill. The star cluster went off, dripping through the sky like a fiery flow of diamonds, and the training was on once again.

As usual, there was a lot going on all at once. He turned his attention to the approaching vehicles. They rumbled down the snow-covered road, tires popping on snow, crunching through the frozen ice and salt. The gunner in the lead vehicle scanned his sector, his head on a swivel, watching all avenues of approach.

He almost missed Reza sprinting toward the back of the convoy, dressed like a local national, but the next thing he knew, Lieutenant Engle's vehicle broke off from the rest of the convoy and headed after him. "What the hell is she doing?" Evan mumbled.

Evan saw the flash at the back of the convoy a split second before the concussion of the blast slammed into him. The gates of hell broke open as the convoy opened fire. Evan had a brief moment to be impressed that they'd gotten blank rounds for their M240B machine guns and one of those puppies was rocking, then everything got twisted up in chaos and smoke. Bursts of muzzle fire melted deep pits into the banks around the road as more flashes went off, followed by far too realistic explosions.

Someone started screaming. Real screams, ringing with real pain.

Sounds he'd all heard before but it still took him a moment to realize that the screams echoing off the walls of the fake houses were not part of the simulation.

He sprinted to the end of the intersection, his boots not carrying fast enough toward the chaos. He was living a nightmare where he ran as fast as he could and got nowhere.

Finally he rounded the first truck. His gaze sharpened

instantly on the scene and he mentally began forming the situation report.

Lieutenant Engle was laid out next to the driver's side of her truck, her left arm bent at an awkward angle, twisted and unnatural. The front end of the truck had smashed into one of the buildings, and the smell of burning diesel seared the insides of his nostrils along with the reeking odor of spent sulfur.

Engle was fighting the medic, thwarting his efforts to stabilize her and probably doing a hell of a lot more damage than had already been done. Blood poured down her face from a gash in her forehead, but Evan couldn't identify the source of the wound.

Claire bolted around the corner a moment after him. His eyes met hers across the chaos. She nodded once and they both moved forward. He kneeled near Engle's feet, while Claire gripped her shoulders and forced her to the ground, stabilizing her head. Evan evaluated the LT's legs for injuries as best he could, considering that she was still thrashing around. Once he was sure that she didn't have any major injuries to her legs, he pinned her down.

Reza appeared out of nowhere and started directing the medic, a girl who couldn't have been more than twenty, but whose hands were straight and steady as she stabilized Engle's damaged arm.

Engle screamed like a wild animal and it took four of them to hold her down until they could get her secured to the stretcher and prepared for movement. The MEDEVAC helo from a nearby hospital landed about a hundred yards away at the edge of the training site. Somewhere in the distance, Evan heard someone start setting up security around the landing zone. Someone clearly hadn't gotten the memo that this exercise had just turned into a real-world emergency.

And then it was over. Just like that, a hush settled over the entire formation.

◈

SARAH APPROACHED, CARRYING THE REMNANTS OF HER ASS with her. Claire had watched from a distance as Colonel Danvers had chewed her friend out for her lieutenant's lapse in judgment. Sarah had been a trooper, standing straight and proud throughout the ordeal. She smiled weakly at Claire.

"It's too bad that ass-chewings don't literally take meat off your ass. I could stand to lose about ten pounds." Sarah ran her hand through her sweat-soaked hair. "I cannot believe that Engle disobeyed the brigade commander and authorized the use of pyrotechnics. She's lucky she's the only one who was hurt."

"Do you still have a job?" Claire tucked her hands in her pockets. "Does she?"

"I'm not sure yet, to either question. I do know the only reason Engle hasn't been fired yet is because she's in the hospital and the boss isn't that much of an asshole to fire her while she's in the emergency room."

Claire flinched at her friend's words. "So she is going to get fired?"

"Maybe. Maybe not. He's pissed right now but when he calms down, he'll look at all the facts."

"What are the facts?" Claire asked, afraid of what she suspected. Reza had been nowhere to be seen since Engle was transported to the hospital. She ignored the nagging voice in her head that suggested what she'd rather ignore.

"Engle cooked up a different scenario. She wanted to see how her sergeants did when she was taken out of the fight so instead of staying in the convoy, she veered off to chase after Reza as if she were chasing down someone they'd caught planting a bomb. Except that when her vehicle rounded the corner, instead of an open road, she found it blocked by burning tires. That's not why he's mad. He's really pissed about the unauthorized pyro. She violated a boatload of policies getting that stuff." Sarah rubbed her eyes, her skin red and raw from the cold. "He's pretty pissed at you, too, Claire. Half the time he was grilling me, he wanted to know whether you'd told the LT to deviate from his training guidance or not."

"Me? What the hell did I do?"

"The other day in the briefing? This is exactly what Engle was talking about doing and Danvers specifically told her not to do. He's holding you responsible for disobeying his guidance, particularly since you admitted to wanting to change the training plan and add in pyro, too."

"Just because I *wanted* to do it doesn't mean I actually *did* it," Claire whispered. Her heart felt like a stone in her chest. Cold slithered up Claire's spine but she said nothing for the longest time, unable to find any words to shape the chaos inside her. "What did you tell him?"

Sarah smiled wickedly. "That you were a stellar officer who would always execute the commander's intent and never willfully disobey a lawful order."

Claire choked back a horrified laugh. It was either that or cry. "How much of that did you actually get out before he cut you off and called you a liar?"

"About two thirds of a sentence, which is two thirds more than I thought I'd get out." Tight lines appeared on Sarah's forehead. "He thinks you planted the idea for Engle to violate the training guidelines."

Claire said nothing, unable to fight back the sinking feeling in her gut.

⁂

Evan and Claire drove back to the lodge together. The ride was quiet, filled with an awkward silence that for once was not the result of an argument between the two of them. It was worry about a friend. A friend whose demons had gotten someone hurt today.

The exercise had been halted for the rest of the afternoon while Colonel Danvers' staff conducted an inquiry into the accident. They'd been held at the training site for five hours while they were questioned about why Lieutenant Engle had deviated from the training plan. Normally, it would have been a single officer asking questions, but Danvers wanted answers yesterday, so the staff had a sense of urgency.

There would be more questions tomorrow and throughout the rest of the weekend.

Claire said nothing as she drove them back to the lodge. Evan hadn't seen Iaconelli since Engle's transport, though not for lack of trying. He deeply suspected that Engle had not cooked up this plan on her own. Claire's silence was an unbreachable wall, a blockade Evan could not break.

"Did you talk to Iaconelli?" he finally asked, his question grating over the awkward silence.

"I haven't seen him." Her voice sounded unused to sound. "I assumed he took one of the other trucks to the hospital to see Engle." She glanced at him before turning down the long, winding road toward the lodge. "Why?"

"Just wondering." It was a coward's answer, but it was the only thing he could think to say at the moment. "How's Sarah?"

"Worried about Engle. She might be going downrange without a platoon leader because of this stunt." But there was no recrimination in her voice. No, what he heard there was fatigue. Bone-crushing weariness from too many years at war and not nearly enough time to recharge between deployments.

Evan said nothing.

But that didn't stop the scene from playing itself out in his head, over and over again, blame and recrimination for the accident pressing in on him until he thought he'd choke on it.

Claire turned the truck down the narrow road leading to the lodge. Trees hung over the road, weighted down with the snow and ice. They could have been driving through a winter wonderland, filled with promise and holiday memories instead of back to the hotel after a bad training exercise.

Instead, Evan felt tired. Drained.

The truck stopped in the parking lot at the lodge. The silence of the cold winter dusk wrapped around them.

"I have to see Colonel Danvers day after tomorrow," Claire said quietly. "He's going to question me, personally."

"I do, too." He studied her, the way her jaw tensed in the fading daylight. "Why do you have to go?"

"He blames me for this. Engle didn't stick to the training plan, and he knows I disapproved of his plan, too."

He shifted so he could see her more easily in the fading light. He wanted to ask her if she thought Reza was involved. If he'd planted the idea to use the pyro in Engle's head. But he couldn't find the words, knowing that they would just add another worry to the weight around her shoulders. "What are you going to tell him?"

"I don't know." She looked out beyond the steering wheel and the snow-covered parking lot, as though she were searching the forest at the edge of the property for an answer. "Half of me feels like covering for Engle because she's been working so hard out here to try and get better. The other half feels like a hypocrite because I would have done exactly what she did. Unauthorized pyro and all."

He followed her out of the truck, not letting her put

space between them, but she was quick and he wasn't going to make an issue out of running after her. At least not yet.

He finally caught up to her in front of the door to her suite. Or rather, she finally stopped. She stood there, her body tense. He had the distinct impression that she'd suddenly stopped fighting.

She stepped into his space but didn't touch him. Didn't cross that last breath of distance to actually contact his skin. She opened the door to her room and stepped back.

When she looked at him, when she lifted her face toward his, what he saw knocked him back, hitting him low and hard.

Invitation.

❧ 15 ❧

Inviting Evan in was stupid, but then again, everything she did with Evan was stupid. If Colonel Danvers had already called Colonel Richter back at Fort Hood, her career was probably down the drain. She might as well soothe the loss of her military career with hot sex and try to forget the wreckage of her life, if only for a little while. And yet his mouth hovered a breath above hers, as though waiting for her to span the distance that separated them.

The few others who had stepped into her territory had always played by her rules. And yet, at this very moment, Evan challenged her. Standing close enough that she could see his nostrils flare slightly, feel the warm kiss of his breath against her skin, he dared her to make a choice.

To let herself feel or to walk away from the one man who inspired a need in her that she'd buried long ago.

She moved. A hesitant, almost-there movement. But that tiny gesture was all it took. He nudged her lips with his, teasing her with the slightest breath of contact. She glanced up to find him studying her, his coffee eyes the color of the desert at midnight. Her fingers curled into his forearms. A soft touch, the only acknowledgement of what this was.

Permission to start fresh, to lance the poison that still stood between them. Or at least set it aside.

Yet it terrified her that he had come to mean so much to her in such a short period of time. She wanted to pull away from that comfort, afraid to let herself crave it. She wanted violence, an answer to the hungry need that rose inside her. She started to turn away, to walk deeper into her room, unsure if he would release her or simply follow.

He shocked her when he captured her, his arms snaking around her, pulling her flush against him. Her back cradled against his chest, in a haphazard, desperate embrace.

She hated the choices she was being forced to make. And she hated having to weigh desire against self-preservation. But for tonight, desire won. She relaxed against him, her bones sagging in relief.

She surrendered.

To the heat curling down her belly to snake between her thighs. To the strength of this man at her back. And to the riot of emotions thundering inside her, hammering at her veins, demanding release. She shifted and Evan traced the sides of her body with his palms, his chest pressed full against her back.

"RELAX," HE WHISPERED AS HE PEELED OPEN THE VELCRO of her jacket. Capturing her jaw with one rough palm, he urged her neck back until she rested against his shoulder. With the other thumb, he traced a line from the bottom of her chin down her throat to the collar of her T-shirt. Slowly, so slowly, he dragged the zipper open, scraping his knuckles against the cotton between her breasts. Again, he traced the line of her throat with feather-light strokes, his fingertips teasing her skin, sending shivers of pleasure flowing over her. He pulled her against him, her rear curved against his hips.

Never had a simple caress moved him so deeply. He was so used to Claire being in control that her surrender, when it came, stunned the hell out of him and made him long for more. This woman, this fierce warrior who gave as good as she got, was pliant and soft beneath his hands now.

He wanted nothing more than to take his time and learn more about this fascinating woman who trembled as he peeled open her bra, never once relinquishing contact between their bodies.

He looked up to find her watching him in the hotel mirror. He was surprised by how small she looked in front of him. He slid his hands over her shoulders, down her ribs. He continued to trace his path, watching as her gorgeous nipples pebbled beneath his touch. Felt the imperceptible arch of her back, an offering.

Evan wanted more than this from her but right now, he'd take what she could give. He wrapped his arms around her, one arm snaking around her belly, the lush weight of her breasts heavy against him, the other sliding up over her collarbone to cradle her throat.

She made a small noise of protest. Evan smiled darkly, watching her in the mirror.

And bit down on her shoulder, just above the edge of a scar. Her gasp was the sweetest pleasure, rocketing straight down his groin to throb in his cock. She arched back against him, rubbing against his erection and making him want to beg. He nudged her neck to one side and captured her earlobe between his teeth at the exact moment he pinched one pearled nipple between his fingers. He traced his tongue over the scars on her back.

She trembled and jerked beneath his touch, arching and

squirming in a way that had him ready to explode before he really got started.

"Like that?" he murmured. He wanted to run his tongue over every single inch of her back. She was taut, wired tight as a rip cord.

"If you don't stop screwing around . . ." She reached behind her, the movement arching her breasts, and found him rock solid and throbbing beneath his uniform. "Poor baby. That feels painful." But she squeezed him, driving him closer to the edge.

He pulled her hands away, guiding her down onto the bed, encircling her body with his own. She resisted until he pressed flat against her, sweeping her hands over her head, his chest against her back, his hips intimately flush with hers. "Trust me, Claire," he whispered against her ear.

Her name on his lips sparked something deep and primitive and needy. She didn't do trust. What he was asking for was more than she was ready or able to give.

He pressed a gentle kiss to the cool skin between her shoulder blades, his hands gently holding hers above her head. One cheek pressed into the cool, crisp sheets, her nipples aching from the cool kiss of cotton. Again, he pressed his lips to the back of her neck, gentle and soft.

"Trust me," he whispered, sliding his hands down her wrists, over her shoulders and framing her ribs, his touch gentle and slow.

He traced his thumbs down her spine, trailing with his tongue. He licked the edge of her uniform pants, slowly urging them down over her hips, revealing the body he'd admired on one too many late deployment nights. He'd fantasized about having her just like this, open, exposed and completely subject to his desire.

He traced his hands up the back of her thighs, slipping his thumbs into the crease between her cheeks before placed a soft kiss on the small of her back. She whimpered and squirmed beneath him. He smiled. He wanted her to beg, to hear her whisper his name.

৩৫৩

CLAIRE COULDN'T SAY WHERE TIME ENDED AND EVAN began. The slow, lazy strokes up and down her scarred back, over her buttocks, down her thighs. He drove her wild with his hands. Every so often, his tongue replaced his finger, leaving cool, wet skin in its wake.

She shifted, spreading her thighs a little more, offering him access to her most intimate flesh. A sound of raw male appreciation emboldened her. She arched her back, shifting her thighs wider, looking at him over her shoulder. "Evan . . ." Her voice was a growl, feral with barely restrained need.

৩৫৩

HE LAUGHED LOW AND DEEP IN HIS CHEST AS HE ROLLED her panties down over her hips, leaving her completely naked, completely gorgeous.

He cupped her cheeks, pressing his open mouth to the sweet flesh right above the dip in her lower back as his fingers finally sought her slick, damp heat.

She jerked, and if he hadn't had one arm across the small of her back, she might have dislodged him. She tried to rock back against his touch, demanding more. "Evan . . ."

"Shh." Slowly, so slowly, he dragged his fingers through her heat, parting her, stroking her. He wanted to taste her, to suckle her where she was hot and swollen and so very wet, but it was too much for him to handle. His cock was steel against the buttons of his uniform. Still, he stroked her, driving her closer to the edge, backing off each time to prevent her climax.

"I swear to God . . ."

"Say please," he whispered.

She arched her hips off the bed, damn near throwing him off, but instead, he seated two fingers deep, deep inside her and she came apart so completely he thought he'd die from the sheer beauty of her release.

He stroked her slowly, prolonging her pleasure until she damn near begged him, capturing her gasps in his mouth.

He stripped, rolling the condom on in some kind of land speed record. He kissed her then, urging her onto her back, forgetting for a moment her panic, her fear. He wanted to feel her body beneath his, to kiss her as she wrapped her thighs around his back. But she wiggled and squirmed until he was pressed to her back. He lifted her thigh, draping it over his, and angled his hips until he was there at the opening of her beautiful sex.

And then she arched backwards and Evan sank home, deep into her lush, wet heat. He reached between her thighs as he drove into her from behind, stroking her pleasure until she shattered and came apart around him.

And when his own pleasure took him over the edge, he was sure he heard his name on her lips, the sweetest cry, as he tumbled into ecstasy.

❧

Claire was nestled against him, her body soft and relaxed in sleep. He shifted now in the pale morning light and pressed his lips to the scars on her back.

The worst of them were deep and ragged. Others were pale, thin lines on her skin. He was on his side now, his head propped up in his palm, tracing the path of those harsh furrows in her skin. Beside him, she sighed.

He stiffened, braced for her to pull away. She'd pulled away so often and so regularly. But this morning was full of surprises, and she simply nestled closer.

Maybe she wasn't fully awake yet.

He hadn't let himself want this. This simple morning, lying in bed, Claire warm and sleepy next to him. He leaned down and pressed a gentle kiss to the center of her shoulder blade. He'd denied himself a happily ever after, had never planned on someone touching the frozen core of his soul. A self-imposed penance for the death of his sister.

But maybe he'd been lying to himself all along. Maybe he'd been denying himself this because he knew he wouldn't be able to handle it. This intense wave of emotion. This connection. There was no control here. This was chaos. This was burning, aching desire that could flare out and consume him.

"Hmmmm."

"Oh good, you're awake," he said, smiling against her skin.

"No, I'm not." She grumbled the words but there was no harshness to them.

Evan skimmed his fingers over her ribs until she shivered beneath his touch. He wanted to challenge her defenses, to tear down her barriers one by one.

One in particular nagged at the edge of his sleep- and sex-filled brain. They still hadn't slept together face to face. He'd wanted to cradle her face in his palms as he'd slipped inside her last night. He'd wanted to feel her orgasm shatter around them both and capture her sighs in his mouth.

But that simple act had eluded him. She'd pushed away, urging him to take her from behind again. And dear lord, it was the singularly most erotic experience he'd ever had with a woman. She was wild and passionate, and used her pleasure to drive him over the edge. But it still wasn't enough for him.

He traced his tongue over her back and urged the sheet that was tangled around them down until her back was exposed. She sighed, and he felt her legs relax. He stroked his fingertips down her ribs, lightly. Teasing.

"If waking me up without coffee is your idea of a joke, I'll warn you, I've neutered men for less." But she shifted, a tiny, subtle movement that gave him access to the warm sweetness between her thighs.

"I can make it worth your while," he whispered, sliding his fingers over the smooth curve of her ass, skirting closer to her center and flitting away, denying them both.

"How?"

"Let's play twenty questions."

"Before coffee?" She sounded pained.

"Yeah." He skimmed his fingertips along the edge of a silver-pink scar, wanting to do more than savor this slow, sexy waking. "Why did you join the army?"

"This really isn't fair. I'm not conscious yet." He nipped her shoulder and she cried out before she could stop it, the sound pure pleasure. "I wanted to do something different."

"Different than what?" He licked the spot where he'd bitten her, leaving a faint pink mark.

"Working at McDonald's, hell, I don't know. Whatever there is to do in a rural Iowa town."

"You're from Iowa?"

"The last two years before I joined the army, yeah. We were never anywhere for long, though." She stretched her arms over her head, pushing the curves of her breasts against the bed. He wanted to shape them in the palms of his hands, but that would require him to shift positions entirely and he was feeling too content to move.

"Why did you move around so much?"

"My dad was a welder. We went where the jobs were."

"No mom?"

"Not exactly." She twisted and pulled the sheet higher over her body. "When exactly will this game be over? I need caffeine or bad things will happen."

She was evading him, he noticed, as he traced the pattern of a star-shaped scar with the pad of his thumb. Her entire left shoulder and upper back bore the physical reminder of secrets she had yet to share. It hurt that she still held so much of herself away from him. "Tell me about these," he whispered, tracing one with the tip of his tongue.

She stilled, any trace of sensual energy fleeing on the edge of her tension. "I fell into a coffee table once."

There was more to the story. He could hear it in her voice, in the quiet hitch in her words. Evan changed tactics, massaging the soft skin between her neck and her shoulder, pressing his thumb against a knot. "You should take better care of these."

"You know an awful lot about taking care of people." She kept her eyes closed. It was nice to see her face so relaxed.

Claire nestled against him, pulling his arm around her body. She traced her fingers over the branches twisting over his biceps. "Why a tattoo?" she whispered.

Evan closed his eyes, surprised that she'd turned the conversation back to him so suddenly. But this, he could answer. "Because I didn't want to forget."

"She was your sister. How could you possibly forget the night she died?"

He shifted and rested his head on his bent arm. "If you lie to yourself long enough, it becomes true." He swallowed, barely daring to continue. "My mom and dad never came to visit me when I was at West Point." He closed his eyes, felt Claire's fingers curl into his skin. "We never had much of a relationship after Casey died. And I was willing to let them go because I couldn't stand how much they blame me. I couldn't let go of Casey, though." He released a quiet sigh. "My parents let me go because they wanted to forget. I refused to let go of my little sister. I got the tattoo right after I graduated."

"You sound so . . . resigned." She traced her fingers over the edge of his jaw.

"Maybe I am. But I can't force a relationship where there isn't one."

Her fingers danced over his shoulders. "Your tribute is beautiful, Evan." She kissed the dark branch over the center of his heart. "Your sister was lucky to have you."

He stiffened. "Claire, I killed her. She wasn't lucky. She was cursed."

Her fingers were cool against his cheeks. "You were seventeen. You made a bad choice. And you've been punishing yourself ever since." She pressed her lips to his. "You can regret the end of her life forever. Or you can remember her and honor the life she lived." Her words pressed around the damaged remains of his heart, a salve. A bandage. And it was too much, all at once.

He turned the conversation back to her. Attempted to lighten it.

"So Claire joined the army. Then what happened?"

"Claire went to college at night and earned her degree and learned to shut her mouth long enough to make it through Officer Candidate School."

His hands were wandering beneath the sheet she'd pulled between them. She wasn't good at this sort of thing. She struggled avoid his dark eyes, afraid he'd see the tragic, lonely little girl that she'd been. But she didn't look away.

And what she felt with this man was warm. And safe. And deeply, deeply arousing. She let her own hands wander, sliding over his torso and chest, loving the feel of his dark chest hair crinkling beneath her palms. His belly was tight, his skin hot and smooth. This big, gorgeous body was hers.

She let her hands wander lower and his body tensed beneath her touch. She chuckled deep in her throat, loving the feeling of power that surged inside her at his tacit admission that she aroused him. She teased the evidence of that arousal with the tip of one finger and his erection jerked beneath her light stroke.

She surrendered to a rare feeling of playfulness and leaned closer, breaking away from the hypnotic grip of his gaze to drag her teeth over the rough skin of his jaw, nipping closer to his ear as her fingers circled his erection and stroked him. Slowly.

He exhaled sharply, his breath cutting off as she squeezed him. "Are you torturing me on purpose?"

"No more than you waking me up without coffee." She traced her thumb over the head of his cock, spreading the warm, moist liquid over the thick, wide tip.

"I might have to get rid of all the coffee in Colorado if this is my reward." His voice grated against her ear.

He encircled her with his arms, tugging her closer.

Her lungs shut down instantly. She tried to push away the sudden panic but failed, and she reacted the only way she knew how.

She turned away from him. Offered herself to him with a deep, sensual arch of her back and the slight spread of her thighs.

He said nothing to acknowledge her panic and for that she was immensely grateful. He stroked her body, his palms cradling her breasts as he slid his erection between her thighs from behind, teasing her with it.

A crinkling of plastic and then beautiful, tight pressure as he pressed against her core. She lifted one knee, opening her body, protecting her soul.

And when he slid deep and slow inside her, she cried out at the relief spreading through her veins like a warm, hot drug, sedating the panic. He wrapped his arms around her, cradling her against him as he moved an anodyne balm to ragged remains of her soul. She loved the stark, harsh contrast of his tattooed arm against her own. It was deeply moving, erotic and sensual all at once.

She surrendered then to the pleasure, giving herself over to the power of his touch. Dragging him with her into a sensual haze, reveling in the desire, hiding the strength of her reaction from the man loving her body. Because the truth was that she was no longer in control. Somehow, Evan had wormed his way past her defenses. He'd snuck in and nestled near her heart.

And that scared the hell out of her.

It was barely noon, but Evan was not at all surprised to find Iaconelli at the bar. For once, he was not even halfway to half-cocked. The big man was nursing a single beer, a fat lip, and a piss-poor attitude.

"I'm not in the mood right now," Reza said when Evan pulled up a seat and ordered a beer.

"Yeah, me neither." Evan ordered a beer, waiting until the bartender slid it in front of him before he spoke. "Did you get the pyro for Engle?"

Reza's silence was enough of an answer. Evan swore viciously. "What the hell were you thinking, Iaconelli?"

Reza sniffed and scrubbed his hand along the scruff of his unshaven jaw. "I was in Kuwait in late '02. We weren't going to war, the President said. We hadn't made up our minds. Diplomacy and blah, blah, blah." He took a long pull off his beer. "We sat in Kuwait for weeks. Went to ranges and talked about how easy Desert Storm was, how unprepared the Iraqi Army was. Then the balloon went up and we were heading north." He shifted and pinned Evan with a hard look. "Do you know what it feels like to cross into a war zone, knowing you could have prepared better? Trained harder. Worked longer hours."

"Ike, none of us is ever really prepared," Evan said quietly. Every time he deployed, he felt like there was more he could have done. "And now Engle may be out of the fight because you couldn't play by the rules the one time it mattered."

"Engle knew the risks. It wasn't her first rodeo." Reza drained the bottle. "And she knew what she was doing. She's a hell of a lot smarter than you give her credit for."

"Yeah well, using unauthorized pyro and deviating from the training plan isn't very smart when it gets you taken out of the fight. Now her team is probably going downrange untrained and without one of the few people who actually have combat experience." Evan scraped his thumb over the label on his beer. "Her ass is going to fry because of the pyro." He swallowed and met his longtime platoon sergeant's eyes. "Were you drinking?"

"One time," Reza snapped, sticking his finger up. "One time I screw up pyro in my entire career and you're going to assume I was drunk?"

"You sent a lieutenant to the hospital. And that's not even the worst of it. Claire has been covering for you for years and you've been letting her." Reza's dark skin blanched, but Evan drove on. "So asking if you were drinking is a fair question, given the circumstances."

"This isn't about me."

Evan slammed his fist on the bar. "This is absolutely about you! Do you care how much you're hurting Claire and everyone else who cares about you?"

"You know what pisses me off?" Reza shoved the stool away from the bar. "You and Claire and every single person I know thinks I've got PTSD or some bullshit. You all talk about me like I'm one step away from killing someone in a drunk driving accident when I've never, ever gotten behind the wheel of the car when I've been drinking and I don't plan to start anytime soon."

"No, but you're not above drinking in a combat zone or during training exercises."

"Fuck you, Sir." He snarled the words an inch from Evan's face. "I didn't ask either one of you to try and save me. But you're right about one thing." Evan could not remember Reza ever being so furious. Not downrange. Not back at Hood. Never had he seen the depth of the anger flashing from Reza's dark eyes. "This *is* about Claire. And it's about you, too. The two of you are pretending that I'm the thing holding you together because you're too scared to have a grown-up relationship based on, hell, being adults."

Reza took a pull from the glass in front of him, then slammed it down, remembering it was already drained. "Claire has never trusted anyone for as long as I've known her. She's always been one of the guys and that's it." He yanked his wallet out of his front pocket. "Until you came along, I've never seen her relax enough to just be with someone. And you're wasting this chance because you're using me as a third wheel when what you need to be doing is figuring out how to hold on to her all by yourself."

Reza slammed a twenty onto the bar to pay for his beer. "This isn't about me. This is about whether you're man enough to love her without me or the war or anything else between you as a buffer. Just you. Just her."

He left and Evan let him go, stunned at how a simple question had nearly turned into a barroom brawl. It was a long time before Evan left the bar.

"SO THE EVAL WAS A DISASTER AND OUR DEPLOYMENT HAS

been canceled," Sarah said by way of greeting as she walked into Claire's suite early Monday morning.

It usually took an act of God to cancel training, but one bad explosion and a broken arm had done the trick this time. Almost everyone else had been sent home after the incident. Claire had been going through the motions for most of the time since Evan had left her room. She hated the room she'd once thought of as opulent luxury. Now it felt like a prison while she waited for her appointment to see Colonel Danvers. The walls closed in on her. She wasn't forbidden from leaving, but she felt locked in nonetheless.

Claire managed a smile. "Really?"

"No. And if you believed that, then I have this bridge in Arizona you might be interested in. I just came by to see how you're doing."

Claire sniffed and palmed her forehead, leaning against the table. "Surviving. Sorry your eval sucked."

"Oh yeah, 'cause five more days practicing being miserable was high up on my to-do list. It's fine." Sarah pulled out a chair and sat next to her. "We're still deploying, regardless of whether the evaluation sucked or not. No commander in the world would tell their boss they're not ready to go to war."

Claire stared longingly at the small fridge, wondering if she dared to have a drink. Maybe if she had a few drinks, she'd be over the worst of her anxiety. Probably wouldn't help much with the saving-the-career part. She swallowed and realized her problems were nothing compared to what her friend was preparing for. "How are you holding up with the idea of leaving Anna?"

Sarah sank into the couch. She didn't answer for a long moment as she pulled her knees up to her chest, resting her cheek on them. "It'll be okay. My mother-in-law loves her. And Anna's little. She won't even remember this in the grand scheme of things."

"Hon, you sound like you're trying to convince yourself," Claire said gently. She moved to sit next to her, resting her head against Sarah's shoulder.

"Maybe I am." Sarah's voice was barely above a broken whisper. "But I don't want to talk about it because I don't want to start bawling. Anyway, what's up with you?"

Her appointment with Colonel Danvers was in two short hours. She seriously contemplated taking a trip to the doc and asking for some anti-anxiety medication. She hadn't eaten at all that morning and the coffee she'd attempted to drink had twisted and writhed in her guts like a live thing. It was not a good way to start off a meeting that was sure to end with an epic ass-chewing.

"You okay?"

"I should ask you the same thing," Claire asked.

"I'm fine. Engle's arm was broken in two places, but she should be healed up enough to still deploy with us." Sarah sounded relieved. Tired, but relieved. "She may or may not still get fired."

"That's good. Listen—"

"Don't you dare. I don't want to hear a word about an apology or anything. It was fun having you up here, my folks learned a lot—no matter what Colonel Danvers says—and that's the long and the short of it." Sarah's voice broke, and with it, her composure. "I'm more worried about you."

Claire blinked rapidly. Sarah was one of her best friends in the world. Her only real girl friend, and at that moment, it struck her forcibly just how much she missed having her around. She tried to sound flip. She failed. "I'm really going to miss you."

"You, too. You have no idea."

Claire glanced at her watch. "I've got to go. I might need some help writing that résumé."

"Not funny."

"Not joking." Claire smiled. "I'll be fine. I've landed on my feet before."

But as she drove onto the main post at Fort Carson alone, Claire was not so sure she was going to survive this one. Colonel Danvers was not her brigade commander, but Claire had no doubt that Colonel Richter had already been informed.

Before they'd left Fort Hood, Colonel Richter had told her not to screw anything up. He'd warned her. And despite the fact that she hadn't put Engle up to changing the training plan and getting the unauthorized pyro, Claire felt responsible.

Because she'd told Evan the truth: she would have done exactly what Engle had done. So the question now was what she should tell Colonel Danvers. Should she deny everything and let LT Engle take the fall by herself? Or should she stand in front of the lieutenant and defend her to a commander who would not appreciate a captain telling him how to train his officers?

She parked the rental car and walked into the Palehorse headquarters. Lifting her hand to knock on Colonel Danvers' door, she had no idea that the questions she was about to face would challenge every facet of her loyalty. Loyalty to a man she would die for and loyalty to a man who'd touched something sacred inside her.

Claire faced Colonel Danvers.

And that loyalty was tested.

❧ 17 ❧

Later that same morning, Evan knocked on the brigade commander's door, hating the fact that his guts were clenched so tight. He should be better at taking an ass-chewing by this point in his career, but the simple fact was that he didn't get lit into that often. He was a good soldier. Still, as the officer in charge of this now epic training disaster, he was the one on the chopping block to see Colonel Danvers.

The evaluation was a disaster. Training cancelled, Engle was still in the hospital. And worse? As he approached Colonel Danvers' office, Evan wasn't even remotely thinking about the brigade commander. Instead, he was focused on the much more personal disaster of his relationship with Claire. He hadn't been able to get Reza's words out of his mind. He should be able to be with Claire without Reza standing between them. Couldn't he? He tried to think of a single regular conversation they'd had that hadn't involved Reza or the army. There had been very few.

Evan knocked on the solid mahogany door.

"Come in, Captain." Danvers' use of his rank was not a

good sign. "I won't waste either of our time with small talk. Here."

Evan reached forward and flipped open the cover of the manila folder Danvers had slid across the desk. The paperwork from range control expressly forbidding the use of pyro on the range.

Signed by Lieutenant Engle and Reza Iaconelli. He skimmed through the paperwork, realizing with aching clarity that he was looking at career-enders. Reza had not been legally certified to use the pyro on this range. Engle had not had the authority to sign for it, let alone authorize its use. Disobeying orders was one thing, but Reza's carelessness had gotten someone hurt. And worse, he'd roped Lieutenant Engle into the fiasco with him. The training plan had been ignored, the prohibition against pyrotechnics violated.

All because a lieutenant thought she knew more about training soldiers than one very irate colonel. Every life Reza had saved now seemed pointless. Every mission he'd ever run, a waste of time. All that experience was now useless against the rage of a furious colonel.

Evan closed his eyes, aching memories twisting through him. Reza stepping out of his truck as sand swirled around him. Dragging his boys out of a burning tank. Spending days on the range just to teach one kid how to shoot. Reza's career was over. A tragic hero to the very end.

Evan breathed deeply as the brigade commander slid one last piece of paper in front of him. A sworn statement signed by Claire Montoya saying that she'd ordered the change in plan. Taking responsibility for the pyro.

The floor tilted beneath Evan as he read her words taking responsibility for everything.

"Did you know about this deviation from the training plan?" Danvers asked.

Evan looked up at Colonel Danvers and felt the last bit of control being yanked from his hands.

❧

CLAIRE STEPPED OUT OF THE WORKOUT ROOM AND FELT THE shadow fall across her back long before she saw it. She turned, and there he was—the cold and closed off Evan that she knew so well. His eyes were dark and lined with anger, his shoulders tight and tense.

"You lied to Colonel Danvers."

Claire swallowed and met his gaze. The raw fury radiating from his eyes killed any trace of kindness. Now the old Evan was back. Cold, calculating Captain America, his voice low and dangerous.

At least she knew how to deal with this Evan. Shuttering the hurt at the betrayal in his voice, she swallowed and braced for his verbal assault. She'd expected him to be hurt. She hadn't expected to see the hurt looking back at her now. She avoided his eyes, not wanting to acknowledge the intense disquiet she felt at his proximity.

He shifted and when he spoke, his voice was low. "Or did you know all along what Engle and Reza had planned?"

She shook her head and folded her arms over her chest, lifting her gaze briefly before settling on a spot over his shoulder. "I stand by my statement."

"So you lied to me? You let Reza and Engle deviate from the training plan?" The cold disdain in his eyes sliced into her soul. "You think this is a joke? Claire, Colonel Danvers is looking to have people fired. That career you wanted to save? You can cancel Christmas, because he's already called our brigade commander back at Fort Hood. And Colonel Richter is furious."

She swallowed the news with a sinking heart. She took a

step backwards, needing distance between them. No sound made it past the blockage in her throat.

"You're lying to me, Claire. You had nothing to do with Engle and Reza's harebrained scheme, did you?"

"I'm not answering that." She stopped backing up, feeling the threat skittering up her spine from the close proximity of his anger.

"Why not? Why can't you tell me the truth for once in your life?"

"What do you want me to tell you, Evan? That I thought Reza was drinking? That I'm pretty sure he'd do anything for that damn lieutenant and I can't for the life of me figure out why? Or do you want me to admit that for once in her life, Engle tried to do something brave? It might have been stupid but it was brave. And I'm not willing to let her drag Reza down with her. Everyone already thinks I'm a screw-up. I might as well live up to my reputation."

"That's the stupidest thing I've ever even heard. You don't even like Lieutenant Engle."

"You're right, I don't. But maybe I realized that she's not as bad as I thought. And maybe she needed someone to kick her in the ass to make her better."

"So you're going to throw your career away over that?"

"You don't get it, Evan. This is about keeping people in the fight who want to be there, who can make a difference."

"*You* make a difference."

"I *made* a difference. Right here. Right now. If my statement keeps Engle and Reza—" *and you*, she added silently —"out of trouble, then it's worth it. Sarah doesn't need this investigation hanging over her head. This ends it. Nice and easy."

"I'm not going to let you do this."

"No one will believe you, because everyone wants to see me as the screw-up." She stepped close, resting her hand on the rough fabric of his uniform. Right over the carved black lines covering his heart. "You don't get to set conditions here, Evan. It's already done."

"Neither do you. This isn't just about the army." His voice was quiet, but beneath the soft tone was a hard edge that cut straight through her. His words dripped across the skin of her throat, threatening to choke her. "Do you know why it bothers me so much that you'll fuck me, but you won't let me touch you?"

Claire swallowed the dryness in her mouth. She didn't want any painful revelations. She didn't want to psychoanalyze her trust issues or the fact that everyone in her life always let her down. He was hitting too close to the mark, striking at the core of her that she'd kept hidden from everyone, even Reza, her best friend. She opened her mouth to speak but he pressed his thumb to her lips. His skin was hot and rough, hard against her mouth.

"Because for the first time as an adult, I've met a woman who is strong and confident and gorgeous and she doesn't think she's worth the price of the uniform she wears. She's so invested in being a soldier, she doesn't think she's worth anything outside of her rank." Evan pushed against her, sliding his hand around her neck until his lips were a breath from her ear. Until his voice was so low she could barely hear him. "You're better than what you'll let yourself be. You're more than the rank on your chest." He nuzzled her ear and she shivered violently with arousal and awareness. "I don't know what the war did to you, Claire, but you won't let anyone get close. Won't trust anyone."

"Since when do you care?" she whispered.

"Since I saw something different this week. Something special. But you know what else I saw? A woman who's afraid. Afraid to trust. Afraid to let her hair down." He threaded his fingers through her hair tightly. "You told me once you thought I was too uptight but the truth is, you're the one who never relaxes. You never trust anyone. And that's a hell of a way to live. "

"You have no idea what you're talking about," she whispered, her voice cracking in the silence. She closed her eyes against the fury in his voice.

"You're wrong." His breath traced over her ear. "I've got you dead to rights. You just don't want to admit it. Who hurt you, Claire? Who broke you so badly that you don't trust me enough to look me in the eyes when I'm inside you?"

She said nothing, refusing to meet his gaze. After a long moment, he released her. "So that's the way it is, then." His words were not a question. The door closed quietly behind him, leaving her cold to the bone, hollowed out and empty.

Leaving her alone. Just like always.

෴

IT WAS A LONG TIME BEFORE CLAIRE GAVE UP ON HER SELF-imposed house arrest. She couldn't find Reza, hadn't been able to find him since the accident two days ago. And Evan? She was pretty sure Evan would never speak to her again. The loss ached against her heart, and she did her best to ignore the wound that still bled from his harsh words. She wouldn't tell him why she'd done it. He didn't need to know that Danvers had been gunning for Evan, too.

Restless, Claire walked into the hospital and her soul recoiled from the sterile smell of antiseptic and floor polish. She hated hospitals. She hated the memory of being in another hospital, long ago, but she pushed past her own tormented history, needing answers more.

She steeled herself with a deep breath and walked to the reception desk, asking for Lieutenant Engle's room. She let the rank on her chest lie for her, as the woman smiled and assumed she was Engle's commander. But when she climbed the stairs and passed the nurses' station, her stomach started a familiar flip.

She straightened. She wasn't that scared teenager anymore. She hadn't been for a long time. She knocked on Engle's door. She wanted to be angry with the LT for the stupid stunt that had landed her in the hospital and a lot of people Claire cared about in a world of hurt. Instead, she found herself wanting to know why she'd done it.

"Come in!"

Engle's eyes widened as Claire rounded the corner and approached the bed. She swallowed nervously and Claire took in the extent of her injuries. Which honestly did not look that bad. "You looked like you were in a hell of a lot worse shape the other day on the range," Claire said by way of greeting.

Engle offered a hesitant smile. "I've been better." She swallowed again and the silence stretched between them. "I didn't mean for anyone to get hurt," she whispered. "I just wanted to train my team."

Claire searched for the right words. For anything she could say to ease the young lieutenant's mind. "No one ever means for someone to get hurt," she said after a long moment. "Whose idea was the pyro?"

"Mine."

Claire pinned her with a hard look. "Then why is Reza's name on the paperwork?"

"I didn't ask him to help," Engle said quietly. "He said he knew someone who could get him the pyro. And so much of the other training was such a waste of time. I needed to know I'd done everything I could to train my team. I just wanted to do what you'd do. You're always so headstrong, so confident. I know we've had our differences, but I kind of want to be like you when I grow up. You know, when I'm a captain."

Claire scoffed quietly. "No. No you don't. My life is one disaster after another." She smiled wryly. "But thanks for saying so."

The echo of Claire's own words rang in her ears. She was uncomfortable that Engle had been looking up to her while Claire had been . . . Claire had been a bitch. "You're in a lot of trouble, LT."

Engle flinched. "Is Reza—I mean Sarn't Ike?"

Unexpected anger flashed through Claire, brilliant and white hot. "Yeah, he is. He was already in trouble before he came to Fort Carson. And now thanks to your stupid infatuation with him and his with you, you two are in trouble."

"Ma'am, there's nothing going on between me and Reza." Engle's mouth opened, then closed abruptly. "He's just a friend."

"Bullshit. What were you doing in his room? Ever since Iraq you've had a thing for him."

"I don't have a thing for him." Engle's skin blanched and she looked away. Her words were so quiet, Claire doubted what she heard. "Ma'am, I'm gay," she whispered.

Claire sank into the chair as embarrassment crawled, hot and prickly, over her skin. "Huh." It was not her most eloquent moment. She searched for something to say, but "I'm sorry" seemed so unbelievably inadequate. She'd judged this woman. Harshly and wrongly.

"Sarn't Ike, he looked out for me. I let everyone think things were going on because, well, you know what it's like being a young lieutenant."

"No, actually, I've never been a young lieutenant," Claire said dryly. "So you let everyone think you were with Iaconelli to avoid . . ."

"I wanted to avoid attention from the captains and majors so I could do my job." Engle's face was drawn, her skin tight.

"Please don't tell. I don't want to get thrown out under Don't Ask, Don't Tell."

Claire's mouth opened but nothing came out. All of her assumptions were wrong. Not just wrong. Horribly wrong. "I'm sorry." It was weak, but it was the only thing she had.

"You're not going to tell?"

"No." Claire smiled sadly. "I'm sorry I assumed . . . a lot of bad things about you." She swallowed. "I was wrong."

Engle's mouth formed a soft oh. Silence stretched between them. "Do I have a chance of saving my career with Colonel Danvers?"

"I wish I knew."

"I'm going to tell Colonel Danvers it was all my idea. I don't want anyone else getting in trouble for me," Engle said quietly, lifting her chin slightly.

"It's a little too late for that," Claire said. "The best thing you can do is own up to what you did. Don't make excuses, okay? Put on your big girl panties and own up."

"Roger, Ma'am." She paused, looking up at Claire with huge brown eyes. "Thanks for checking on me."

Claire nodded once and left, unable to stand there looking at someone she'd judged so harshly. It was humbling to see the evidence of her error look up at her with something akin to hero worship.

It was not a comfortable feeling. Claire wasn't a hero. Not even close. And as she rode back to the lodge, she wracked her brain for a way around the obstacle that was threatening to end Reza's career. Engle? She hadn't expected to care about Engle or her career, but she did. Turned out she was a good kid. She'd made a tough decision, hiding who she was and letting people think the worst about her.

Claire doubted she could ever make it up to her but as she turned into the parking lot of the lodge, she knew she'd done the right thing by taking the blame for the pyro. It wasn't much, but it was all she had at the moment.

A tiny piece of penance paid.

Claire parked the rented vehicle and stepped into the brilliant, sunny afternoon that was Fort Carson in November, determined to go for a walk and push aside the melancholy that threatened to choke her.

She started to head upstairs, but she couldn't face the aching silence coming from Evan's room. The kind of silence that suggested he'd checked out and headed back to Fort Hood. Which would be for the best, because she didn't think she could face the scathing recrimination in his eyes when he looked at her.

He'd looked at her with such disappointment. He didn't know whether to believe her or not. And there was nothing he could do about it. She'd made her choice.

It was the right thing to do. He never had to know she'd kept him from being investigated with her statement.

Which was fine. It didn't matter. None of it did. She had a meeting with Colonel Richter scheduled for the day after she returned to Fort Hood. She was so tired of fighting for her career, for her credibility. If her signed sworn statement got Reza out of the hot seat and kept Engle in the fight, then so be it. If it kept Evan from ever being tainted by having known her, then good. Claire's career would end quietly with an honorable discharge and she could go about her life as a civilian while Evan kept leading soldiers. If Reza was still in the fight, still leading soldiers in combat, well, then it would all be worth it.

Which meant her career, the only thing in her life that she'd ever been good at, was over.

Funny, she should be more panicked than she was. Instead, there was a strange, twisting calm inside her, an eerie quiet, like the waves pounding on the shore of the ocean. Steady. Constant.

She turned down a trail and started walking away from the lodge.

Screeching brakes shattered the snow-covered morning.

She spun toward the parking lot she had just left, crouching down in a reflexive reaction to the sound. A full-size black SUV careened over the center median and into one of the ski racks at the edge of the parking lot.

The world went absolutely still. Fear gripped her for one soul-crushing moment as she froze, unable to move. She recognized that SUV. One of the rental cars. Fear pulsed through her veins as she sprinted to the scene of the accident. *Please let me be wrong.*

She didn't know how she was the first to reach the SUV. She grabbed the door handle and ripped it open.

Smoke billowed from the mangled front of the SUV and the driver was trying to extract himself from the air bag. Blood gushed down Reza's face. One eye was already swollen shut and a massive gash split the skin across one cheek. He smiled when he recognized her, his teeth stained with blood. "Hey, can you find my seat-belt slicer? I seem to be stuck."

Her eyes burned. And then she shoved it aside.

She would cry for him later.

$\mathscr{H}$ 18 $\mathscr{H}$

Evan sprinted into the emergency room, his heart pounding in his throat, the fear threatening to choke him. He'd feared the worst when the phone call had come in, saying one of their team was in the hospital. That one of their rental vehicles was involved.

The memories of bloody snow had slammed through him until he thought he would break. He couldn't say how he'd reached the hospital. The only thing he knew was blinding, punishing fear as he raced through the double doors.

Evan's heart skipped in his chest, clenching tightly, his relief so palpable it nearly dropped him to his knees when he saw her.

Claire sat hunched over in the waiting room chair, arms wrapped tight around her stomach. If he lived a hundred years, he knew he'd never forget how Claire looked in that moment. Broken and wrung out from crying.

But alive. And unhurt.

He approached her slowly, not wanted to startle her, worried that the emotions twisting inside him were beyond his control. She looked up at him, her eyes green pools of sadness and worry, her mouth lined with fear. His throat closed off as he sat next to her, not waiting for an invitation that might never come.

If it wasn't Claire in the hospital . . .

"He swears he wasn't drinking," Claire whispered.

"Pretty sure we don't need a toxicology screen to tell us the truth on that." He kept his voice low, quiet. As if he was afraid he'd spook her if he moved too fast.

Claire said nothing and hunched back over. "They're only letting in family and the chain of command."

She shifted, folding her hands in front of her and twisting her fingers together. Evan sat down in the chair next to Claire's, afraid to reach for her. "I'll go with you. To lay out his options to him."

She looked at him then, heartbreak filling her eyes. "There's only one. He's got to self-refer to alcohol counseling. He's got to go to rehab." Her voice cracked on the end of the word.

"Rehab isn't a dirty word, Claire. It's not going to change who he is. At least not in a bad way." He wanted to cradle her face in his hands, to soothe the ragged grief he saw in her eyes. "He'll still be Reza. Just hopefully a sober Reza."

She shrugged and looked down at her hands and he knew she still wasn't being completely honest with him. For now, he let it go. He didn't think she was up for a fight. "I know that. Even if the company commander supports him, battalion and brigade might still push to throw him out for the alcohol-related incident."

Evan shook his head, even as a deep disquiet slithered in and whispered that she might be right. "I have to have more faith in our leaders than that."

"Then you have more faith than I do. If he were more senior, he'd be moved to another job and shuffled around. But he's only a sergeant first class. He's replaceable." She offered him a rueful smile.

"Men with Reza's experience are not replaceable." He shifted slightly, angling his body toward her. He'd never seen her looking as utterly lost as she did now. She bruised his heart, shattering the wall he'd been attempting to erect around it since he'd walked away from her. He hadn't wanted to need her, hadn't wanted to crave her. But the fear he'd felt was a crushing acknowledgment of what she'd come to meant to him.

"I've seen it happen time and time again. It's not what you know, it's who. And Reza may be connected to a few of us around here, but no full-bird colonel is going to stick his neck out on the line for an enlisted man." Her voice cracked a little. "He's just another expendable soldier."

Evan folded his fingers together. "You don't know that."

"Yeah, I kind of do." Her whispered words held a wealth of knowledge and dark certainty. "He has to get help."

He looked down at her folded hands, her bowed head. She sounded defeated. Like she was tired of fighting. Maybe she was. He almost reached for her, though terrified she would shatter beneath his touch.

The wide double doors opened and a white-coated doc walked out. They stood as she walked up to them. "You're here for Sergeant Iaconelli?" She stuck out her hand. "I'm Colonel Pillai."

"Tell me you have good news?" Claire said.

The doctor smiled and warm relief prickled over Evan's skin. "He's incredibly lucky. He shattered his collarbone in two places. Seventeen stitches in his forehead. But considering how bad the accident was, it could have been much worse."

Claire pressed her lips together and nodded. "Is there any chance we can see him, Ma'am?"

"Is there any chance either of you are in his chain of command?"

"Do past commanders count?" The words rolled easily off Evan's tongue. He hadn't been Reza's commander in over a year, but the difference didn't seem to matter nearly as much as it might have once.

Dr. Pillai smiled. "Sure. It's got to be quick, though. We're probably going to be moving him up to the ICU in the next hour."

The doctor walked back to the front desk and buzzed them in. Claire lingered closer to Evan.

"She didn't say anything about the toxicology screen," Evan said softly.

"Even if he was drinking, she probably wouldn't tell us." She sounded resigned, as though it was a foregone conclusion that this was going to end Reza's career.

Evan didn't push the issue. In the end, seeing his former platoon sergeant nearly broke him. Half of Reza's face was bruised and his left eye was swollen shut. His dark skin was splotchy black and blue. He offered a lopsided grimace that Evan supposed was meant for a grin.

"You look like shit." Reza's words were slurred, his smile a little too cheerful. "I know what you're going to say."

Claire folded her arms across her chest, straightening slightly. "I'm glad you're okay," she said softly.

Reza attempted to frown but winced as the movement jarred his stitches. "Okay, that wasn't what I expected you to say." He sighed, the smile fading. "I wasn't drinking."

"You're going to have to do better than that," Evan said.

"I was up driving around half the damn night from not drinking. I couldn't sleep and the walls were closing in on me." He sighed and looked away. "I fell asleep behind the wheel."

Claire plucked at the sheet on the edge of the bed,

looking miserable and out of sorts. Evan rested one hand on her shoulder. Claire stiffened slightly, then relaxed beneath his touch.

"Reza, I love you like a brother but this has to stop. You—"

"I don't need any lectures right now."

"Yeah, well maybe it's time you got a lecture," Claire snapped. "I'd take a fucking bullet for you but you've gone too far. You need help, Reza. Before you kill someone."

"Been there, done that, got the shitty T-shirt and the Bronze Star to boot," he ground out. "I'm not in the mood for your shit, Claire."

"Watch your mouth," Evan said softly. He squeezed Claire's shoulder gently as he chose his words carefully. "You've got two choices. You self-refer. The minute you're released from the hospital, you get yourself back to Fort Hood and over to substance abuse and enroll yourself in rehab."

"And option B?" Reza had long ago given up smiling.

Claire's voice was flat. "There *is* no option B. You self-refer."

⛌

"THAT WENT WELL." EVAN PUSHED HIS SUNGLASSES ON AS they stepped outside. It took him a minute to realize that it was dark and he didn't actually need the shades.

"If by well you mean he's no longer speaking to us, it went swimmingly." Claire stuffed her own glasses in the front of her uniform, between the Velcro and the zipper.

Evan put his hand on her shoulder, stopping her, briefly surprised when she didn't pull away. "It needed to be done," he said quietly.

"I know that." She refused to meet his gaze, looking out

instead over the parking lot, which was illuminated by flood-lights. "I suppose one of us should call back to Fort Hood and tell Colonel Richter. The hospital is bound to report it to the command. Because Colonel Richter needs one more thing to have kittens about."

She started walking again, only to stop a moment later. His heart broke a little more for her. "Hey."

She glanced at him, then looked away, as if afraid to hold his gaze long enough to let him see into her soul.

He dared to reach out and touch her jaw, urging her to look at him. For the life of him, he could not find the anger he'd harbored toward her since she'd slapped at him with hard realities and hurtful words. Now all he felt was sadness for her hurt. Regret that she was so closed off and distant that she couldn't even trust him to be there with her. "You scared me today," he whispered. "I thought it was you in the hospital."

She said nothing, her eyes shimmering in the low winter light. She looked like she was going to spend the entire night lying awake and damn it, he wasn't going to let her do that by herself. Not tonight. "You don't look like you should be alone right now."

"I can't do this with you." She met his gaze. "I can't be the woman you need, Evan."

He slipped his fingers down her neck, his thumb caressing the soft skin at the edge of her jaw. "I didn't ask you to marry me. Just stay with me tonight. Just tonight. Because honest-ly?" He leaned in, brushing his lips against hers and not giving a damn who saw. "I don't want to be alone, either."

THEY SAT IN THE CAR IN THE PARKING LOT OUTSIDE THE lodge. Cold seeped in through the doors and windows, freezing the silence around them. "When I was fifteen, my father tripped and fell on me. He'd been drinking." She swallowed and stared into the darkness.

"The coffee table?" Evan murmured. "The scars on your back. Shattered glass?"

She nodded silently then pushed out a deep breath. "When I finally got to the hospital, I told them what had happened. They took me away from him because he admitted to drinking too much. They said he wasn't responsible enough to take care of me. I spent the next three years in and out of foster homes. He died two weeks after I joined the army." Claire sat in the dark, her boots resting on Evan's dashboard, her chin resting on her knees. "My tenth-grade English teacher helped take me away from my dad. I trusted her. I talked to her about things at home. And she helped take me away from the only home I had."

Her heart ached for the girl she'd been. So naïve. So trusting in the wrong people. "I was eighteen the first time I met Sarn't Iaconelli."

"It sounds weird hearing you call him 'Sarn't.'" His voice was a low rumble beneath the hushed blanket of night.

She smiled. Evan's face was lit by the parking lot lights outside the lodge. "Yeah, well, he was Sarn't Ike a lot longer than I was a sergeant." She took a deep breath, letting the words come out without a filter. She'd held onto them for long enough.

"We were stopped just outside of Basra. Things had been quiet. Mostly. Little flare-ups but nothing major. We thought one division would win the entire war in less than a month." She looked away. "I worked on the plan with my battalion commander. I trusted him. Looked up to him. God, I was such a fool."

She opened the door of the truck, needing the crisp, cold

night air to ease some of the pressure burning in her lungs. He followed when she climbed out.

Funny how she'd gotten used to having him around. Iraq. Fort Hood. Fort Carson. Somehow, Evan had wormed his way past every single one of her defenses until she found herself scanning the faces in a room looking for him. He tormented her dreams. Teased her with a hint of what could be.

It scared the hell out of her.

Evan followed her into the lodge, then into her room, and he closed and locked the door behind them. She felt him move toward her and she managed not to brace herself when he rested his hands on her shoulders. "Keep going," he urged.

She took a deep breath. Then started talking.

"Reza and his platoon were pinned down just outside the Baghdad Airport. My commander shocked the hell out of me when he said he wasn't going to let anyone go after them because we needed to capture the airport first." She swiped at her cheeks to hide the tears. "You asked me who broke me? It was the battalion commander who I trusted, who I admired, who refused to let me go after my friend. Who tried to court-martial me when I did it anyway. It was my father, who wasn't man enough to be the dad I needed. Everyone in my life I was supposed to be able to trust has let me down. Except Reza." She sniffed. "It's killing me to watch him waste his life at the bottom of a bottle." She offered a watery smile. "You asked me once why I wouldn't face you when we're having sex? Because I'm afraid, Evan. I'm afraid you're going to be just like everyone else in my life."

"That's pretty harsh," he said gently.

"Not really." She sniffed again. "I mean, you turned me in to Colonel Richter after the range fire." She swiped at her cheeks again, trying to smile at her own weak attempt at a joke. "Our track record with each other sucks."

HE PULLED HER AGAINST HIM AND STROKED HIS HANDS UP and down her back, tracing her spine with his thumbs, unable to deny the harsh truth of her words, no matter how gently they were spoken. Up and down, again and again, he stroked her. Softly. Hoping to gentle the fierce violence of emotion raging through him. Too much raged inside him. Fear. Loss.

But it was the utter hopelessness he saw in Claire's eyes that terrified him.

She was on the verge of giving up, of forgetting everything she'd fought so hard to become. Her stubborn need to hold the line, to do the wrong thing for the right reasons—all of it was what drew him to her. And tonight, she looked as though she'd lost her will to fight.

She lifted her head away from his chest. Her eyes were red and they threatened to spill. "Don't cry," he whispered. "Please don't cry."

She tried to smile but he stopped her, nudging her lips gently with his. He rubbed his nose against hers, lashing back the intense hunger he wanted badly to satiate. She met him halfway, opening her mouth beneath his. Her tongue darted against his, a warm, wet slide of heat against heat. It was Claire who deepened their kiss. Claire who stepped closer to rub her hips against his. Claire whose fingers traced beneath his T-shirt and caressed his skin.

Claire who spanned the distance between them.

"It's okay to be afraid," he whispered against her lips.

She closed her eyes, resting her cheek over the hard black lines covering his heart. "I don't want to be alone."

This time, it was Evan who crossed the space between them. "You're not," he whispered.

They stayed that way a long time. Kissing. Petting. Quiet strokes, soothing the ragged emotions in each of them. Curled on the bed, fully clothed, their bodies touching, for once, only for comfort. The shift came quietly, a soft transition from soothing to sensual.

Evan's fingers pressed up the back of her neck and tugged her hair free from the knot she wore. He threaded his fingers through her hair, rubbing her scalp gently. After an impossibly long silence, she shifted against him, relaxing into his touch, some of the sadness and grief and sacrifice burned away by its heat.

"You have magic fingers," she murmured.

Evan stopped, lowering his head to the cradle of her neck, his entire body shaking. She frowned and turned to see him wiping his eyes. He looked at her then and laughed out loud.

"What?" Her lips twitched into an almost smile.

"Magic Fingers . . . it's a sex toy company."

Claire bit her lip but the laugh bubbled free, unexpected and welcome. "Do I want to know how you know this?"

He offered a nonchalant shrug, a smile lingering on his lips. "There's a lot of time to kill on deployments."

"With sex toys?"

"All I'm going to say is the source of the chlamydia in my company all those years ago was not a soldier." His voice lowered just a little, his eyes darkening in the shadows of her dimly lit suite. "And no, I never spent any quality time with Magic Fingers, in case you were wondering."

She dragged her palms over his chest, savoring the feel of his hard muscles beneath her touch. He was solid. Real. She smiled. Evan made her laugh when all she wanted to do was cry. "I'm not so well acquainted with sex toys that I know their brands."

"Well, thanks to my time in the trenches as a tank

company commander, I learned all kinds of interesting things. Things you never expect to learn as an army officer."

He stopped her as she parted the zipper on his uniform jacket, grasping her wrists gently. He rubbed his thumbs along the inside of her wrists. "Are you sure this is what you want tonight?"

"Do you just want to cuddle instead?"

"I could draw you a picture of a bunny. You could hang it on your fridge." He released her wrists and shrugged out of his jacket as she pushed it off his shoulders.

She wrapped her arms around his neck and pressed her lips to the side of his throat, feeling his pulse beat against her skin. His arms tightened around her waist and she felt his breath on her neck.

"You can draw me the bunny later." She nuzzled his shoulder where the tattoo covered the scars he'd borne on his soul long before he'd etched them into his body, then reached between them, sliding her hand into his pants. "I'd much rather spend some quality time with your cock."

He made a low growl in his throat, his fingers gripping her wrist. "Not funny."

"It's a little funny." She laughed but then he nipped her ear, his breath a rush against her skin. And suddenly, she didn't feel like playing anymore. Serious now, she met his gaze. "Make me feel, Evan. Make me forget."

Claire tugged her hands free and pulled her uniform T-shirt over her head. Evan's mouth went dry.

"Mother of God."

She wore a tiny black demi-bra. It cradled her breasts and looked like it was struggling just to stay in place. He could see the dark of her nipples behind the thin black lace. He framed her ribs with his palms, slipping them higher. The woman was drop-dead gorgeous wearing army uniform pants and a lacy bra.

"This isn't very functional," he murmured, dropping to his knees so that her breasts were at eye level. "But it's sexy as hell."

She threaded her fingers into his hair, smiling down at him. "Sometimes I like to wear something other than functional cotton. Not that cotton doesn't have its own virtues as a fabric, but—"

She hissed sharply as he traced his tongue over her nipple, fabric and all. His fingers danced over her back, pressing her closer, and he felt her arch beneath his touch. He stifled a groan as her nails dug into his scalp. A dark desire shot through his blood and the lingering thrill built to a fierce inferno.

He suckled her, tugging her nipple between his teeth. She moaned low in her throat and slowly slid down the length of his body until she straddled his bent knees. She looked between their bodies and smiled.

She reached between them, tugging at his belt. She frowned when it didn't slip free immediately. "It's just an army belt." He laughed and pulled it all the way off, leaving his pants gaping at the waist.

Claire didn't waste a moment before she slipped her hand into that gap. She loved the feeling of the crisp hair against her palm before she encircled him, squeezing gently. "I think this might be better than your magic fingers," she whispered. "I see that you're wearing panties today."

"Underwear. Men don't wear panties."

He traced her ear with his tongue, and her breath hitched when he blew gently on the moist heat he'd created.

He pulled back suddenly, still cradling her neck in his palm.

She flicked open the buttons of his pants, freeing his erection. When she traced her thumb over its head, she felt him stiffen and swell beneath her touch.

Claire pushed to her knees and spanned the tiny space between them. A thrill of power shot through her when his gaze swept over her body, his jaw pulsing as he looked at her. She slid her palms up over the rough fabric of his uniform, then gripped the edge of his T-shirt as she continued her explorations.

She dragged the T-shirt off and kissed him. Her fingers traced the lines on his chest, sliding around his back to dig into the solid muscles clenching beneath her touch. The ragged scar on his deltoid was smooth and soft beneath her fingers, his muscles satin on steel. She wrapped her thighs around his waist and urged him onto his back.

"This is a much better position," he said against her lips as he cupped her breasts, teasing her nipples until they stiffened.

She shivered beneath his touch, closing her eyes and arching into his palms. He moved suddenly and stood, lifting her easily. She lowered her legs but he urged her to wrap them back around his hips. She was distracted enough by the pleasure of her heat rubbing against his erection that when he suddenly released her, she actually tumbled onto the bed without catching herself. "That was not cool."

While she pulled off her pants and shoes, he stripped off the rest of his clothing, then knelt at the edge of the bed near her feet. He captured one of them, gently massaging the sole of her foot with his thumb.

"I'm really not interested in what you think of my feet," she said, trying to tug her foot free.

He held her foot firmly, tracing his fingers up her calf, rubbing her skin in soft, easy circles. He followed his thumb with his tongue, leaving a trail of moist, warm heat on her skin. She trembled as he slipped farther up her body, a slight smile teasing her lips.

"What?" he asked.

She opened her eyes to see him looking up at her from the apex of her thighs.

"I'm glad I shaved my legs today."

"Hmm." He kissed her inner thigh, then bit down gently at the seam where cotton met flesh. "Shave anything else?"

She swallowed and shifted, relaxing her thighs a little more. "Only one way for you to find out."

CLAIRE'S BODY WAS TENSE AS A DET CORD BENEATH HIS touch. She was beauty and sensual energy bound together in one woman who could send him into the darkest rage or draw him into the fiercest passion.

Her thighs clenched against his forearms but he kept stroking that impossibly soft skin between the edge of her thigh and her intimate heat. He'd dreamed of her like this.

He barely restrained the urge to tear her panties off, instead dragging them slowly down her thighs. "Oh my God."

His mouth went dry. She was completely bare except for the tiniest stripe of the deepest copper red at the very center of her.

He looked up at her. She smiled sheepishly. "Surprise," she said weakly.

"Oh, you've got to explain this," he said when he could speak. He nuzzled the soft skin of her inner thigh, kissing her gently, then blowing on the moist skin. "Later."

And when he tasted her, long and slow and smooth, Claire's entire body tightened. He stroked her with his tongue, teasing her until her body was tight beneath him.

Her orgasm was beautiful against his lips. She trembled beneath his mouth, her cries pure balm to his ragged soul. He didn't stop stroking her until she was tight and tense once more.

Only then did he crawl up her body, teasing her with his thumb. He was darkly aroused by the sight of his dog tags resting between her breasts.

She tried to turn like she always did. He gripped her hands, threading his fingers through hers and dragging her arms over her head. "Don't." He brushed his lips against her cheek. "Trust me, Claire?"

She turned her face away from his, closing her eyes. He released one hand to cradle her cheek in his palm. *Please don't turn away.* But he didn't say the words. Reality had crawled into bed with them and Evan wanted to kick the bastard out into the cold.

He kissed her sweetly, coaxing. Soothing. Doing everything in his power to relax her, to keep her from turning away and shutting him out. "Claire."

He whispered her name, his lips near her ear. "Look at me."

She didn't open her eyes.

"Claire. Please look at me." His words were ragged, his voice shredded, his control shattered.

Finally. Finally she met his gaze. Iridescent shards of emotion glinted back at him. Releasing her hands, he cradled her face in both palms. Her fingers clenched his as her thighs wrapped around his hips and urged him home.

"I love you," he whispered, holding her gaze as he pushed deep inside her.

She tried to turn her face away. Closed her eyes so she wouldn't have to meet his gaze. He gently urged her chin back.

He slid fully inside her again, a slow, deliberate stroke. "I love you."

She gasped quietly as he sank fully inside her and she closed her eyes, arching and opening for him.

❦

His breath was hot on her ear, his words a whisper against her skin. Everything rioted inside her, violent fear mixed with insecurity. This wasn't supposed to have happened. She wasn't supposed to care about this man. Not like this. She was a good friend. A good soldier. A terrible lover.

"Look at me," he whispered again, not moving inside her, denying her the release she needed.

She rolled her hips, digging her fingers into his skin and urging him to move. He refused and she opened her eyes, looking into the depths of Evan's own dark need. Her breath caught in her throat, desire welling up from deep, deep within her.

She met his gaze and he moved inside her, bringing her pleasure toward an intense, unreached peak.

"I love you," he murmured against her mouth and she captured his words inside her.

"Evan—" Her breath caught as gripped both her hands in his so he could cradle her cheek with his other hand.

He kissed her then, as he drove them both closer to the edge of no turning back. The abyss spiraled wide and inviting, urging her to take the leap, to embrace everything he offered.

She shattered, her name on his lips the last thing she heard as she tumbled into the chaos.

❦ 20 ❦

"I have to see Colonel Richter when we get back."

Claire was nestled against him, his chest strong and hard against her back. His dog tags were warm beads of metal against her spine. Every inch of her body was surrounded by him and one arm had snaked around her waist to hold her hand.

He nuzzled her neck, placing a soft kiss over one of her scars. "You don't have to say anything. Invoke your Article 31 right to remain silent."

She sighed deeply and closed her eyes, letting the weight of his words surround her. "I can't."

"Why not?" His words were rough against her neck.

She said nothing for a long time, searching for the right words to give voice to the chaos rumbling inside of her. It was time to let go of all of it. The fear of keeping the secret of Iaconelli's drinking from everyone. Her constant conflict between loyalty and duty.

None of it was worth the price she'd paid.

It was time to face reality. Life wasn't fair. She rolled over to face him, the quiet rustle of sheets the only sound besides their breathing. He sighed and pulled her to him, twining his legs with hers and wrapping his arms around her. She rested her cheek against his shoulder and stroked the soft hair on his chest.

"My career is over, Evan." Her voice broke but she continued. "You were right. Cutting corners is the wrong way to go. Good people got hurt along the way. People I care about," she whispered. "I never wanted Engle to get hurt, either. Turns out, she's not as bad as I thought she was."

His arms tightened around her and he kissed her forehead. She pressed her lips against his heart. "I want this over. I want Reza in rehab and I need to go to sleep knowing that you're out there in the world, protecting us."

Evan said nothing as he pulled her more tightly against him. He was no longer relaxed—his body had gone tense and stiff. His thumb idly stroked the scars on her shoulder and Claire wished he'd say something.

Anything at all to ease the fierce awkwardness between them. But when he spoke, he shattered any illusions that she'd been fooling anyone but herself.

❧

"How far were you willing to let this go, Claire?"

"What are you talking about?"

He rolled her until she was flat on her back, her thighs spread out on either side of his hips. His body was hard and rough against hers. Her panic flared but the anger in his eyes was not, for once, directed at her.

"You had no idea what Reza was doing with Engle." His words were harsh with the brutal truth. "You're lying. You're lying to Danvers and you're lying to me. Why?"

She stilled, her words a crushed whisper. "Get off me."

He let her go. But he followed her out of the bed they'd

shared, refusing to back down. She pulled on a T-shirt, searching for sweat pants, needing something, anything, as a shield between them.

"Why are you willing to throw away your career for a worn-down soldier who's going to drink himself into an early grave?"

His words were a slap, harsh and brutal. He stepped in front of her, his hands gentle on her shoulders. "Reza is not your father, Claire. And he needs to want to be saved," he whispered.

Claire bit her bottom lip until she tasted blood. Anything to keep it from trembling. "That's really rich coming from you. How many years has it been since you called home? I would give anything to have my father back. And you're wasting all these years because you think your parents blame you for your sister's death."

"That's not fair. They do blame me."

She shook her head. "It's been almost two decades. Long enough for them to remember they still have a son." Her voice broke. "A son they should be damn proud of." She tried to pull away from his touch but he just tightened his grip. "I'm not doing this for Reza. I'm doing this for the kids he's saved. For the soldiers he'll still lead through combat. I'm just a renegade officer who can't follow orders. Reza's a warrior. A real-deal warrior. He needs to be in this fight." She shook her head, unwilling to admit that she was doing this for him, too. "I want to be a good soldier but all I ever do is break the rules."

The tears that threatened to spill finally overflowed, soaking her cheeks. She swiped at them with the back of one hand. "I'll take the fall for this because everyone expects it to be me who screwed it up anyway. Reza goes to rehab and stays in the fight."

"And you lose the thing that's defined you for your entire adult life," Evan whispered.

"It's worth it. If one life is saved because you or Reza is in the fight then it's worth it." She turned away before he could see the truth of her words in her eyes.

He stopped, his pants halfway up his thighs. "This isn't about me, Claire. And it isn't about Reza." Hitching his pants over his hips, he crossed the space between them, kissing her fiercely until she leaned back against the table to stay upright. "This is about you trying to prove your worth."

She shook her head, but he pressed his thumb against her lips. "I know what you're doing," he whispered harshly. "And I'm not going to let you."

And then he was gone.

EARLY THE NEXT MORNING, CLAIRE KNOCKED ON REZA'S hospital door, hoping she didn't look as bad as she felt. She'd slept fitfully the night after her fight with Evan and this morning, he wasn't answering his door. Which was just as well. She didn't know how to handle the legion of dark emotions Evan dredged up.

He'd said he'd loved her right before he'd walked out on her. Even the memory of those whispered words were enough to send a shiver tracing across her skin.

Reza had been furious the last time she'd seen him, but she couldn't leave Colorado without seeing him again. She didn't know what to expect as she walked into the hospital room and she hesitated at the corner, afraid to take that last step closer. Reza sat in the hospital bed, watching TV. He started to offer a weak smile but it immediately turned into a frown. "Who kicked your puppy?"

Claire smiled as relief crawled over her skin. Just like that, they were back to normal. Something unlocked inside her, sliding back into place. "No one important," she lied. "You look terrible. That black eye should be good with the ladies."

Reza cleared his throat roughly and Claire laughed. "You already found someone here, didn't you?"

"None of your business," he said roughly. "Are you okay?"

She shrugged and looked down at her feet. "Everything about this sucks."

"Tell me about it." He narrowed his eyes at her. "Claire." She breathed deeply before she met his gaze. "I wasn't drunk."

She swallowed. "But you'd been drinking."

This time, it was Reza who looked away, flipping the remote control over and over in one hand.

"It's probably better if you don't answer that," she said softly. "Ah hell, Reza."

Her voice broke and she swiped angrily at her cheeks. "When are you going to stop?"

Silence stretched between them, awkward and full of pain-filled regrets. The only sound was the steady beep from the heart monitor and Claire's quiet sniffs as she tried to rein in her emotions.

"So are you finally going to admit to what's been happening with you and Evan?" he said quietly. She looked up at him, waiting to see the accusation, the blame. He shook his head with a slow smile. "You're so obvious."

Claire sighed and looked around the room, avoiding his gaze. If it were anyone else asking, she'd tell him to pound sand. But this was Reza, which made the conversation all the more difficult. "We slept together a few times. No big deal."

"Bullshit. That's a very big deal in the world according to Claire."

Claire shifted, not liking the third degree, even if it was

from Reza. "No, it's not." But even she didn't sound convinced.

Evan's whispered words in the dark of her suite pressed in on her, squeezing her chest. She didn't want to care about someone so much it hurt. She'd done that before and it had always turned out badly for her. It was hard enough losing friends in combat. Her throat tightened at the thought of standing in Evan's memorial ceremony and she blinked suddenly.

"You're an ass, you know that, right?" Reza said, tossing the remote with a rough exhale.

Claire smiled, jolted out of her melancholy. "Of course you mean that in the most loving way, right?"

"No. I mean it just how it sounds." Reza glanced at the now black TV, then back at her, his expression hard and serious. "I've known you for years and you're a great friend. You've never let anyone get close to you. Why are you so scared of a relationship?"

"I'm not hiding some deep psychic harm from my dad, if that's what you're getting at."

"Bullshit."

"Holy crap, Reza, I don't really need this right now." She turned to go but his words dove in front of her, stopping her retreat.

"I'm not actually finished."

Claire narrowed her eyes and turned back, braced for Reza's onslaught. Instead, he patted the bed. She looked at him as if he'd lost his mind. "I'm not one of your groupies."

"Shut up and come sit down," he snapped. "Pretend I'm your grandfather and you're going to read to me or something."

She released a laugh, then approached the bed, leaning against it near his hip. She was shocked when he grabbed her hand and tugged her down until she couldn't escape. His hand was big and warm on her wrist but she felt nothing. Nothing like when it was Evan holding her.

"You can't keep pushing away everyone who cares about you, Claire. You don't even have a dog or a cat." His voice softened. "I get it. Your dad didn't take care of you the way he should have. People you trusted let you down. But that's not an excuse. You can't avoid caring for people because you think they're going to die or let you down or run off on you."

"Thanks for the pep talk. It really helps." She tried to stand but his grip was like iron. She looked at her longtime friend, noticing for the first time the lines that were etched into his smooth, dark skin. He'd done a good job of hiding the wear and tear of the war but at that moment, she saw all of it. All the strain, all the fatigue he'd tried to smother with drinking and good times.

She stopped pulling away and sat. "You scared the shit out of me last night," she whispered.

She clenched her fingers into a fist beneath his hand. He squeezed gently.

"Look at me, Claire." She met his gaze. " I won't make you worry about me like that again. But you've got to promise me something."

"I'm not going to give up the army, get married and live happily ever after." Although, if her conversation with Colonel Richter went like she expected, she'd be doing the giving up the army part a hell of a lot sooner than she'd ever planned.

His lopsided grin was pure Reza despite the fat lip. "Look, I've known you a hell of a lot longer than I've known Loehr. But if he's willing to put up with your bullshit and still wants to be with you, then that's a hell of a lot of points in his favor."

"Gee, thanks."

"You're a hard woman to care about, Claire." He loosened

his grip on her wrist. "If I go to rehab, you have to promise me you'll give things a shot with Evan. You deserve someone to make you happy."

"That's a shitty bargain," she grumbled.

"Take it or I head to the bar after I get out of the hospital and get hammered."

"No, your happy ass is going to rehab if I have to fly back up here, handcuff you and drag you there in a police car."

He laughed out loud and released her hand, rubbing his jaw. "Yeah, well, I had to try."

"It's not as simple as you make it sound."

"Yeah, actually it is. You walk up to Evan and say, 'I'd like to give whatever this is a shot. I promise not to be psychotic and stare at you while you're sleeping or anything but I've got some stuff to work through.'"

She laughed out loud, mildly horrified. "Yeah. Wow, that's so sexy."

"Or how about this: 'I'm kind of crazy but I'd like to keep having sex with you while I work through my crazy.'"

She was laughing so hard, she doubled over to keep from peeing her pants. She swiped her fingers beneath her eyes and looked at her longtime friend. "Thanks. I really needed that laugh. And none of those options are on the table. Evan's not talking to me right now."

"Why?"

"Because I'm me and I'm a champ at screwing things up," she said dryly. She breathed deeply. "I don't know how to do any of this," she admitted finally.

"Then you tell him that. For once in your adult life, you start with honesty and go from there. One day or one step at a time. It doesn't matter. Evan matters."

Reza shrugged, but his lips were curled in an easy smile that hid nothing. She'd never hid anything from him either, and she wasn't about to start now. "Yeah, he does."

"That's a start. I know where to get a set of handcuffs, too. You two figure this out or I'll use them." He glanced at the clock and gave her hand a tiny squeeze before he released her. "Don't you have a flight to catch?"

❧

IACONELLI HAD BEEN MOVED OUT OF INTENSIVE CARE AT some point and Evan had a hell of a time finding out where he'd been moved. He was still furious with Ike. For drinking. For the screw-up with the stupid pyro. And most of all for hurting Claire.

After going to every other floor in the hospital, he finally found him on the second floor. Evan's flight back to Fort Hood was later that day and he was short on time for the mission he needed to accomplish before he got on that plane. Claire had already left for the airport a few hours ago—he'd heard her door swing shut. He wanted to stop all of this, but Claire was determined to take one for the team.

Evan had never been angrier with her than he was as he stalked through the halls, looking for Reza. The TV blasted out into the hallway the moment Evan opened the door, not caring if he was welcome or not.

He stopped short and coughed loudly.

A dark-haired nurse jerked away from Reza, her mocha skin flaming deep red. She adjusted her top and ducked out of the room.

Reza fiddled with the remote, lowering the volume. Finally he cleared his throat. "Your timing sucks."

Evan couldn't find the energy to smile. "Glad to see you're feeling better."

"High as a kite and about as good. Nice to see you, too."

"Is she part of your pain management plan?"

Reza grinned and idly scratched his chest near the edge of the cast that was holding his arm immobile. "Maybe."

Evan shook his head and folded his arms over his chest, leaning against the wall. Reza tossed the remote onto the bed. As furious as he was, Evan couldn't find the words he needed. How did you tell a man that someone he cared about was about to ruin her life for him? "You scared the shit out of a lot of people."

"I don't need another lecture."

"I'm not giving you a lecture. I'm merely commenting on the facts as they stand."

Reza sniffed and shifted, wincing as he moved, trying to get comfortable. It was the only outward sign that he was hurting as bad as he was. Evan approached the bed. "Need help?"

"Yeah. Can you grab that damn pillow?"

"It's stuck under your ass."

"Ha ha ha. That's why I need your help."

Evan fixed the pillow, then swore viciously. Iaconelli waited in heavy silence. Finally, Evan spoke. "Claire is taking the fall for your stupid stunt."

"She didn't even have anything to do with that change in the plan. Engle came to me and asked me for help. Claire didn't know anything about it."

"Yeah, well, she's already signed a sworn statement telling Colonel Danvers—you remember, the guy who already told her not to screw it up—that she approved the change in the plan." Evan pinned him with a hard gaze. "She's going to ruin her life over her loyalty to you."

Reza said nothing for a long time. His jaw tightened and he looked away. "She's an idiot. Who told her to do that?"

"No one told her to. She's got some screwed-up idea that taking the fall for this will somehow keep you from getting thrown out of the army." Evan pinned him with a hard look. "She's already on her way back to Fort Hood."

Reza scrubbed his hand over his jaw, careful to avoid the bandage covering one cheek. "Why is she doing this?"

"Apparently she's got some pretty strong notions about what good officers do." He didn't share the secrets he'd unearthed. He wouldn't expose her weakness to her friend. But it killed him to think that she thought so little of herself that she would throw her career away for some stupid notion of loyalty or courage. It wasn't courage when the cause wasn't worth fighting for. And Iaconelli? He was a good soldier, a leader of men, a man who'd saved Evan's ass. He could ask him to tell the truth, to stop Claire's stupidity before it was too late. But that would end Reza's career and as much as he hated what the man was doing to himself, he was a good soldier. He looked up to find Reza studying him thoughtfully. "What?"

"I've got a solution to your problem. You're not going to like it and Claire may never speak to you again, but it solves your problem."

Evan settled back against the sink, crossing his arms over his chest. "I'm all ears."

❧

LATER, EVAN WALKED INTO HIS HOTEL ROOM, A SINKING feeling in his guts. He didn't know if Reza's solution was going to make a damn bit of difference, but it was a chance he had to take. He packed the last of his bags, acutely aware of the silence from the room next to his. There were still a couple of hours before his flight.

Claire's words echoed against his soul. She'd called him a coward because he didn't call home. She didn't know what it felt like, to have his parents look at him with blame in their eyes. He wasn't a coward.

Was he?

He glanced down at the cell phone he'd tossed onto the bed when he came in. His hand trembled as he picked it up and scrolled through the contacts until he found his mother. His father. And the home phone number he rarely called.

He pressed a single button.

The ring filled his ears, blocking out all other sounds. He sank to the bed, his hand gripping the phone hard enough to shatter the glass. His breath stuck in his chest. A solid lump of fear. Of longing.

"Hello?"

His voice caught in his throat. Finally, he forced the words past the stone against his heart. "Hi, Mom."

❧ 21 ❧

A day later, Claire flashed her ID card at the desk sergeant, then walked into the long corridor that lead to the Reaper command group and Colonel Richter's office.

She tried not to feel guilty about not calling Evan. But being home in her own space had made her crave silence, for once, instead of trying to drown it out with exercise or constant activity. She'd taken a hot bath. She'd had a couple of glasses of wine. And when she'd finally crawled into her bed, she'd struggled not to feel like it was swallowing her up instead of welcoming her home. Her bed felt empty now that she'd spent a night curled in Evan's embrace.

He said he loved her. She frowned, pushing away the disquieting thought that he had no idea what or who she was. He couldn't love her. He loved the woman he thought she was. Shoving away her melancholy, she straightened her spine and prepared to face the judge, jury and executioner that was Colonel Richter.

The Reaper headquarters was nothing like the Palehorse headquarters—the building was old and polished whereas

Palehorse was new and shiny. Despite the circumstances, Claire felt welcome in the Reaper corridor. She was tied to the history here. She was a part of that history. A history that mattered.

She traced her fingers beneath the framed plaque that was inscribed with the names of the fallen from each of Reaper's deployments. It choked her up each time she walked past it and she supposed that was the intention behind hanging it here. So that no one would ever forget.

She never would. Not every name represented a loss that had touched her personally, but the ones that did?

They had scarred her as badly as the glass that had pierced her skin so many years ago. Maybe worse, because until now she hadn't realized just how much she'd been holding the people in her life at arm's length, even good friends like Sarah and Reza.

She blinked rapidly and shoved the emotions down ruthlessly.

Whatever was going to happen was going to happen.

The command group offices were empty, so Claire approached the door and knocked, standing at attention until she heard Colonel Richter call for her to enter.

"Stand at ease, Captain Montoya."

She wasn't used to seeing Colonel Richter behind the commander's desk. He was rarely in his office since returning from downrange. He was the kind of commander who preferred responding to emails on his BlackBerry so he could be out with the troops. She admired his dedication and he was the kind of leader she'd follow anywhere. Knowing how badly she'd screwed up was hard enough, but it was even worse to think that she'd disappointed a man whom she respected.

"So we've got a small problem," Colonel Richter said, folding his hands across his lap and rocking back in his chair.

His dark hair was salt and pepper at the temples, his face weathered and lined from years in the sun.

"Sir, the pyro—"

"Stop talking, Captain. Until I give you permission to speak." His voice never rose, but Claire felt like she was five years old. One expected a brigade combat team commander to be many things, but soft-spoken was not one of them. People listened to Colonel Richter because they wanted to, not because they had to.

She said nothing, but she clenched her fists together behind her back.

"I've dealt with many things over my twenty-six-year career but I've never seen an officer go to such lengths to protect a noncommissioned officer." He sighed, and that sigh held the weariness of a man who'd seen far too much in far too short a time. "Did you know the extent of Sergeant Iaconelli's drinking problem?"

Claire's mouth fell open but she snapped it closed quickly. This wasn't about the pyro. She met his steady gaze, swallowing the sudden lump in her throat. "I suspected, Sir," she said quietly.

"Did you know he made a habit of drinking on duty?"

Claire's palms were slick and she could feel sweat rolling down beneath her armpits. This was not what she expected. Not at all. She said nothing.

"Sergeant Iaconelli and I served together at Sand Hill." Colonel Richter stood and crossed the room to a small, black book. Claire stood rigid, trying to look but not daring to move. He approached and held up a picture of a much younger Captain Richter and several men wearing the brown round hat of the drill sergeant. She recognized Reza standing at parade rest next to the captain. "He was the youngest drill sergeant on the trail. Most junior, too. So when I became a battalion commander getting ready to invade Iraq, I looked for that young sergeant to see if he was still around."

Claire forced herself to breathe. She didn't remember a Lieutenant Colonel Richter back in 2003. It didn't mean he wasn't around. Just that she didn't know him.

"See, here's the problem I'm facing. Reza Iaconelli finally stepped in it. And he's a senior noncommissioned officer. You realize that means I don't get a vote in what happens to him."

"Sir?"

Richter dropped the black book on his desk, irritation flashing in his eyes when he turned back to her. "The division commander withholds authority for the misconduct of all senior leaders. I may not be able to protect him this time."

Claire said nothing, not really sure what she was supposed to say.

"So now I'm stuck because I think you did what you did for the right reasons. You've got an integrity problem, but your bigger problem is your loyalty."

She flinched as his words hit her square in the sternum. She opened her mouth to protest, then snapped it shut, remembering that while she might admire Colonel Richter, she was not on that level of familiarity with him. He slid a sworn statement across the desk to her. She glanced down and read it quickly, her stomach sinking. Reza's statement countered hers on every single point. He took complete responsibility for the accident at Fort Carson. She smiled when she read *"Captain Montoya didn't know shit about the change in the plan and don't let her lie to you and say she did."*

She blinked fiercely as her eyes filled.

"You were incredibly loyal to do what you did, Claire," he said softly. "But you should have trusted me enough to talk to me off line about Iaconelli's problem. I thought you had more courage than that."

He slid a sheet of paper across his desk toward her. She

glanced down and her heart sank. Chills prickled over her skin and she shivered despite her best effort.

Conduct unbecoming. False official statement. Violation of a Lawful Order. Dereliction of Duty.

Her throat tightened. "Letter of reprimand, sir?"

"Yes. I managed to keep the fiasco at Fort Carson from the division commander, so I'll deal with you. Iaconelli's incident, however, hit the police reports. I'll do what I can to keep the division commander from crushing Iaconelli's nuts. I hear he's already enrolled in alcohol counseling at the hospital at Fort Carson."

She couldn't breathe.

"I wanted your ass for covering for Iaconelli and making a clusterfuck out of the exercise at Fort Carson." Colonel Richter tossed a pen on top of the paper.

Her mouth was dry and she swallowed several times to make her lips actually form coherent words. He slid another sheet of paper toward her. "On orders report?"

"You're leaving the brigade. The question is where you're going." He set the two papers next to each other. "You have two choices."

She frowned. "Sir, this is just across post to the Armored Cavalry Regiment. They just redeployed from Iraq."

"I generally don't make it a habit of making decisions while I'm angry." He leaned against the desk, folding his arms over his chest. "When you screw up, you damn sure don't do it in half measures. I was disappointed in you for going at it with Lieutenant Engle in Iraq," he said softly, and Claire wanted to crawl into a hole and die. "I still am. But you were willing to take the fall for this harebrained stunt she pulled with Iaconelli because you care more about her staying with her team than you do about holding a grudge." He slid a pen across his desk. "If you sign this and don't fight it, it stays here. It won't make your permanent records. But I can't let this go unpunished. Your evaluation report is going to be average, but it won't reflect this letter." He smiled, and his blue eyes glittered beneath the office lights. "Primarily because your loyalty should be commended, not destroyed. But next time, do something before somebody gets hurt."

She breathed deeply, reading the letter of reprimand along with her evaluation report. Not a glowing report. Her first middle-of-the-road report since she'd been commissioned. It hurt. Badly. But it could be worse.

She straightened. "I understand, Sir."

"If you don't want to go to the Third Armored Cavalry Regiment, there's a command opening up in the military police brigade. They're deploying to Afghanistan in three months." She lifted her gaze to Colonel Richter's, her blood pounding in her ears, not daring to voice the answer to his unspoken offer.

He was giving her a chance to leave the brigade and in doing so, offering her the chance to salvage her career.

She couldn't speak, her mind tumbling over the possibilities and the reality. She could deploy and get far and fast away from Evan and the complicated feelings he stirred in her. She could lead soldiers again. If she chose the job across post, she would stay here and there would be no guarantee of success. The Armored Cavalry Regiment was a hard unit, with a reputation for crushing poor performers.

Choosing the ACR meant staying at Fort Hood. It meant that she could see Evan at the end of each day. Providing she could get him to talk to her again. Never once in her life had she chosen a lover over the job. She simply wasn't wired that way.

She hesitated over the choice. Her fingers trembled as she lifted the pen. But she did not hesitate as she made her selection.

THE LETTER OF REPRIMAND SAT ON THE SEAT NEXT TO HER as she turned her car toward Stillhouse Hollow and the small house Evan rented there.

The reprimand was nowhere near the price she'd thought she'd have to pay and she suspected that Evan had somehow influenced what had happened. The sun was low in the afternoon sky, the wind cooling the warm air. November in Texas was pretty nice when it wanted to be. Better than Fort Carson, that was for sure.

She checked the directions on the pink sticky pad one more time and took the next right, mildly impressed when she drove through a gate that made her think of a ranch rather than a subdivision neighborhood.

A huge red barn stood in the middle of a pasture and there were at least five horses grazing around a pile of hay. A stock pond was off to her left and there was a little white house a couple hundred feet away from it. Nestled against a small mountain, the tiny ranch house was flush against a patch of trees.

She knocked on the front door.

"Hello, Claire."

She spun at the sound of Evan's voice. He padded up the steps to her, his skin slick with sweat. He wore a dark blue T-shirt and lightweight pants. Sweat darkened the shirt between his broad shoulders and she caught a glimpse of skin between his pants and his shirt as he lifted a black water bottle to his mouth.

A thousand emotions flashed over his face before it shuttered closed. "I don't suppose you know anything about Reza writing a second sworn statement?" she asked.

"Maybe." His expression didn't budge. "Did it make a difference?"

"I'm on assignment. Does that answer your question?"

"Not entirely." His voice was low, dangerous. "Where did he put you on assignment?"

She thrust the letter of reprimand at him and felt like a fool for doing it so quickly. He glanced down but didn't raise his hand to accept the piece of proffered paper. "Answer the question, Claire."

"He offered me a second command in the military police brigade. They're deploying in three months."

Evan wiped his hands on his T-shirt and turned away, but not before she caught the flash of hurt on his face. "Good for you. Congratulations. I'm sure you'll love being a commander again."

"I'm turning it down, Evan."

He stopped. His shoulders rose with a shuddering intake of breath. It was a long moment before he turned back slowly to face her. "What?"

"I'm turning it down."

"Why? A successful second command will practically guarantee your promotion." His voice was tainted with disbelief and something else she couldn't identify.

"I'm going across post. To the Armored Cavalry Regiment." She smiled weakly. "Ai-ee-yah," she said, the regiment's slogan feeling strange on her lips. "I'm staying on at Fort Hood. I report to the ACR next week." Evan's eyes were dark, his expression unreadable, and she barreled on, afraid she'd lose her courage. "Maybe keeping my career isn't everything that's important," she said quietly. "Maybe I've been worried about the wrong things. Maybe the thing that's the most important has been missing from my life the entire time." She paused, watching emotions flicker across his face. "Until there was you, there was no reason for me to try and make a home out of anywhere the army sent me. I didn't even realize what I was doing.

"My dad couldn't stop drinking." She swallowed past the lump in her throat. "I always thought that if I'd been a better daughter, if I'd done better in school or kept the house cleaner . . . maybe he'd have loved me more." Her eyes filled and she blinked rapidly, but she didn't wipe away the tears that poured out of her. She shrugged. "You know the rest," she whispered, biting her lip. "Reza said I should just tell you I'm crazy and ask you to put up with me." She pressed her lips together, biting back the sting of emotion. "But that's not really the entire truth." She breathed deeply, smiling tremulously. "I miss your cock when it's not around. And the rest of you isn't half bad, either."

He choked suddenly, then broke out laughing. Relief raced over her skin and she let herself smile. He walked toward her then and wrapped his arms around her. She rested her head against his chest, the warm, wet T-shirt clinging to her cheek.

"My cock comes with conditions," he said against her hair.

She tipped her face up to his and dragged his mouth down to hers. "Are you going to tell me what they are?"

She didn't give him the chance. She kissed him, pouring everything she couldn't say into the stroke of her tongue, the glide of her lips against his.

༄

Capturing her jaw with one rough palm, he urged her neck back until she rested against his shoulder. With the other thumb, he traced a line from the bottom of her chin down her throat to the collar of her T-shirt. Again, he traced the line of her throat with feather-light strokes, his fingertips teasing her skin, sending shivers of pleasure flowing over her. He nibbled on her ear, sucking gently as he finally peeled her T-shirt over her head, revealing all that was not sensible about her.

She'd turned down the second command, a job he knew she'd craved, a job she should have taken. He had a chance to make a life with her. He was going to hold on to this as long as he could. He lifted her against him, carrying her the short distance into his home. He didn't give her a chance to look at the mess of his kitchen or the unmade bed. He simply laid her down on the twisted mess of his sheets and stripped her with fevered urgency.

He couldn't name the moment when Claire had become the object of his dreams, only that she had. It was a chance at happiness he'd done nothing to deserve but he was going to take it. For as long as he had it, he'd take it.

She rolled until she straddled him, then threaded her fingers with his and slid her heat against his erection with a tiny movement of her hips.

After a moment she pulled back, stroking his cheek with one hand, loving the scrape of his two-day shadow against her palm. She cupped his cheeks in her palms. "I love your cock, Evan." She traced her tongue against his bottom lip. "But I love you more."

He laughed and she felt it deep, deep inside of her. "I'm asking you to give me a shot. I'm not an easy person to love and I don't really know how to do this whole relationship thing, but I'm asking you to take a chance on me. To help me learn to trust."

And then she moved and Evan sank home, deep into her lush, wet heat, and in that moment, he held her tight in his arms, no barriers, no walls. Just him. Just her.

She brushed her lips against his as she slid down his length once more. "Because I do love you. I don't know how to do that, but I want to try and learn."

Beautiful and unbound, Claire rose over him, her hips twisting in the darkest pleasure until she shattered and came apart around him.

LATER, WHEN HE HELD HER AGAINST HIM, HER HANDS stroked idly over his chest and shoulder. They lingered on the scar over his shoulder before drifting down beneath the sheet that covered them. Her hand drifted lower again, finding him already aroused. "So about these conditions your penis comes with?"

"Why don't we talk about those later?" He grinned against her mouth and cradled her face in his hands, marveling that this woman was finally his. "I think we have time."

"Yeah. I think we do."

Claire walked into the house and dropped her body armor next to Evan's near the front door. Every muscle in her body ached from spending all day on the range during the last day of a two-week-long field training exercise and she wanted nothing more than to collapse into a heap and sleep for a week.

"Evan?" Silence greeted her shout and she frowned. His truck was in the driveway so he couldn't be far. Figuring he was somewhere around, she walked into the bathroom and stripped off her sweaty uniform. Her bones creaked as she stepped into the shower, holding her head beneath the steady steam. Pulsing heat penetrated her sore muscles and she rotated her neck, trying to ease away some of the soreness.

She'd been gone to the field for a week with her new squadron and she was flat-out wrecked. She'd thought there were some grade-A pricks in her previous team, but they had nothing on the first-class assholes she was working with now.

She loved it. It was a challenge, and Claire loved nothing more than a challenge.

The shower stall opened and she glanced up, a smile pouring over her. "Hey."

"Hey." Evan left the door open and started stripping in front of her. She marveled at the beauty of the man, watched the fresh black ink of Casey's name ripple across his back as he moved.

"How's the tattoo?" she asked as he pulled off his boots.

"Healing well." He looked up at her, his gaze dark and intense. "I talked to my parents today."

She smiled, feeling a starburst of joy that he'd managed to finally reconnect with his family, followed quickly by terror at his next words. "They're coming down next weekend." He finished getting naked in three seconds flat and he stepped in behind her. His fingers sought her shoulders, instantly finding her sorest spots. "They want to meet you."

She rolled her neck at his ministrations. "You have no idea how terrifying that is for me to hear."

"You'll do fine." His quiet laugh rumbled through her body as his hands continued to explore. "So later, I have something for you."

"Oh yeah? That's not fair. I didn't get you anything." She frowned, tipping her head back to lean it against his shoulder. "Wait, what are we celebrating?"

"Couple of things," he murmured, nipping her ear. "Me getting you to move in, for one. You not freaking out for a full six months." He cupped her breasts, nibbling on her neck. "And me asking you to marry me."

His arms tightened around her as she stiffened. "Don't freak out," he whispered, holding her close, his body cradling hers. "It's only a matter of time before one of us comes down on orders. The army doesn't recognize life partners."

He turned her gently, cupping her face. "This isn't just about the army, Claire. I like coming home to you. I like knowing you're there, even if you're better at blowing shit up than you are at cooking chicken."

"That's not fair. I followed the instructions," she said, her voice breaking.

"And no one died from food poisoning." Evan smiled as water sluiced between their bodies. "I want you in my life, Claire. Today. Next week. Next year." He pressed his lips gently to hers. "Say yes?"

She smiled against his mouth, fighting to keep her voice from breaking. "What if I say no?"

"You won't." He leaned back. "Will you?"

Shaking her head slowly, she reached between their bodies. Slowly she slid her hand over his erection. "Does this mean I get to keep your penis around?"

"You can do whatever you want to it, so long as it doesn't involve hot wax or shaving."

"I shaved for you."

Evan laughed. "You've never seen a bald cock. It looks like a plucked chicken."

In all her life, she'd never imagined laughing during a marriage proposal. She'd never imagined any marriage proposal. Still smiling, she wrapped her arms around his neck and kissed him fiercely. "Yes, Evan, I'll marry you."

THANK YOU FOR READING CARRY ME HOME! I HOPE you loved Claire & Evan. Keep reading to find out what it takes to break through a heart made of stone. Find out more in **A PLACE CALLED HOME**.

Nothing good comes from caring about someone. Love has always let him down. So what happens when this stone cold soldier runs into the one thing he cannot control - a woman bold enough to love him? Can he let go of his past and let his guard down?

ONE CLICK A PLACE CALLED HOME, an emotional enemies to lovers romance NOW!

Turn the page for an extended excerpt from Ike and Emily's story.
Carry Me Home was previously published as ALL FOR YOU

EXCERPT FROM A PLACE
CALLED HOME

PROLOGUE

Fort Hood, Texas

Spring 2009

"Where the hell is Wisniak?" Reza hooked his thumbs in his belt loops and glared at

Foster.

Sergeant Dean Foster rolled his eyes and spat into the dirt, unfazed by Reza's glare. Foster had the lean, wiry body of a runner and the weathered lines of an infantryman carved into his face, though at twenty-five he was still a puppy. To Reza, he'd always be that skinny private who'd had his cherry popped on that first run up to Baghdad. "Sarn't Ike, I already told you. I tried calling him this morning but he's not answering. His phone is going straight to voicemail." Reza sighed and rocked back on his heels, trying to rein in his temper. They'd managed to be home from the war for more than a year and somehow, soldiers like Wisniak were taking up the bulk of Reza's time. "Have you checked the R&R Center?"

"Nope. But I bet you're right." Foster pulled out his phone before Reza finished his sentence and started walking a short distance away to make the call.

"I know I am. He's been twitchy all week," he mumbled, more to himself than to Foster. Reza glanced at his watch. The commander was going to have kittens if Reza didn't have his personnel report turned in soon, because herding cats was all noncommissioned officers were good for in the eyes of Captain James P. Marshall the Third, resident pain in Reza's ass.

Foster turned away, holding up a finger as he started arguing with the doc. Reza swore quietly, then again when the company commander started walking toward him from the opposite end of the formation. Reza straightened and saluted.

It was mostly sincere.

"Sarn't Iaconelli, do you have accountability of your troops?"

"Sir, one hundred and thirty assigned, one hundred and twenty-four present. Three on appointment, one failure to report and one at the R&R Center. One in rehab."

"When is that shitbird Sloban going to get out of rehab?" Captain Marshall glanced down at his notepad.

"Sloban isn't a shitbird." Reza squared his shoulders, staring hard at his commander, daring Marshall to argue. "Sir."

Marshall looked like he wanted to slap Reza but as was normally the way with cowards and blowhards, he simply snapped his mouth shut. "Who's gone to the funny farm today?"

The Rest and Resiliency Center was supposed to be a place that helped combat veterans heal from the mental wounds of war. Instead, it had become the new generation's stress card, a place to go when their sergeant was making them work too hard. Guys like Wisniak, who had never deployed but who, for some reason, couldn't manage to wipe their own asses without someone holding their hands abused the system, taking up valuable resources from the warriors who needed it. But to say that out loud would mean agreeing with Captain Marshall, something Reza would be dead before he ever did in public.

Luckily, Captain Ben Teague approached, saving Reza the need to punch the commander in the face. The sergeant major would not be happy with him if that happened. Reza was already on thin ice as it was. He was holding steady, but there was no reason to give the sergeant major an excuse to dig into his fourth point of contact.

He was doing just fine. One day at a time, and all that.

Too bad guys like Marshall tested his willpower on a daily basis.

"So you don't have accountability of the entire company?" Marshall asked. Behind him, Teague made a crude motion with his hand.

Reza rubbed his hand over his mouth, smothering a grin. "Sir, I know where everyone is. I'm heading to the R&R Center after formation to verify that Wisniak is there and see about getting a status update from the docs."

Marshall sighed heavily, and the sound was laced with blame, as though Wisniak being at the R&R Center was Reza's personal failing. Behind him, Teague mimed riding a horse and slapping it. Reza coughed into his hand as Marshall turned an alarming shade of puce. "I'm getting tired of someone always being unaccounted for, Sergeant."

"That makes two of us." Reza breathed deeply. "Sir."

"What are you planning on doing about it?"

He raised both eyebrows, his temper lashing at its frayed restraints. His mouth would be the death of him someday. That or his temper.

He didn't really care.

He started ticking off items on his fingers. "Well, sir, since you asked, first, I'm going to stop by the shoppette for coffee, then take a ride around post to break in my new truck. I'll probably stop out at Engineer Lake and smoke a cigar and consider whether or not to come back to work at all. Around noon, I'm going to swing into the R&R Center to make sure that Wisniak actually showed up and was seen. Then, I'll spend the rest of the day hunting said sorry excuse for—"

"That's enough, sergeant," Marshall snapped and Teague mimed him behind his back. "I don't appreciate your insubordinate attitude. Accountability is the most important thing we do."

"I thought kicking in doors and killing bad guys was the most important thing we did?" Reza asked, doing his damnedest not to smirk. He failed. Miserably. Time to crack open a cold one and kick his boots up on his desk.

Except that he'd given up drinking. Again. And this time, it had to stick. At least, it had to if he wanted to take his boys downrange again.

The sergeant major had left him no wiggle room. No more drinking. Period.

"Sergeant—"

"Sir, I got it. I'll head to the R&R Center right after formation. I'll text you..." He glanced at Foster, who gave him a thumbs-up. Whatever the hell that was supposed to mean. Wisniak was at the R&R Center, Reza supposed?

"You'll call. I don't know when texting became the Army's preferred technique for communications between seniors and subordinates. I don't text."

Reza saluted sharply. It was effectively a fuck off but Marshall was either too stupid or too arrogant to grasp the difference. "Roger, sir."

"Ben," Marshall mumbled.

"Jimmy." Which earned him a snarl from Marshall as he stalked off. Teague grinned. "He hates being called Jimmy."

"Which is why you've called him that every day since Infantry Officer Basic Course?"

"Of course," Teague said solemnly. "It is my sacred duty to screw with him whenever I can. He was potty trained at gunpoint."

"Considering he's a fifth generation Army officer, probably," Reza mumbled. Foster walked back up, shaking his head and mumbling creative profanity beneath his breath. "They won't even tell you if he's checked in?"

"I practically gave the lady on the phone a hand job to get her to tell me anything and she pretty much told me to kiss her ass. Damn HIPAA laws. How is it protecting the patient's privacy when all I'm asking is if the jackass is there or not?"

Reza sighed. "I'll go find out if he's there. I need you to make sure the weapons training is good to go." Still swearing, Foster limped off. Too bad Foster wasn't a better ass kisser; he'd have already made staff sergeant.

But Marshall didn't like him and had denied his promotion for the last three months because Foster was nursing a bum leg. Granted, he'd jammed it up playing sports, but the commander was being a total prick about it. It would have been better if Foster had been shot.

"Damn civilians," Reza mumbled, glancing at Teague. "I get that the docs are only supposed to talk to commanders but they make my life so damn difficult sometimes."

"They talk to you," Teague said, pushing his sunglasses up on his nose and shoving his hands into his pockets.

"That's because they're afraid of me. I look like every stereotype jihadi they can think of. All I have to do is say *drka drka Mohammed jihad* and I get whatever I want out of them."

"A Team America: World Police reference at six fifteen a.m.? My day is complete."

Teague laughed. "That's so fucking wrong. Just because you're brown?"

Reza shrugged. Growing up with a name like Reza

Iaconelli had taught him how to fight. Young. With more than just the asshole kids on the street. He'd learned the hard way that little kids better have a whole lot more than attitude when standing up to a grown man.

"What can I say? No one knows what to think of the brown guy. I'm sure if I was smaller people would think I was Mexican." He started to walk off, still irritated by Marshall and the unrelenting douche baggery of the officer corps today. They cared more about stats than soldiers. It was total bullshit. The war wasn't even over yet and it was already all the way back to the garrison Army bullshit that had gotten their asses handed to them from 2003 on.

"Where are you heading?" Teague asked.

"R&R. Need to check up on the resident crazy kid and make sure he's not going to off himself." He palmed his keys from his front pocket. Reza slammed the door of his truck and took a sip of his coffee, wishing it had a hell of a lot more in it than straight caffeine.

He'd rather have his balls crushed with a ball peen hammer than deal with the R&R Center. He hated the psych docs. They were worse than the bleeding heart officers he seemed to find himself surrounded with these days. Just how he wanted to start off his seventy-fourth day sober: arguing with the shrinks.

Good times.

"I don't really think you understand the gravity of the situation, Captain."

Captain Emily Lindberg bristled at the use of her rank. The fact that a fellow captain used it to intimidate her only irritated her further.

She inhaled a calming breath through her nose and spoke

softly, deliberately attempting to keep her composure. "I'm sorry, Captain, but I'm afraid you're the one who doesn't understand. Your soldier has experienced significant trauma since joining the military and his recurrent nightmares, excessive use of alcohol to self-medicate, and his inability to effectively manage his stress are all indicators of serious psychological illness. He needs your compassion, not your wrath."

"Specialist Hendersen needs my size ten boot in his ass. He sat on the damned base last deployment and we only got mortared a few times. He's a candy pants who has a serious case of *I do what I want-itis* and now he's come crying to you, expecting you to bail his sorry ass out of a drug charge." Emily could practically see smoke coming out of the big captain's ears.

Once upon a time, she would have flinched away from his anger and done anything to placate him. It was abusive jerks like this who thought the Army was all about their ability to accomplish their mission. The mouth breather in front of her didn't care about his soldiers.

It was up to folks like Emily to hold the line and keep the Army from ruining yet another life. There had already been more than fifty suicides in the Army this year and it was only April. "What Hendersen needs, Captain Jenkowski, is a break from you pressuring him to perform day in and day out. My duty-limiting profile is not going to change. He gets eight hours of sleep a night to give the Ambien a chance to work. And if you don't like it, file a complaint with my boss. He's the full-bird colonel in charge of the hospital."

"You fucking bitch," he said. His voice was low and threatening. "I'm trying to throw this little motherfucker out of the Army for smoking spice and you're making sure that we're stuck babysitting his candy ass. Way to take care of the real soldiers who have to waste their time on this little weasel instead of training."

The door slammed behind him with a bang and Emily sank into her chair. She had a full three minutes before her next patient and it wasn't even nine a.m.

A quick rap on her door pulled her out of her momentary shock. "You okay?"

She looked into the face of her first friend here at Fort Hood, Major Olivia Hale. "Yeah, Olivia. I just..."

"You get used to it after a while, you know," Olivia said, brushing her bangs out of her eyes.

"The rampant hostility or the incessant chest beating?" Emily tried to keep the frustration out of her voice and failed.

"Both?"

Emily smiled. "Well, that's helpful."

Moments like this made her seriously reconsider her life in the Army. Of course, her parents would be more than happy for her to take the rank off her chest and return home to their Cape Cod family practice. The last thing she wanted to do was run home to a therapy session in waiting. Who wanted to work for parents who ran a business together but had gotten divorced fifteen years ago? At least here she was making a difference, instead of listening to spoiled rich kids complain about how hard their lives were or beg her for a prescription for Adderall so they could prepare for their next exam.

Here she could make a difference. Do something that mattered.

Her family wouldn't understand.

Then again, they never had.

Yeah, she'd pass, thanks.

"Can I just say that I never imagined that I'd be going toe-to-toe with men who had egos the size of pro football linebackers? Where does the Army find these guys?"

"Some of them aren't raging asshats," Olivia said. "Some commanders actually care about their soldiers."

An Outlook reminder chimed, reminding her that she had two minutes. Emily frowned then clicked it off. "It must be something special about this office, then, that attracts all the ones who don't care."

She'd recently moved to Fort Hood because it was the place deemed most in need of psychiatric services. They had the unit with the highest active-duty suicide rate in the Army. She was trying her damnedest to make a difference but the tidal wave of soldiers needing care was relentless.

Add in her administrative duties on mental health evaluations and sometimes, she didn't know which day of the week it was.

"Does it ever end?" she whispered, suddenly feeling overwhelmed at the stack of files on her desk. Each one represented a person. A soldier. A life under pressure.

Lives she did everything she could to save.

Olivia shrugged. "It doesn't." She glanced at her watch. "I've got a nine o'clock legal brief with the boss. You okay?"

She offered a weak smile. "Yeah. Have to be, right?"

Olivia didn't look convinced but didn't have time to dig in further. In the brief moment she had alone, Emily covered her face with her hands.

Every single day, Emily's faith in the soldiers she'd wanted to help weakened. When officers like Jenkowski were threatening kids who just needed to take a break and pull themselves together to find some way of dealing with the trauma in their lives, it crushed part of her spirit. She'd never imagined that confrontation would be a daily part of her life as an Army doc. She'd signed up to help people. She wasn't a commander, not a leader of soldiers. She was here to provide medical services. She'd barely stepped outside her office, so all she knew was the inside of the clinic's walls.

She'd had no idea how much of a fight she'd have on a daily basis. Three months in and she was still shocked. Every single day brought something new.

She wasn't used to it. She doubted she would ever get used to it. It drained her.

But every day she got up and put on her boots to do it all over again.

She was here to make a difference.

A sharp knock on her door had her looking up. Her breath caught in her throat at the single most beautiful man she'd ever seen. His skin was deep bronze, his features carved perfection. There was a harshness around the edge of his wide full mouth that could have been from laughing too much or yelling too often. Maybe both.

And his shoulders filled the doorway. Dear lord, men actually came put together like this? She'd never met a man who embodied the fantasy man in uniform like this one. The real military man was just as likely to be a pimply-faced nineteen-year-old as he was to be this...this warrior god.

A god who looked ready for battle. It took Emily all of six-tenths of a second to realize that this man was not here for her phone number or to strip her naked and have his way with her. Well, he might want to have his way with her but she imagined it was in a strictly professional way. Not a hot and sweaty way, the thought of which made her insides clench and tighten.

She stood. This man looked like he was itching for a fight and damn it, if that's what he wanted, then Emily would give it to him.

It was just another day at the office, after all.

"Can I help you, Sergeant?"

Reza glanced at the little captain, who looked braced for battle. She was cute in a Reese Witherspoon kind of way, complete with dimples, and except for her rich dark hair and silver blue eyes. If Reza hadn't been nursing one hell of a bad attitude and a serious case of the ass, he would've considered flirting with her.

Except that the sergeant major's warning of *don't fuck up* beat a cadence in his brain, so he wouldn't be flirting anytime soon. Besides, something about the stubborn set of her jaw warned him that she was ready for battle. She didn't look tough enough to crumble a cookie, and yet she'd squared off with him like she might just try to knock him down a peg or two. This ought to at least make the day interesting.

Reza straightened. She was the enemy for leaders like him, who were doing their damnedest to put bad troops out of the Army. People like her ignored the warning signs from warriors like Sloban and let spineless cowards like Wisniak piss on her leg about how his mommy didn't love him enough.

This wasn't about Sloban. He couldn't help him now and that fact burned on a fundamental level. He released a deep breath. Then sucked in another one. "I need to know if Sergeant Chuck Wisniak signed in to the clinic."

"I'm sorry but unless you're the first sergeant or the commander, I can't tell you that."

Reza breathed hard through his nose. "I'm the first sergeant."

Her gaze flicked to the sergeant first class rank on his chest. He wasn't wearing the rank of the first sergeant, so his rank was missing the rocker and the diamond that distinguished first sergeants from the soldiers that they led. Sergeants First Class were first sergeants all the time, though.

Her eyes narrowed. "Do you have orders?"

Reza's gaze dropped to the pen in her hand and the

rhythmic way she flicked the cap on and off. He swallowed, pulling his gaze away from the distracting sound, and struggled to hold on to his patience.

"First sergeants are not commanders. We don't have assumption of command orders." He pinched the bridge of his nose and sighed. "Ma'am, I just need to know if he's here. Why is this such a big deal?"

"Because Sergeant Wisniak has told this clinic on multiple occasions that his chain of command is targeting him, looking for an excuse to take his rank."

"Well, maybe if he was at work once in a while he wouldn't feel so persecuted."

The small captain lifted her chin. "Sergeant, do you have any idea what it feels like to be looked at like you're suspect every time you walk into a room?"

Something cold slithered across Reza's skin, sidling up to his heart and squeezing tightly. "Do you have any idea what it feels like to send soldiers back to combat knowing they lost training days chasing after a sissy-ass soldier who can't get to work on time? Or cries every time his sergeant yells at him?"

A shadow flickered across her pretty face but then it was gone, replaced by steel. "My job is to keep soldiers from killing themselves."

"And my job is to keep soldiers from dying in combat."

"They're not mutually exclusive."

Silence hung between them, battle lines drawn.

"I'm not leaving here without a status on Sarn't Wisniak," Reza said.

Captain Lindberg folded her arms over her chest. A flicker in her eyes, nothing more, then she spoke. "Sergeant Wisniak is in triage."

"I need to speak with him."

Lindberg shook her head. "No. I'm not letting anyone see him but his commander. He's probably going to be admitted to the fifth floor. He's extremely high risk. And you're part of his problem, Sergeant."

Reza's temper snapped, breaking free before he could lash it back. "Don't put that on me, sweetheart. That trooper came in the Army weak. I had nothing to do with his lack of a backbone." Reza turned to go before he lost his military bearing and started swearing. She'd already elevated his blood pressure to need-a-drink levels and it wasn't barely past nine a.m.

He could do this. He breathed deeply, running through creative profanity in his mind to keep the urge to drink at bay.

Her words stopped him at the door, slicing at his soul.

"How can you call yourself a leader? You're supposed to care about all your soldiers," she said, so softly he almost didn't hear her.

He turned slowly. Studied her, standing straight and stiff and pissed. "How can I call myself a leader? Honey, until you've bled in combat, don't talk to me about leadership. But go ahead. Keep protecting this shitbird and tie up all the counselors so that warriors who genuinely need help can't get it. He doesn't belong in the Army." He swept his gaze down her body deliberately. Trying to provoke her. Her face flushed as he met her eyes coldly. "Neither do you."

Emily sucked in a sharp breath at Iaconelli's verbal slap. In one single slap, he'd struck her at the heart of her deepest fear.

It took everything she had to keep her hands from trembling.

Her boss appeared in the doorway, saving her from embarrassing herself.

"Is there a problem, Sergeant?"

The big sergeant turned and nearly collided with a full-bird colonel who looked suspiciously like Johnny Cash.

Sergeant Iaconelli straightened and his fists bunched at his sides. "You don't want me to answer that. Sir."

"I don't think I appreciate what you're insinuating."

"I don't really give a flying fuck what you think I'm insinuating. Maybe if your doctors did their jobs instead of actively trying to make my life more difficult, we wouldn't have this problem."

"What brigade are you in, Sergeant?" her boss demanded.

She watched the exchange, her breath locked in her throat. The big sergeant's hands clenched by his sides. "None of your damn business."

Colonel Zavisca might be a medical doctor but he was still a full-bird colonel. Emily had never seen an enlisted man so flagrantly flout regulations.

"You can leave now, Sergeant. Don't come back on this property without your commander."

The big sergeant smirked and stalked off.

Emily wondered if he'd obey the order. She suspected she already knew the answer.

Her boss turned to her. "Are you okay?" he asked. Colonel Zavisca's voice was deep and calming, the perfect voice for a psych doctor. It was more than his voice, though. His entire demeanor was something soothing, a balm on ragged wounds. His quiet power and authority stood in such stark contrast to Sergeant Iaconelli.

She had experience with rough men like Sergeant Iaconelli. He was energy and motion and hard angles. And he was rude. Colonel Zavisca was more like some of the men at her father's country club. He was familiar.

"I'm fine, sir. Rough morning, that's all."

Emily stood for a long moment, Sergeant Iaconelli's verbal

slap still ringing in her ears. He had no idea how much his comment hurt. She didn't know him from Adam but his words had found her weakness and stabbed it viciously.

In one single sentence, he'd shredded every hope she'd held on to since joining the Army. She'd wanted to belong. To be part of something. To make a difference. He'd struck dead on without even knowing it: Her family had told her she'd never fit into the military. She fought the urge to sink into her chair and cover her face with her hands. She just needed a few minutes. She could do this.

The big sergeant's opinion did not matter. Her parents' opinion did not matter.

If she kept repeating this often enough, it would be true.

Her boss glanced at the clock on her wall. "It's barely nine a.m."

She smiled thinly. "I know. Shaping up to be one heck of a Monday. Is triage already booked?"

He nodded. "Yes. I need you in there to help screen patients. We need to clear out the folks who can wait for appointments and identify those who are at risk right now of harming themselves or others."

"Roger, sir. I can do that. I need to e-mail two company commanders and I'll be right out there."

"Okay. Don't forget we have the staff sync at lunch. And if you have time, please confirm that we have *Talarico's* reserved for the hail and farewell."

She raised both eyebrows. "I'd forgotten about that. Will do." Reservations for functions were normally taken care of by the civilian secretaries, but this was a purely military event, so as the most junior member of the team, the rose had been pinned on Emily to make it happen. She didn't mind. Not in the least.

Even this early, the day showed no sign of slowing down and all she wanted to do was go home and take a steaming hot bath. She'd been trying to work out a knot behind her left shoulder blade for days now and things just kept piling up. She needed a good soak and a massage. Not that she dared schedule one. The risk of cancelation was too high.

"There's that smile. Relax. You're going to die of a heart attack before you're thirty. The Army is a marathon, not a sprint."

"Roger, sir." She waited until he closed the door before she covered her face in her hands once more. She could do this. She just needed to find her battle rhythm. She'd get into the swing of things. She wasn't about to quit just because things got a little rough.

Her cell phone vibrated on her desk. Oh, perfect. Her mother was calling. Not that she was about to answer that phone call. She couldn't deal with the passive aggressive jabs her mother was so skilled at. Besides, she was probably just going to press Emily to give up on—as she put it—slumming in the Army and come home.

She'd worked too hard to get where she was and she damn sure wasn't about to go limping home. How could she? They'd looked at her like she was an alien when she'd told them about Bentley. As though she had somehow been in the wrong for her fiancé's betrayal. As though, if she'd been woman enough, he never would have strayed.

There was no way she was going home. Not on their terms. If she ever went home again, she would do it on her own terms. She'd walked away from everything in her life that had been hollow and empty.

She was rebuilding, doing something that mattered for the first time in her life. Every day that she avoided calling home or being the person her father and his friends wanted her to be was a victory. No one in her family had had her back when she'd needed them. She might not have found her place yet in the Army but just being here was a start. It was something new and she wasn't about to give up, no matter how much Monday threw at her.

Tuesday really needed to hurry up and get there because, as Mondays went, this one was already shot all to hell.

One click CARRY ME HOME now!

THANK YOU

Dear Reader,

Thank you so much for reading. If you'd like to make sure you never miss a new release, sign up for my newsletter at http://jessicascott.net/subscribe and please like my Facebook page at https://www.facebook.com/JessicaScottAuthor/. You can also join my reader room, affectionately known as The Pint for exclusive first looks at new releases.

If you enjoyed the story, please consider leaving a review. Word of mouth is incredibly important for helping other readers discover new authors. I appreciate any and all reviews (whether positive or negative or somewhere in between).

Until next time!
Jess

ACKNOWLEDGMENTS

It truly takes a village for me to write. The people who supported me through this book are legion and I'm sure I'll forget some (because I always do), but please know that your support, encouragement and most of all, the boot on my fourth point of contact, is not only needed but appreciated. Julie Kenner, as always you are a wonderful mentor and friend. I somehow thought I wouldn't be standing on the ledge anymore when I published. Guess I was wrong about that. Allison Brennan, you are my rock and someone whom I can always count on to kick my butt and make me put on my commander panties. Thanks for not letting me mope too long. Roxanne St. Claire, your solid advice through thick and thin is invaluable to me. Robyn Carr, thanks for letting me pick your brain and letting my kids take over your book signing!

To my sisters in Loveswept, Ruthie Knox and Elisabeth Barrett: all I can say is thank you. You were there for late-night phone calls, plot overhauls and some serious crisis management. Friends like you are few and far between. Sarah Frantz, you have been my go-to gal on all things editing for ages now: thanks for being there in a pinch and helping make this story so much better. Nick Franklin thanks for helping me war-game the training stuff. I bet you never expected to see your name in print in a romance novel.

Last and most importantly, to my husband: thank you for not getting upset when I spent more time fighting deadlines than spending time with you. Thank you for grocery shopping and most of all, thank you for the research and development help. To my daughters: I am so lucky to have such cool kids. Yes, we're going to write the hamster book.

This book may have taken a village, but all mistakes are purely mine.

Author's Note

The Coming Home series and Homefront series were originally published as separate series. I have rebranded them to get things organized as they were originally intended.

Come Home to Me: A Coming Home Novella* was originally published as part of the Homefront series

Carry Me Home* was originally published as Until There Was You as part of the Coming Home series

A Place Called Home* was originally published as All for You as part of the Coming Home series

Take Me Home* was originally published as It's Always Been You as part of the Coming Home series

Last One Home* was originally published as Find My Way Home as part of the Homefront series

Jessica Scott is an Iraq war veteran, an active duty Army officer and the USA Today bestselling author of novels set in the heart of America's Army. She is the mother of two daughters, too many animals, and wife to a retired NCO.

She's also written for the New York Times At War Blog, PBS Point of View Regarding War, and IAVA. She deployed to Iraq in 2009 as part of Operation Iraqi Freedom (OIF)/New Dawn and has had the honor of serving as a company commander at Fort Hood, Texas twice.

She holds a Ph.D. from Duke in sociology and she's been featured as one of Esquire Magazine's Americans of the Year for 2012.

Photo: Courtesy of Buzz Covington Photography

Find her online at http://www.jessicascott.net

For more information,
www.jessicascott.net
jessica@jessicascott.net